I0699707

Certain Sensibilities

a love story

SONDRA RICE NEWMAN

Helping talented writers
publish exceptional books.

www.AcornPublishingLLC.com

For information, address:
Acorn Publishing, LLC
3943 Irvine Blvd. Ste. 218
Irvine, CA 92602

Certain Sensibilities

Cover photo by Tetyana Lyapi
Line art sketches by Eleanor Kohloss
Cover design by Damonza
Interior design and formatting by Debra Cranfield Kennedy

Printed in the United States of America

ISBN-13: 979-8-88528-093-8 (hardcover)
ISBN-13: 979-8-88528-092-1 (paperback)
Library of Congress Control Number (LCCN): 2024902661

For Matthew

Table of Contents

Chapter
One

The New Arrival

It was midafternoon when Cary Branscombe logged into the employee portal at the Fairfield Nursing Home. He looked up to see Marge Cochran, RN, waiting to speak with him.

Marge was the unit supervisor on the 3 p.m. to 11 p.m. shift and overworked; she had little time to inform him of his assignments.

"We're shorthanded tonight," she announced. "Marva has a sick child at home and won't be coming in. I couldn't get anyone to fill her shift on short notice, so we're all going to need to take up the slack."

Cary showed no sign of surprise. It had been this way since he began working there as a Certified Nursing Assistant. Such was the nature of the beast, and he accepted it as a condition of his job.

"You'll be responsible for rooms A-14 through A-22, and you'll need to pick up a new admission we have in A-26," said Marge, a short, stocky blonde in her mid-forties.

"Her name is Elizabeth Gardner, and she requires a wheelchair and transfer assistance."

"Anything else I should know?" Cary asked.

"It's her first time in a care facility. Kind of a rough day for her," said Marge. "Told one of the CNAs on the day shift that she saw this as the end of the line for her. Maybe you can cheer her up a bit."

Cary, an unmarried man in his early thirties, was a day student at the community college and worked the evening shift at the nursing home.

He was by no means an Adonis. However, despite showing no interest other than being polite and sometimes humorous, he had to fend off occasional come-ons from the young women employed at the facility.

Clean-shaven with neatly trimmed wavy hair the color of dark roast coffee beans, he stood just under six feet and gave off a surfer appearance, even in the basic burgundy scrubs that all the CNAs wore.

He began his shift by looking in on Daisy Carpenter in A-14.

"How are you feeling today?" he asked the bedridden eighty-five-year-old former florist. "Is the arthritis a little better today?"

Daisy was assigned a private room, as were all of the patients on "A" wing. It was because all the patient rooms were too small to accommodate a second bed. A miscalculation had been made in the architectural plans years earlier, and the management decided it was too late to make any changes.

Daisy was one among a majority of patients who rarely received visitors. Sometimes a relative would drop in briefly at Christmas.

"Oh, I'm gettin' by," Daisy replied. "How you doin'?"

"Okay. Just starting on my shift. Press the call button if you need anything," Cary said. "Dinner's in two hours."

One by one, he checked on his patients, always exchanging light banter in an effort to lift their spirits.

When he reached A-22, Brooks Washington greeted him with a smile.

"Hi, champ. What's cookin'?" Cary asked.

Brooks was almost always in an upbeat mood. A dyed-in-the-wool sports fan, he subscribed to almost every cable sports package available. His son, a mid-level City of Tucson administrator, paid the upcharge so his father could watch sports anytime he wished.

Upwards of ninety percent of the patients at the Fairfield Nursing Home were Medicaid patients. The average monthly nursing home cost in Arizona was $6,000 to $7,000 a month, an amount that few families or individuals could afford to pay out of pocket.

To qualify for assistance, each recipient was required to sign over to Medicaid their monthly Social Security checks and any pensions or other income. The recipient was then provided with a modest monthly stipend to cover the cost of items for personal hygiene, haircuts, snacks, and sundry purchases.

"Did you see last night's Diamondbacks game?" Brooks asked.

"I understand it was a whopper for the home team," Cary replied. "Read about it in the paper, but I was working, and they kept me busy here. Gotta go. We're shorthanded again this evening."

When Cary reached A-26, there was a new name card in the small cardholder on the door. It read "Elizabeth Gardner."

He knocked gently on the open door and waited to enter. After a moment, a soft, almost inaudible feminine voice responded, "Yes, please come in."

When he entered, his first impression was that the new patient was a refined lady, like those that he had read about in Victorian-era classics.

Clad in a hospital gown, the new patient, wearing reading glasses, sat propped up in bed. She held a hardback copy of John Steinbeck's *The Pastures of Heaven*.

Elizabeth Gardner had a patrician look about her and had been blessed with classic bone structure. Cary could imagine her likeness on a coin. Her hair, unlike that of so many of the women patients, appeared to have no tinting of any kind, but was cloud-white. She had a smooth complexion, though unnaturally pale.

"Good afternoon. My name is Cary. I'll be looking after you between now and eleven tonight. Could I ask how you'd prefer to be addressed? By last name—Ms. or Mrs.? Or first name?"

"Elizabeth will do," she answered. There was no power in her voice. It was weak and unsteady.

Cary turned to his iPad and brought up her chart.

"I see you don't have any food allergies. Either I or a volunteer will be taking you to the dining room for dinner at about five o'clock. We'll have a wheelchair for you," Cary said. "Before then, one of our LPNs will come around with your meds.

"I see that you're reading Steinbeck's second published work. Not many folks have read it. I remember it's all short stories, but they're wonderful. I can't forget one of his characters, Junius Maltby."

As they spoke, out of the corner of his eye, Cary caught sight of a 5×7 black-and-white photo in a frame on her night table. In the photo, a young woman, likely Elizabeth, in a smart English riding outfit, stood holding a horse by its bridle.

"You strike me as someone who enjoys good books," said Elizabeth.

"Can't get enough," replied Cary.

At that moment his pager vibrated.

"Oops, that's my pager," he said, looking at it to see which patient required his assistance. "I've got to go, but I'll see you later."

Cary quickly strode down the hall to A-18, where Harriet Oesterle was waiting for someone to assist her to the room's small private bathroom. As he waited in the visitor's chair for Harriet to summon him for a return to her bed, he reflected on his first meeting with the new patient in A-26.

Her chart showed that she was eighty-nine years old, non-ambulatory, and suffering from congestive heart failure along with a less severe case of rheumatoid arthritis. She had been admitted to Fairfield as a Medicaid patient after a social worker determined that she could no longer manage in her one-bedroom apartment.

His brief conversation with Elizabeth played on his mind. It was as if this woman was coming into his life not unexpectedly. It was something he couldn't immediately put his finger on. Neither could he dismiss it.

At that moment, he spotted one of the nursing home's volunteers walking in the corridor outside Harriet Oesterle's room. He wasted no time in calling to her as he kept an ear open for Harriet's call.

"Hello, Mrs. Stiglitz," he said to the matronly volunteer. "I'm so glad to see you. We're shorthanded this evening, and I've got two patients who take their dinner in the dining room, and I was hoping that you might be able to assist one of them. I have a new patient who arrived today, and I need to attend to her."

"No problem, Cary. I'm always pleased to help you. You work so hard. I believe I can manage it. Just let me know who and at what time," she replied.

An hour later, Cary was pushing Elizabeth in a wheelchair toward the dining room. She wore a nursing-home-provided robe and appeared to have freshened up in preparation for dinner.

As they entered the dining room, which resembled a school cafeteria, Cary pointed out, "The dining room here is divided into three sections. On your right is for patients who require hand feeding. Straight ahead is for those who need less assistance, and on your left is for those who can manage independently. The folks in that group are very sociable and it's an opportunity to find yourself in some interesting conversations."

"Can I take my dinner there?" asked Elizabeth.

"I don't see why not," came the reply as Cary wheeled her to her seating choice. "The food here's not gourmet, but it's pretty good."

Cary explained that due to his other responsibilities, they were arriving after many of the patients had already been served.

"But I'll make sure that tomorrow evening I'll get you here early enough to have a choice of where you take your dinner," he said.

Cary wheeled her past a community table toward a vacant smaller table. He handed Elizabeth one of the menus that lay on the table.

"I'd suggest something easy to digest. You wouldn't want the pork chops or Swedish meatballs on your first night. You need some time for things to settle," Cary said. "I'd recommend the spinach and cheese soufflé. It's light and always well prepared.

"Give me a moment, and I'll be right back," he said.

Cary returned with a tray that held a small cup of chicken and rice soup and set it down before her.

"The soufflé will be ready in ten minutes. I'll pick it up," Cary said.

"So far, it seems that you've handled this transition quite well," he remarked. "I know it's not easy coming here after you've been on your own."

"It's been a very long time," Elizabeth replied.

She went on to tell him about how she had come to move to Tucson from the East Coast after her husband died almost fifty years earlier, adding that she had a master's degree in English literature and taught briefly at one of the colleges in the Boston area.

"I had no reason to remain in Boston," said Elizabeth. "My husband was gone, and many of my friends had moved away. But I had a friend in Tucson, so I came here."

When she arrived in Tucson in the 1950s, she said, she quickly discovered there was little chance of being hired to teach at a college or university as the major growth had not yet begun. However, there was a librarian position open at what was then the main library, where, though overqualified, she was immediately hired. She worked there and later at one of the branches until reaching the age of 65, when she was eligible to retire.

Things went well for a while, but after a few years of contending with boredom and loneliness, everything began to go downhill, she said.

"It seemed like there was a new medical problem every week. It came to where I couldn't do my own grocery shopping anymore, and cooking meals was a real challenge. I became depressed," she said.

"Worse yet, I had outlived what few friends remained. When it came holiday time, my mailbox was empty except for a Christmas card from my insurance agent.

"Fortunately for me, a very kind and conscientious social worker took note of my plight and arranged for me to come here. It will take some getting used to, but I can't say I miss the loneliness."

"You won't be alone here, that I can guarantee you," Cary responded. "On the contrary, it can get a bit hectic at times."

"I might find that a welcome change," said Elizabeth.

Later, as she finished eating her soufflé, Cary described a small group that met for dinner most nights.

"There's this one table where I know you'll fit in," he said. "I'll introduce you tomorrow evening. You'll feel right at home with these people."

The following afternoon, Cary arrived at work a few minutes early. He went straight to the desk of Marge Cochran.

"Marge, I need a favor," he said.

"What is it?"

"The new patient in A-26. I'd like to be regularly assigned to her. She's a kindred soul. We speak the same language," he said.

"Okay, Cary. I understand. It's all that classical music, art, and books. Right?"

"Yeah, right. You know me," he replied with a smile.

"You can start today. I'll move Mrs. Jethroe over to Connie, and you'll still be working the same number of patients."

"Thanks, Marge. You always come through for me," Cary said.

After logging in, Cary began his shift by checking on his patients. Some would need to be bathed, others helped to the toilet, and some transferred from their beds to their wheelchairs.

An hour later, he arrived at Elizabeth's room. She was seated in a chair, engrossed in a book. It was a mystery novel titled *The Cat Who Played Brahms*.

"I'm surprised to see you reading mystery paperbacks," Cary said.

Elizabeth put down her book and looked up at him.

"I know you may be disappointed, but one can't exist on a steady diet of the classics," she replied.

"Today I decided to lighten things up a bit." Elizabeth said. "I once met Lilian Jackson Braun, the author of the famous 'The Cat Who . . .' mysteries. I was visiting a friend in Tryon, North Carolina, and she was doing a reading in the public library. She lived in Tryon and died only a few years ago. She made it to ninety-seven."

"Well, I can't promise you Lilian Jackson Braun or Steinbeck, but I believe you'll really like the folks I'm going to introduce you to at dinner. I won't be able to hang around, but I'll make the introduction and get your dinner for you," Cary said.

"I'd also like to see you get outside during this nice weather. Problem is that CNAs aren't allotted any time for such duties, and the only way is for one of our volunteers to take you out."

He walked to the window, looking out. "The gardens are nice at this time of year, but finding an available volunteer is the problem. This nursing home was begun as a nonprofit, but they couldn't make it financially. So it was sold to Fairfield, which is just a spoke in the wheel of a large, for-profit corporation. It's hard to recruit volunteers at a for-profit. We still have a few volunteers who were here when it was a nonprofit. I'll see what I can do."

"Cary, you've been awfully kind," said Elizabeth. "I don't know what I can do to reciprocate."

"Not a thing," answered Cary. "The folks I talk to these days don't seem to have an interest in much beyond the mundane. So this is a privilege for me."

Cary departed for his rounds, returning about an hour later to transport Elizabeth to the dining room.

"I have a couple of patients I need to help feed first, but I'll have time to get you settled. You can look over the menu while I'm away," he said as he handed her a printed sheet listing the evening's offerings.

As they arrived in the dining room, Cary swung Elizabeth's wheelchair in the direction of the space set aside for independent diners. He wheeled her toward a table for four where two men and a woman were in deep discussion.

"Churchill was never under any illusions about Stalin," declared one of the men, who Elizabeth would later learn was Gordon. "It was the Americans who bought this 'Uncle Joe' stuff. Stalin had us hoodwinked for a time."

The conversation stopped as Cary wheeled Elizabeth to the table and prepared for an introduction.

"Hi, folks, I'd like you to meet Elizabeth. She's a new patient," said Cary. "I was hoping she could join you."

All three greeted her, almost in unison.

"Of course," responded the woman, a gray-haired intellectual type, her hair put up in a bun and speaking Queen's English. "I'm Vivien, and my friends here are Max and Gordon."

"Vivien is an anthropologist. She worked out of the British Museum," said Cary. "Gordon's a journalist. He traveled the world for the Associated Press. And Max was a makeup artist in Hollywood. He's also a writer, and some of his scripts were made into movies that we've all seen."

To which Gordon added, "I guess it's obvious that all of us here are 'former this and former that.' So maybe you'd like to tell us a little bit about yourself."

Elizabeth shrugged. "You've all had illustrious careers. I just taught English literature at a small liberal arts college in New England, and when I came here I took a job as a librarian."

"Bottom line, it's 2015, and we're all has-beens here," said Max. "Please join us. The night is young. We've already looked over the menu and made our choices. Elizabeth, why don't you take a look, and we can submit all of our orders at the same time."

After briefly studying the menu, Elizabeth chose the baked whitefish and opted for a glass of white wine, as did the others.

"Management is very progressive," said Gordon. "Penelope, the nurse practitioner here, convinced the management that a glass of wine is thera-peutic. It also doesn't hurt that Vivien's niece is CEO of a company in Silicon Valley and when she comes to visit, she always brings along a wine gift. Last time, it was a bottle of 2009 Pichon Lalande. We have a rule at this table—we always share. I can assure you that it made for a memorable experience."

"I'll pick up your orders," said Cary, "but after that you'll have to excuse me as I have two patients waiting to be helped with their dinners."

For the next hour, Cary table-hopped taking care of patients who required feeding assistance. He kept an eye on the group and observed that Elizabeth was an active participant in the conversation.

After taking the two patients back to their rooms, Cary returned to the now near-empty dining room and approached Elizabeth's table where a spirited conversation was in progress.

"Come now, Gordon, you must admit that you don't know everything even though you are a veteran reporter," declared Vivien. "Santorini is in Greece, not in Italy."

Addressing the others seated at the table, she asked, "Isn't that right?"

They all nodded in unison.

Cary stepped forward to a position behind Elizabeth's wheelchair. "Sorry folks," he said, "but I've got to take Elizabeth back to her room. I can see that all of you are having a good time. Tomorrow you can resume where you left off."

The new friends bade Elizabeth good night.

When they reached her room, Cary asked Elizabeth if she might prefer to sit in her chair or perhaps read or watch TV.

"If you like, I can check to find out what's on PBS tonight," he said.

"Thank you. I can find it if I decide to watch TV," she replied. "You must take care of your other patients. I'll press the call button if I need anything."

"Okay," said Cary. "I'll be back before I go off duty and help you get settled for the night."

With that, Cary was off down the hall and immersed in fulfilling the needs of his other patients.

A few days later, Cary stood in front of Marge Cochran's desk. It was an hour before the start of his shift. Marge had finished speaking with another worker and turned to Cary.

"What brings you in this early?" she asked.

"I need to give you a heads up so you won't be caught flatfooted if anyone asks," he replied. "I've been trying to find a volunteer who's available to take Ms. Gardner outdoors for some fresh air and sunshine, but no luck. I'd like to do that myself on my own time before I start work today."

"I can't see any problem with that," she said. "If volunteers can do that and family members and friends can do that, I can't see why you can't, so long as it's on your own time." She studied him with curiosity. "But can I be so bold as to ask why?"

"I really enjoy talking with Elizabeth. I can't do that when I'm on duty taking care of other patients."

"Okay then," said Marge. "See you at three."

A few moments later, he was knocking on Elizabeth's door, which was propped open. She was sitting in a chair reading.

Gone was the hospital gown. She wore white ankle-length pants and a navy blue-and-white-striped blouse; visibly more at ease since her two suitcases containing her clothing had caught up with her.

"Why, Cary, what a surprise. You're so early. Has your shift changed?"

"Nope. I came so I could take you out into the garden before I go on duty."

Her face lit up. "Wonderful. I just need a few moments to freshen up. Could you push that little cart with my makeup and hair brush over where I can reach it?"

Moments later, Cary guided Elizabeth's wheelchair out a side door into the garden and onto a paved path.

Cary found a shaded area next to a wooden bench where he parked Elizabeth in her wheelchair and sat down next to her. The garden was situated in a long, narrow area between the east wing of the nursing home and the north wall of the memory care unit.

A paved walkway in the center ran the full length of the grounds. Shorter arterial walkways led off here and there to benches or flower beds or to a well-placed piece of garden statuary, while a ramada in the middle provided shade, as did two mature trees. The tallest was covered with purple flowers, but Cary couldn't identify it by name. The other was a Texas ebony.

"This garden wasn't in the architect's plans," he explained. "It was an afterthought, created only last year."

"Really?" she replied with a smile. "It's lovely. In Boston, they would call this a vest-pocket park."

Cary's idea of showing Elizabeth this part of the campus brought immediate results. She looked relaxed, no longer tense from her moving-in experience.

Once settled, he reached into his knapsack and pulled out a small, gift-wrapped package, which he handed to her.

"It's for you. I hope you like it," he said.

She carefully unwrapped the gift, revealing a thin, undersized book with a slightly worn cover.

"It's a book of Wordsworth's poems," she exclaimed excitedly. "How did you know?"

"It was a hunch," he replied, feeling pleased with her response. "I was fairly certain that Wordsworth would be a poet you'd like. I hope you don't mind that it's a used copy. I buy most of my reading material from a large used-book store. You probably know it. It's Bookman's on Speedway."

The gift was obviously a welcome surprise, and it was reflected on Elizabeth's pale face.

"Would you read me one of your favorites?" she asked, handing Cary the book.

He opened it, leaned toward Elizabeth and in soft tones began reading aloud.

I Wandered Lonely as a Cloud
By William Wordsworth

I wandered lonely as a cloud
That floats on high o'er vales and hills,
When all at once I saw a crowd,
A host, of golden daffodils;
Beside the lake, beneath the trees,
Fluttering and dancing in the breeze.

Continuous as the stars that shine
And twinkle on the milky way,
They stretched in never-ending line
Along the margin of a bay:
Ten thousand saw I at a glance,
Tossing their heads in sprightly dance.

The waves beside them danced; but they
Out-did the sparkling waves in glee:
A poet could not but be gay,
In such a jocund company:
I gazed—and gazed—but little thought
What wealth the show to me had brought:

For oft, when on my couch I lie
In vacant or in pensive mood,
They flash upon that inward eye
Which is the bliss of solitude;
And then my heart with pleasure fills,
And dances with the daffodils.

"That was lovely," Elizabeth said. It was obvious that she was deeply moved and reached over and gently rested her hand on Cary's arm.

"I'll always remember my first time in this little garden with you and Wordsworth for company. I feel that I'm a little alive again."

As time went on, Cary continued to arrive early almost every day so he could take Elizabeth into the garden, where they shared books and conversation.

Sometimes he would bring her that day's *New York Times*, which a patient had already read and passed on to him.

In the evenings, he would see that Elizabeth was always seated at the table with her dining companions.

When she first arrived at Fairfield, Elizabeth had reported difficulties in sleeping. However, Cary discovered that if he read aloud to her, she would fall asleep within a few minutes.

On one particular evening, Cary was reading to her from a Wilkie Collins classic, *The Woman in White*, when Elizabeth interrupted him.

"Cary, I love this story," she said. "And if I were reading the book, I wouldn't be able to put it down. So if I ask you to stop here, will you promise me that we can take it into the garden tomorrow and continue? I'm getting so sleepy now."

"Of course," he replied as he closed the book.

As he spoke, he realized that he had gently covered her hand with his own.

Later, when Cary was in his 2003 Mazda pickup driving home, that one moment when their hands touched kept coming back to him.

On another afternoon, Cary thought that Elizabeth might benefit from a reflexology treatment, but he foresaw some obstacles. When he logged in at the start of his shift, he had a plan.

"Hi, Marge," he said. "I've got something special I'd like to do on my shift—with your approval, of course—and that's to give all of my patients a foot massage."

"And do I know why you're doing this?" she replied with a bit of a smile. "And yes, you're wise to protect yourself and *me* from possible criticism."

"I think you know me better than my mom did," Cary replied with a grin.

Later, after he had performed his regular duties and given foot massages to his other patients, Cary appeared at the door of Elizabeth's room. She had been reading.

"Many who've had this treatment say that afterward they feel as if they've received a full body massage," Cary said. "It's worked that way for me, too. So relax and take it all in. I'll start very gently, and you can give me some guidance if you'd like it to be gentler or a little more firm."

As Cary massaged her feet, Elizabeth told him how relaxed it made her feel.

"I may fall asleep right now," she said.

"That's normal," said Cary. "Among those who introduced reflexology here was a physician in Boston named Fitzgerald. That was about a hundred years ago. Before then, according to history books, it was practiced in ancient Egypt.

"There's no absolute proof, but Fitzgerald and those who followed mapped out charts showing connections between areas of the foot and major organs such as the heart, lungs, kidneys, and a lot of other body parts."

By the time he completed his last sentence, Elizabeth was asleep.

Kindred Spirits

OVER THE NEXT FEW WEEKS, Cary arrived early for his shift and routinely accompanied Elizabeth into the garden. They talked about their favorite books or music. Sometimes the conversation turned to politics, the economy, world events, or the environment. And every now and then they spoke of their lives before they met.

Sundays, however, were special, and Elizabeth regretted that they came only once a week. Sunday was one of Cary's days off, and she could count on his coming to visit her around ten in the morning and staying for most of the day.

Sometimes he would arrive early, then depart around noon to "forage for a tasty lunch," and return with a carryout for both of them.

On this particular Sunday, assisting Elizabeth in dressing was a CNA named Nadine, who confided that she loved clothes. She coaxed Elizabeth to wear an outfit that hung in the room's tiny closet. It was a white cotton Guatemalan peasant blouse with a modest scoop neck and colorful embroidered flowers around the neckline.

"What about this one, Ms. Gardner?" asked Nadine, holding it out for approval.

Elizabeth frowned slightly and wrinkled her nose. "Oh, dear . . . I loved that when I bought it, but I always feared it was too youthful for someone my age."

"Remember, Ms. Gardner, age is only a number. Dress for how it will make you feel. With the temperature today expected to be close to 90 degrees, you'll look and feel cool. I'm positive," Nadine said.

After a few minutes of doubt, Elizabeth acquiesced and chose a lightweight pair of cornflower-blue capris and white sandals to complete the ensemble. She added small silver hoop earrings. Then sunscreen for her face, neck, arms, and hands, which she had forgotten to apply before getting dressed. She finished with a light brushstroke of blush to her cheekbones and a natural shade of lip gloss, applied with the tip of her little finger.

Surveying herself in the full-length mirror—wheelchair and all—Elizabeth didn't think she looked badly put together. To the contrary. She smiled at her own image and said to the CNA, "You were right, Nadine. I'm fortunate to have you as my fashion consultant."

Cary arrived on time and, following a few compliments on her attire, he wheeled Elizabeth outside and halted at one of their favored spots, a bench beneath the tall tree in bloom with an abundance of purple flowers.

"If it gets too warm for you, we can always go inside and I'll find a place where we can talk," Cary said.

"And miss this?" Elizabeth raised her arm, stretching it out in front of her. "This is one of the most magnificent jacaranda trees I've ever seen."

"Jacaranda. Is that what they're called?" asked Cary.

"Yes, and they're one of my favorites," replied Elizabeth.

"It's really beautiful, Elizabeth, and I hate to admit this, but I never paid much attention to the plants or trees until I met you. I'd come out here on my break for some fresh, non-nursing-home air and stretch my legs, but the garden was just there until you came along."

"Could it have been, Cary, that you looked, but you didn't see?"

Cary grinned and nodded.

"Jacarandas are tropical trees," said Elizabeth. "The first time I saw one was in India."

"India?" he asked in surprise.

"Yes, India. It was in the 1960s, and a couple that I was friends with had introduced me to Transcendental Meditation. Bob and Leah were lovely people and great fun and wonderful traveling companions. We were at an ashram, actually, when I saw not one, but many jacarandas. It was a heavenly sight."

"I wish I had been there with you," Cary said softly.

"That's a very nice thing to say." Elizabeth laid her hand on his arm.

"I didn't say it to be nice; I mean it. I wish I could have known you back then."

Elizabeth drew a deep breath and smiled faintly. They sat together for a while longer. Neither spoke, but Cary's hand found hers, and they both felt transported—if not to India, to someplace wonderful.

"Cary, talk to me, please. You are a fascinating individual, especially for a man of your tender years. How did you get to be who you are today?"

"Thought you'd never ask," he said. "Around here, I'm just Cary the CNA. I'm used to it, though. Aside from my mom, nobody's ever wanted to know. As you can imagine, being the curious sort that I am, I find that strange."

"Well, I am interested. I wanted to know from the first day, but I felt it wouldn't have been proper to ask. So please forgive me."

"You're forgiven. How could I not?" he replied.

"Okay. Here goes. I grew up in Northern California in a working-class neighborhood in Milpitas, a town that bumps up to San Jose and back then was still affordable. We rented a single-wide mobile home owned by a trucker and his wife."

"This doesn't surprise me," said Elizabeth. "I didn't have the impression that you were born into privilege."

Cary shrugged. "My mom raised me by herself. She worked all her years as a waitress. They're now called servers. My father abandoned her when he learned she was pregnant. I never knew him, and I have no desire to find him now."

Cary leaned forward, placed one elbow on each knee and stared at the ground.

"My mom was the best mother anyone could ever want. Unfortunately, she was a smoker and died of lung cancer when I was sixteen. I was in high school. I felt so frustrated that I couldn't do anything to make the cancer go away. When she was so sick, I shopped, made the meals, and took care of the house. I tried to comfort her the best I could."

Tears welled in Cary's eyes. Elizabeth took his hand in hers.

"I could tell by the way you relate to your patients that you have a sensitivity and empathy that didn't come from a textbook," she said.

Cary collected himself. "After Mom passed away, her sister, my Aunt Joan, came to California and offered to take me home with her to Arizona. If it weren't for Aunt Joan, I would have been sent to a foster home.

"She's been wonderful. And so has her husband, Eldon. Thanks to them, I was able to finish high school and start college. I attended the community college here and pulled straight A's. But my curiosity took hold of me about four years ago, and after saving some money, I stuffed some jeans and T-shirts into a knapsack, said goodbye to Tucson, and set off to see the world."

He leaned back on the bench, remembering this adventurous chapter in his life with a nostalgic smile. "When I got as far as Newport News, Virginia, I signed on to a Greek coal freighter and washed dishes and cleaned the galley all the way to Rotterdam. From there I was launched on a journey that would take me to some of the most interesting places in Europe. I hitchhiked, landed in some small town or big city, and often found a job someplace where I could work 'off the books.'"

"Where all did you go?" Elizabeth asked.

"Paris, London, Vienna. But I also spent time in some out-of-the-way places like Estonia, the Channel Islands, and Ireland.

"It was in Ireland that I got lucky. Got a job mucking stalls at a small thoroughbred breeding farm near Tipperary. When I say that I 'cleaned up' on the horses, I mean that literally.

"I had a great gig in France. This retired actress—American—hired me as a driver and gofer. She had inherited a fortune from her last husband and lived on an estate outside Aix-en-Provence.

"She told everyone she had hired me because I could make a perfect whiskey sour. Or sometimes she'd say it was because I was good in bed."

Elizabeth, surprised, stared wide-eyed at Cary.

Cary laughed and rapidly added, "No, no, no! There was never anything like that. Honest! When she told people that, it instantly made her the center of attention. That's what she wanted. To have all eyes focused on her. I wasn't there very long."

"Where did you go after that?" Elizabeth asked.

"First to Greece. I always wanted to visit Delphi and the islands that are mentioned in *The Odyssey*. I had learned some Greek while on board the coal freighter. After Egypt and Israel, I started feeling homesick. Got on a flight home the next week."

"So how did you become a CNA?" Elizabeth asked.

Cary glanced at his cellphone. He looked up and said, "It's almost noon and we've got a lot more to talk about. This might be a good time for a break. The sun has moved on us. If I take you back to your room, I can run out and pick up some lunch. We can eat out here under the ramada."

•••┌──┐└•••

In half an hour, Cary returned with a bag containing egg salad sandwiches, iced tea, and brownies for dessert.

Seated in the shade of the ramada, Cary returned to answering Elizabeth's question.

"The general manager here is Paul Giroux. I worked for Paul when he was the assistant general manager at Mountain Brook. It was my first job after returning home. That was during the recession when jobs were scarce. I had seen an ad in the paper, and it mentioned shift work. Training was included. It was perfect for me. It allowed me to take my college classes during the day and work at night.

"When Paul was offered the top spot here, I was among about a dozen workers who followed him. He's a great guy. He stands up for his employees."

"And how did you come to appreciate the arts, if I may ask?" said Elizabeth.

"That started about five years ago," said Cary. "But it really started much earlier. When I was a kid in middle school—I was about fourteen—they called my mom into school, and a counselor told her that she had a gifted child. At the time, I wasn't sure what that meant, but when I got into high school the counselors arranged for me to take courses in what they call advanced placement. I found them not only a breeze, but interesting as well.

"When I enrolled in community college here, I was working full-time.

"One of the electives I chose was art appreciation. It was a class taught by a woman in her early forties. Her husband was an airline pilot and flew transatlantic routes. She taught part-time—only that one course.

"I really grooved on what I learned in the class and was also impressed with the instructor."

He grinned and laughed. "Actually, I was infatuated.

"To provide you with a description is difficult because whenever I think about her a half-dozen adjectives pop into my head. Gracious, cultured, elegant, refined. And contrary to what you might expect, she was unpretentious."

He paused for a moment, drifting back to the past. "You wouldn't describe her as a head-turner, but she was attractive in an intellectual way. I won't mention her name because she's known in this community and I wouldn't want to have any gossip circulating because of anything I might say. So I'll just refer to her as 'Jane.'"

Elizabeth nodded, clearly intrigued by the story.

"I was so taken with her that I would always hang around after class to ask questions related to the evening's lecture or art presentation. I believe that after a few of those after-class conversations, she caught on that my interest extended beyond the academic curriculum.

"At that point, things got more personal. She asked me if I liked French Impressionists, and would I like to attend a lecture on the subject—to which I answered with an enthusiastic 'yes.'

"The lecture was to be held in the evening in a large downtown church where concerts are often given on weekends. I was to meet her there and she would see to it that I had a reserved seat. When I arrived, I was shown to my seat, but it wasn't next to hers. I got the picture right away.

"Following the lecture, there was a punch and cookies reception where she approached me and made some comments about the lecture. I asked if we might go somewhere for coffee as my mind was full of questions.

"Almost on cue, she said that would be nice and suggested a place in Catalina that serves great coffees. You probably know Catalina. It's a good distance from here—about a 45-minute drive.

"Obviously, it was a place where we were not likely to be seen by anyone she knew. Once there, it all came out. She'd been married to her husband for twenty-two years. They had two daughters who were away at college, and her husband had been cheating on her for a long time. He had a mistress in Flagstaff. Not far away from there lived a pilot friend. Both loved fishing. At least once a month he took off for a couple days, saying he was going fishing with his friend.

"Jane told me she was long-suffering but couldn't see how a divorce would make life better for her. She valued her position in the community. Despite the cheating, her husband fulfilled his duties by always accompanying her to important social events."

Cary sighed. "I could see that she desperately needed a man who admired her, wanted her, and would show her some affection. That was me."

He wondered if Elizabeth would be disapproving, but she didn't seem to judge him, merely nodding for him to continue.

"Jane was concerned about her reputation, so every meeting had to be preplanned as if we were agents working undercover for the CIA. Sometimes we were able to stay as long as a week in a cabin on Orcas Island, Washington. Other times, it was a weekend getaway to Mexico. But always it was somewhere where she wouldn't be recognized, and we always traveled separately until we reached our destination."

"So why did the relationship end?" asked Elizabeth.

"It wasn't her husband. He didn't care. He sensed that something was going on, but like Jane, he was of the mind that so long as it was discreet, it wasn't a problem. After all, he knew about a pot calling the kettle black.

"But to answer your question, Jane found her soulmate. She met him at a conference about expanding health care. She was in Denver participating in this seminar which was chaired by the attorney general of a western state. She had asked questions during the seminar and had contributed to some of the discussion. Afterward, she was approached by this gentleman and asked to have lunch with him on the pretext that they would talk about a reform proposal that she had submitted.

"Well, I suppose you can guess what happened. The attorney general was recently divorced and looking to remarry. He had ambitions beyond his current position and wanted a wife who was up to helping him achieve his goals. It also turns out that he was a warmhearted individual, found her very attractive as well as being his intellectual equal. Bottom line: She divorced her husband, moved to the attorney general's state, and they got married. She sent me a letter, which I've kept, after she made her decision. I was happy for her."

Elizabeth gave him a gentle smile. "You're a kind man, Cary."

His cheeks warmed. "I knew our relationship wasn't meant to last, but it was great during the time it did. Since then, there hasn't been anyone I could relate to until I met you."

They were both quiet for a moment. Cary cleared his throat. "Well, now that I've bored you with my life story, I'm hoping you'll share some of yours."

She laughed. "I must admit, when you were telling me about Jane, I was listening carefully. It made me feel as though I had a *doppelganger*."

"How do you mean?"

"It seems I'm unable to escape from the word *extramarital*. It's been my nemesis as far back as I can remember." She folded her hands in her lap. "But let me start at the beginning. I was an only child born into a New England family that claims to trace its history back to the arrival of the *Mayflower*. The family name was Ferguson, although in the original Scottish it was Farquharson. My mother was a Ferguson and wanted everyone to know it.

"She was a dutiful daughter and when it came time for her to marry, it was her parents who chose her spouse, a young man from another old New England family.

"As one might expect, it was a loveless marriage, and before I was born, my father left and immigrated to Australia. They never divorced but did not remain in contact. I was raised by three women—my mother, my grandmother, and a housekeeper. After my father left, my mother legally changed our names back to Ferguson. We never talked about my father."

Cary listened patiently as Elizabeth continued.

"I was always sent to good schools, and after receiving my undergraduate degree in fine arts with a minor in French history, I went on to graduate school and took a master's degree in English literature.

"It was during the time I was a grad student that I met Arthur. He was in one of my classes. Arthur fell for me on our first date. We had attended a performance of *Knickerbocker Holiday* put on by the school's drama department. It was the first time I heard 'The September Song.' It was so beautiful. We went for coffee afterward.

"Arthur did everything that night short of propose."

She smiled, a little bitterly. "But you see, Arthur Keyes was Jewish, so that put a stopper on any aboveboard relationship right there and then. And of course, marriage was completely out of the question as far as my mother and grandmother were concerned. That is not to say that they were anti-Semitic. They were not. But as to my marrying anyone who didn't measure up to their narrow expectations, all Catholics, Jews, and Hispanics were automatically excluded.

"From that time forward, my relationship with Arthur was surreptitious. After a time, I was pressured into marrying Eliot Grayson, an accountant, who possessed the required pedigree. Once married, I had quite a surprise coming—Eliot was bisexual. He had a male lover who lived in Provincetown, a gay-friendly community on Cape Cod, and Eliot did little to try to cover it up."

Cary squeezed her hand. The contact felt so natural now. "I'm sorry, that must have been very hard to cope with."

She nodded. "When Eliot was away, Arthur and I would see each other as often as we could. Arthur was enrolled in law school and received support from his parents. When he received his law degree, he was recruited by a small firm that specialized in product liability law.

"Within a year, he was trying cases that brought the firm six figures and sometimes more. He was set. But not as far as his personal life was concerned. We were still in love. He wanted to marry me."

At that moment, a bright red cardinal flew overhead, breaking the moment. Cary glanced at his cellphone.

"I can't believe it. It's almost 3:30," said Cary. "The time has gotten away from us. You'll need a nap before dinner."

"Oh, must we? The time I'm waiting for you goes by so slowly," responded Elizabeth. "And the time I'm with you always goes much too fast."

A few days later, as Cary was logging in for his shift, Marge Cochran motioned him to her desk.

"The boss wants to see you right away," said Marge. "I know what it's about. You're not in any trouble, but you won't like what you're going to hear. Two of our CNAs quit yesterday. Jay and his girlfriend are moving to California, and Mary Alice got a job with better hours working as a receptionist in a medical office. We're down by two in this wing, and Paul is going to ask you to work double shifts until we can find two replacements."

Minutes later, Cary walked through an open door to Paul Giroux's office.

Looking up from his desktop computer, Paul said, "Cary, come in. Be with you in a minute."

Paul was in his mid-forties, medium height, starting to go gray, and carried an extra twenty-five pounds.

He wore his usual office attire: a bright-flowered Hawaiian shirt, khaki cargo shorts, and a pair of brown Crocs.

He dressed that way, he once told Cary, because it made him more approachable to both patients and staff. "Besides that," he said, "I'm easy to find."

Paul swiveled away from his computer's monitor screen, and before he could get out the words, Cary spoke.

"I already know what you want," Cary said. "The answer is 'yes,' I'll work a double shift, but I want you to let me bring you two replacements so I can get back on my regular schedule. I'm in the middle of the semester at the college and I can't afford to miss any classes."

"Go ahead," Paul said. "But tell me just how you are going to do that."

Cary replied, "I still keep in contact with a CNA I worked with at Mountain Brook. She's at Copper Hills Vista now. It's not a great place to work. She has a cousin who works there, too. I'd like to meet with them as soon as possible. But I need your approval to offer them each a $500 sign-up bonus."

Paul nodded. "Whatever it takes."

"Okay, I should get started," said Cary as he headed toward the door.

"You sometimes amaze me," said Paul, grinning.

En route to starting his shift, Cary stopped at the empty dining room, pulled up a chair, and searched his cellphone contacts for the name and number of the CNA he needed to reach. After a few rings, his call was forwarded to voice mail. He left a message asking his prospect to phone him as soon as possible.

Cary spent the afternoon ministering to his patients. When he arrived at Elizabeth's room, he briefed her on what was happening.

"It will be a grind for the next few weeks, but I'm confident that I can recruit the needed replacements," he told her.

"Anyway, I'll be a rich man with all that overtime," he said jokingly. "I think the first thing I'll do is buy a nice bottle of wine that you can share with your dinner group. They will enjoy it, and you can impress your friends with your knowledge of wine."

"You know I'm not a showoff, Cary," she protested. "But I must admit that it will be fun. My only regret is that you can't be with us."

At that moment, Cary's cellphone rang. It was the callback he'd been waiting for.

"It's good to hear from you, Daniela," he said. "Look, I've got a deal that I'd like to run by you and Maya." There was a pause on Cary's end as he listened.

"Yeah, it's about a job here. Can I meet you both on Saturday at Di Graziano's Pizza? Treat's on me."

With the call ended, he turned to Elizabeth.

"Wish me luck," he said. "Or actually wish us both luck."

It was 2:22 p.m. on Saturday when the landline phone rang in Paul Giroux's home.

"I'm at Di Graziano's Pizza and both women are ready to sign on," Cary announced. "There's only one issue standing in the way."

"And that is?" asked Paul.

"Maya's got a little boy who's eighteen months old," Cary said. "She's a single mom and the cost of childcare is eating up her very modest income and leaving nothing at the end of the month.

"She knows about our on-site childcare facility and is eager to have her boy close to where she's working, but she wants a waiver. I explained the way it works: the first year she gets a 33 percent discount; the second year, 66 percent; and the third year and thereafter it's free.

"She wants it free the day she starts working. Says she can't afford the fee. Daniela, her cousin, has agreed to come on board if Maya does. Daniela has no kids."

There was a brief pause as Paul pondered his decision.

"Okay," said Paul. "Tell her it's a deal. I might get some flak from corporate, but I'll remind them what it would cost in accumulated overtime if we don't fill these slots right away."

"Great. Thanks, Paul."

"No, Cary. Thank *you*. Tell them to report to human resources as soon as possible and let's get them started. I'll contact HR and give them a heads up."

On his way home, Cary stopped at Fairfield and updated Elizabeth. He informed her of his success and how that would enable him to return to his normal 3 p.m. to 11 p.m. shift. He promised he would come back later to read to her at bedtime.

A week passed and Cary had returned to his normal work schedule. Sunday being one of his days off, he spent the morning studying for upcoming final exams and the afternoon with Elizabeth in the garden. He had brought her daffodils, which he placed in a water glass on a window ledge in her room.

Before he left, he made a trip down the hall and returned with the Sunday edition of *The New York Times,* which one of his patients had already read and saved for him.

"This should keep you occupied until dinner," he said as he laid the heavy newspaper on her tray table.

"I'll be reading this for the next week." She smiled. "Thank you so much."

On Monday, before starting his shift, Cary stood in Paul's office and handed him a receipt from Di Graziano's Pizza. "It was only $36.72 for a giant pizza and three beers," he said. "You got off light this time."

"Cary, you are impressive," Paul said. "As I've told you before, when you get your college degree, I could have you here working alongside me. In a few years, you'd have your own facility to manage."

"I know, but when I finish work on my degree, I hope to be inside an R&D lab doing research," Cary replied. "The only thing better than that would be if you were running the lab."

"You know all the right things to say," said Paul. "I'm deeply touched."

Another week passed. It was Saturday, one of his days off, when he arrived to take Elizabeth out for fresh air. They would be unhurried today.

They soon found a perfect shaded spot under a large native mesquite tree. Cary pulled an outdoor chair over close to Elizabeth. He had stopped at a French bakery and bought a couple of chocolate éclairs, which he removed from a white bakery box. From a paper bag, he took out napkins, paper plates, and plastic forks.

"I thought you might like a dessert while you tell me more about yourself," said Cary. "You were recalling your relationship with Arthur."

"So I was," Elizabeth said. "But first I must have a bite of this éclair," she said, setting the plate on her lap. She took a delicate nibble, savoring the rich pastry.

"You'll soon learn that Arthur was the centerpiece of my life for years to come. But it wasn't the way we wanted it.

"Arthur urged me to get a divorce or an annulment. I wanted to, but my mother and my grandmother insisted it would ruin the family's reputation. Desperate, one summer day, I drove to Maine to visit my Uncle Luke. He was the black sheep of the family. He had married a divorced cannery worker, Wilma, who was a single mom. I had to arrange to visit with him under cover of darkness, so to speak."

She paused for another bite of éclair, dabbing her lips with the napkin. Every movement was elegant and graceful.

"Uncle Luke made his living working lobster traps and selling his catch to restaurants," Elizabeth continued. "While his wife worked at her job in the cannery, Uncle Luke taught her son the lobster trade. I hadn't been in contact with him in years, but he was glad to see me. I told him of my quandary and how, though Arthur's family was equally opposed on religious grounds, Arthur was ready to make the break regardless of the consequences.

"I told him that in my case, it also meant divorcing Eliot. Uncle Luke reminded me that he had faced a similar dilemma when he informed my grandmother that he intended to marry Wilma. At the time, he was told that if he married Wilma, it would embarrass the family and that if he did, he would be disinherited.

"It really came down to that," he said. "If Arthur and I wanted to be married, we would have to accept the consequences. He suggested that if we went ahead, we should also consider moving far away to put some distance between us and the families. Often such an opportunity comes only once in a lifetime, he said, and in his situation, he seized it and never has had any regrets."

Cary asked, "So Arthur was prepared to make such a break, but you were not?"

Elizabeth nodded with a touch of sadness. "That's right. It was the biggest mistake of my life.

"But it gets even worse. After I told Arthur that I couldn't do it, he was terribly disappointed. Not long after that, he called to tell me that he had received an offer from a law firm in Tucson specializing in product liability. The offer included a partnership. He said he had accepted the offer and would be leaving Boston at the end of the month. He begged me to come along. I couldn't.

"After Arthur left, I pined for him. I hated my mother and grandmother, who had forced me into a sham marriage and pushed my guilt buttons any time I mentioned Arthur's name."

"Sounds awful," said Cary.

"When Arthur arrived in Tucson, we would talk on the phone at least once a week, and he would send me 'I love you' cards. That went on for several months. But then the calls and the cards stopped coming. I worried, but I didn't want to phone him.

"At about that time, Eliot went on one of his weekend getaways to meet his lover in Provincetown. On Sunday night, it was getting late, and he had not returned. I began to worry, and then the phone rang.

"It was a state police officer calling to inform me that Eliot had been in a serious highway accident and that he had not survived. He was on his way home when he lost control of his car and collided head-on with a moving van. The officer urged me to have a friend or relative drive me to the morgue to identify the body."

"My God," Cary muttered.

"A few days after the funeral, I got hold of myself and phoned Arthur with the news. After offering his condolences, he informed me that he was married and had just returned from a honeymoon in Hawaii."

Elizabeth's face had gone very still, her eyes haunted. "I felt my knees going out from under me. *This all really couldn't have happened,* I said to myself. I didn't know whether to scream or cry. Arthur explained that a senior partner in the firm had invited him to a Passover Seder. The partner's wife, daughter, brother, and sister-in-law were among family members attending.

"The daughter wasn't married, he told me. He said it didn't take long to figure out that there was some matchmaking going on.

"It was a whirlwind courtship, orchestrated by her parents. The two had been to bed a couple of times and they were soon engaged. I asked him if he loved her, and he never answered my question."

Cary said nothing, trying to offer silent comfort with his presence.

"I was devastated. I moped about, often talking to myself. I just couldn't get a grip."

"This is taking a toll on you, just telling me about it," said Cary.

"I'm afraid it has. I need to get a little rest. Can we go back inside?" Elizabeth said, her face drawn. "Thank you for asking about my life," she said.

ONE EVENING JUST BEFORE DINNER, Cary arrived at Elizabeth's room bearing a surprise.

"Is that for me?" Elizabeth asked as he handed her a wine gift bag.

"It's for you," he said. "The money to pay for it came from the spoils of my back-to-back shifts. Remember, I told you I'd be rich after getting all that overtime. The salesman at the wine store told me that it's a very nice Bordeaux. He said it was a Saint-Émilion from the Right Bank. I really didn't understand, but I didn't want to show my ignorance. I hope you'll like it."

"Cary, this is really extravagant," Elizabeth said as she turned to glance at the label.

"You mentioned that often your dinner pals bring a bottle for the table," said Cary. "I thought it would make you feel good if you could contribute, too."

"The wine that you just handed me is the 2007 vintage of Château Canon-la-Gaffelière," Elizabeth said, further studying the label. "There's also Château La Gaffelière, which adjoins the former's estate. At one time, it was a single vineyard, but it was divided in the late eighteenth century and since then has had two ownerships. Depending on the vintage, one of the two might enjoy a slightly higher rating or preference than the other, but both produce quality Bordeaux."

"How do you know so much about wine?" asked Cary, impressed by her knowledge.

"I spent a lot of time with someone who was a wine buff," she replied. "It was Arthur. Arthur and his wine is a story for another time. But I must ask you not to bring me any more such expensive wines."

Later that evening, when Cary went to the dining room to call for Elizabeth, the dinner conversation was just wrapping up. Gordon, in the most effusive manner, said, "Elizabeth, you really know how to pick 'em. Wow! That was some wine. I wouldn't mind drinking that every night."

The others at the table joined in light applause.

"I'm glad you enjoyed it," replied Elizabeth, obviously uneasy about all the fuss.

Once they returned to Elizabeth's room, she was more relaxed.

"I'll be off at eleven and be back to read to you if you're not already asleep," said Cary.

"With the dinner and the wine, I think I'll fall asleep almost instantly," said Elizabeth. "Could you help me get ready for bed now?"

After making sure that she was settled in, Cary bade her good night and headed down the hall to attend to his other patients.

•••┌──┐•••

On Saturday, as usual, Cary called for Elizabeth at about 2:30 p.m. and wheeled her to a shady spot in the garden.

"If you're up to it, I'd like to know what happened after Arthur told you that he'd gotten married. I remember we had to quit there," he said.

"It's something I'd almost like to forget," Elizabeth replied, studying the slow-moving clouds. "I could understand why he acted as he did. He figured I'd never be able to break free, and the opportunity for him presented itself. I blamed myself and my reluctance. I could have been Mrs. Arthur Keyes if I had only had the courage to act sooner.

"Several months passed and we exchanged a few letters. I wrote to him at a post office box that he had secretly rented. His wife didn't have a clue. Then one day he phoned me. It was in 1950, and long-distance calls were still very expensive. He couldn't risk phoning from his law office, so he called from a friend's.

"He told me he couldn't live without me. He asked me to move to Tucson as soon as I could arrange it. He would see that I had a job and a place to live. We could be together often, but it would have to be without his wife's knowledge."

"I assume you agreed, otherwise you wouldn't be here in Tucson," Cary said.

"Yes, and I knew it was wrong," Elizabeth admitted. "But I wanted him as much as he wanted me. So I packed up what I had, didn't tell my mother I was leaving, and drove to Tucson in my old car. I decided I would write to her after I arrived. Otherwise, I feared I'd lose my nerve."

She let out a long breath. "When I arrived, Arthur had leased a furnished apartment for me. The refrigerator was filled with groceries. Wine, stemware, plates, and candles were on the dining room table. I was hoping that this was the start of having a near normal life together."

Something in her grim tone prompted him to ask, "But it wasn't, was it?" Cary asked tenderly.

"No," said Elizabeth. "From that day on, there would never come a time when Arthur could come home to me. There were promises that he would leave his wife that he knew he couldn't keep. I would be hopeful, but only to see my hopes dashed. All the time we spent together over the years was stolen time. We could never be seen together in public.

"As you might imagine, it was a far from ideal situation. Arthur would be required to lie or, at best, stretch or twist the truth to come up with reasons why he wasn't at home. There were purported business meetings with a 'Monty' in Phoenix or a 'Drew' in Prescott that never existed." She sighed. "Those nonexistent out-of-town 'meetings' were precious because there was no hiding, no having to keep our eyes on the clock.

"Back home in Tucson, we were always aware that we had only so many more minutes for love or for talking. And oh, did we talk. Or maybe just another glass of wine. But it was always 'Beat the Clock.' I often referred to those one-hour visits as just that." Elizabeth shook her head ruefully. "It was like being contestants in a race. Having to truncate your deepest feelings, carnal and otherwise, and not express what was in your heart and soul because the miserable clock was ticking away our time together."

"I know how that must feel," Cary commiserated.

"We never, ever had enough time together. Even when he told his wife he was having dinner with a 'client' we could maybe squeeze out three hours for ourselves. Half for dinner, half for making love."

A faint blush rose to her cheeks. It made her look almost girlish. "When I didn't prepare dinner, it was a takeout from a nearby restaurant. On those occasions, Arthur would ask the server which entrée he could get out of the kitchen the fastest.

"He would have to leave eventually—no matter the circumstances—and that was the worst.

"There was the pillow beside mine with the hollow in it where he had rested. The wonderful smell of him on the bed sheets was intoxicating. I wrapped myself in a towel—still damp—that he had used after taking a quick shower before he went home. Anything to prolong the scent of him. To prolong the proof that I hadn't imagined the whole thing. That he really existed."

Cary twined his fingers with hers. The depth of her passion surprised him—though perhaps it shouldn't have. She was a complex woman with many layers. One whom it would take some time to truly know.

At that moment, the two were approached by a well-dressed, middle-aged woman. They quickly disengaged their hands. Cary didn't think the woman had noticed. She looked apologetic as she addressed Elizabeth. "Pardon me, I'm sorry if I'm interrupting, but could I ask you a question or two?"

The woman went on to explain that she was in Tucson to find a place for her mother, who was no longer able to live independently.

"I'm Clarissa Downing, and I'm here from New York for only a few days. My husband and I live in Westchester," she said. "I was wondering if you can recommend this facility. Whatever you can tell me would be helpful."

"I'm Elizabeth Gardner, and this is my friend Cary Branscombe," she replied graciously, extending her hand, which the woman accepted. "Cary works here, but this is his day off."

Cary gave a friendly smile of acknowledgment.

"In answer to your question, I suppose you can say that if one must be in a nursing home, this is probably as good as you're going to find here in Tucson," Elizabeth said thoughtfully. "The management is caring and sensitive to the wishes and needs of its patients."

"I do appreciate this," the woman said. "And I love your floppy hat."

After the woman left, Cary turned to Elizabeth and asked, "Do you know why the woman chose you to ask instead of any of the other patients or their visitors who are sitting out here right now?"

"I have no idea," Elizabeth replied. "Do I appear a soft touch?"

"No," replied Cary. "But the lady knew class when she saw it."

Elizabeth's cheeks pinked again at the compliment.

It was a relaxed weekend during which Cary visited Elizabeth on both days. She shared more of her life story with Cary, detailing how when she hadn't been able to find a college teaching job, she settled for a lower-paying position as a librarian.

"It was at least an opportunity to work," she said. "I could not abide the thought of staying in that apartment all day."

Over the years, and after taking some night courses, she had worked her way up to the position of reference librarian, which she enjoyed. But when she reached retirement age, her job came to an end, and she found herself with a calendar that contained too many blank pages.

"I could live on the pension and Social Security," she said, "but I couldn't handle the boredom, even with Arthur stopping by almost every day. So I began getting involved in volunteer work, tutoring and that sort of thing. I found it rewarding."

But when Arthur died of a sudden heart attack, she was devastated, she said. And because of her advancing years, she detailed how difficult it had become to commute to the volunteer locations.

"I became a prisoner in my apartment. Failing health and nothing I could look forward to," she confided. "That's when the social worker discovered me and arranged for me to come here."

Cary now had a full understanding. Although she had never expressed bitterness or blame, he could see how this woman could feel that she had been cheated and relegated to playing second fiddle in both her marriage and her relationship with Arthur.

On Monday, when Cary reported for work, Marge Cochran flagged him down.

"Paul wants to see you in his office," she said with a knowing look. "I suppose you can guess what it's about."

Moments later, Cary stood before Paul Giroux's desk.

"This won't come as a surprise to you, Cary, but I received a phone call this morning from regional," said Paul. "They were contacted by headquarters, which had received two complaints related to you and Elizabeth Gardner.

"I told them that I was fully aware of the situation. That whatever time you've spent in her company has been on your off time and that you've shown no favoritism as far as allocating your work time between your patients.

"But the answer I received is that although you've done nothing wrong, it's all about *appearance*. I was given no choice but to give you two options. They offered to transfer you to our Arundel Gardens facility on the northwest side. That would allow you to come here and visit Ms. Gardner whenever you wish." He sighed heavily, clearly unhappy. "Or you must resign."

Cary wasn't surprised. He'd been half expecting this for some time, though he did wonder who had filed the complaints.

"Can I give you my answer tomorrow?" he asked calmly. "I need to check on some things when I leave here today."

"No problem," said Paul. "I can hold them off for another day. But, Cary, I don't want to lose you. Please keep that in mind."

• • • ⌐ ¬ • • •

The next day, Cary was back in Paul's office.

"I've made my decision," he said. "I'm sorry, but I'm going to have to resign."

Paul frowned. "But what will you do? How is that going to solve the problem?"

"Well, you know I rent a small casita not far from here," said Cary. "It's owned by a retired couple who live in the main house in front. The wife is related to my Aunt Joan's husband. I spoke with them about it, and they said it would be okay if I wanted to move Elizabeth into my place. I'll give her the bedroom, and I'll sleep in the living room."

He firmed his voice. "As far as the legalities are concerned, there are none. I've spoken about all this with Elizabeth. In principle, we're on the same page, although there are times when she's unsure.

"She's not under guardianship and she has no conservator. She's on her own and free to go wherever she wishes. She knows I'll take good care of her."

Paul leaned back in his chair. He looked profoundly disappointed, but he'd always been a good boss and seemed to realize that arguing would be pointless.

"Cary, it might not be what I'd do, but who am I to second guess you? I don't need to tell you that there's always a job for you here."

He stood up and held out a hand. Cary shook it. "I wish you both well. And please, stay in touch."

Cary went to Elizabeth and broke the news. He had discussed the options with her on the previous evening and though she was in favor of the plan, she had some misgivings. Although she had told Cary earlier that she couldn't bear it if he were to be away from her, she nevertheless felt that she would be imposing on him.

"When I spoke with Barb and Lee last night, they were not only agreeable but very supportive," said Cary. "I need to move some things around and find some furniture. I also want to spruce up the place a bit."

"Wait!" Elizabeth blurted out. "I can't process this so quickly. I need some time to think this through. Can we talk about this?"

"Of course we can. And perhaps you see another option," Cary replied. "I've gone over this in my head a dozen times and can't think of anything better. I've already got a job lined up where I can work from home and not have to leave you alone."

"Cary, you think of everything. I can't tell you how grateful I am," said Elizabeth. "But you must understand that this isn't easy for me. All the years during my relationship with Arthur, I had this feeling that I was a 'kept woman' even though I had a full-time job. I had my pride, and overall, it was uncomfortable.

"I really want to say yes, and if you can help me to do that, I believe I can work my way through this. And please don't answer until you've heard what I'm going to say.

"First, I want to help with the living costs. When I move out of here, I'll be able to again receive both my state pension and Social Security benefits because Medicaid will no longer be paying my nursing home bill. Those living costs include groceries, utilities, rent, and incidentals.

"And as you already know, I don't have an aged mother whom I need to support. If I did, she would be 120 or even older," she said with a smile.

"Maybe that's better for us," said Cary, amused. "I believe I can say with some amount of certainty that your mother would not have approved of me. Anyway, my answer to your conditions is an unqualified 'yes.'"

"I'm so relieved," she said. "I can't tell you how much this was weighing on me." The tension left her face, which lit up with eagerness and new life. "Now I'm excited. Yes, I know it's a bit late and the scope is limited, but there is so much I can now look forward to. You and me—together."

"I'm with you," said Cary. "I'll be grateful for every moment that we can spend together. Sometimes I ask myself where we are in this relationship, and I provide my own answer that says that the overture hasn't yet been played."

"And I have just one more minor issue," she said. "You mentioned renting a hospital bed for me. Please don't. Before I came here, I slept in my own bed in the apartment. It was never a problem. I realize that facilities such as this one must have all its rooms equipped with these beds, but it would be a negative for me if I were to have one at the casita. Should the occasion arise when I would need one, we can consider it at that time."

"It's a deal," replied Cary. "And it makes practical sense, too."

"If nobody's watching, I'd like to give you a hug," said Elizabeth. "You are my prince, and I want you to know that," she added excitedly.

She embraced him. He smelled a hint of her perfume, her downy-soft hair brushing his cheek. It felt like coming home.

Getting Ready

PROCRASTINATION WAS NEW to Cary, and he didn't like it. Here he was on a Saturday morning exactly one week away from Elizabeth's scheduled move-in, and he'd done nothing to prepare. There were things she would need. He wanted her to be comfortable in the casita, but most of all he wanted her to feel welcome.

Those were his intentions, but so far there was no bed for her to sleep in, no chair for her to sit in, and not even a set of new towels just for her.

Setting up to work from home for his new call center job had taken many hours; more hours than he had expected. His employer had provided a desk, a padded, ergonomically-designed office chair, a computer, two monitors, two state-of-the-art headsets—one was an emergency back-up, the technician explained—and so on. And of course, a high-speed Internet connection. The manuals they gave him to read in hard copy and online were voluminous and detailed, requiring his time and concentration as well.

But today, he had to put all of that on hold and prepare the adobe brick casita for Elizabeth's arrival.

By 6 a.m., Cary was on the move so he could work in his run early to beat the desert heat. It took him less than five minutes to reach the path that ran alongside the Rillito River, which was a dry riverbed most of the year. If he ran east toward the Pantano Wash for about half an hour and doubled back, it would be enough for his body to trigger the endorphins that he would need for the day ahead.

He varied his speed as his body dictated, alternating between jogging and running. It was sunrise, and the open space around him made him feel that the world had been revitalized overnight.

What sleep did for Cary, the night had done for nature, and he felt part of it. He connected with the earth as his feet pounded the ground and began to feel invigorated as he breathed hard to fill his lungs. His running became rhythmic, and his exertion triggered the sought endorphins.

World events, politics, strife, problems of all sorts—even his lengthy to-do list—were temporarily set aside.

Cottonwood trees growing on a quarter-horse ranch bordering the river towered over all the other trees in sight. A pair of Cooper's hawks soared above, performing a ballet in the sky. Mexican gold poppies grew here and there, providing spots of color among the strips of green grass and weeds in the middle of the riverbed. Three coyotes on the prowl trotted up the bank and crossed Cary's path, but not close enough to cause him concern.

Cary had it right. While running, and even after returning to the casita, he felt the surge of energy he had anticipated. He downed a couple of glasses of water to rehydrate and then headed for a quick shower. Coffee, a banana, and a blueberry muffin made for his breakfast.

While he ate, he also tapped away on his laptop searching for stores that sold used furniture. There was a slew of listings, and many located nearby. It became clear that the potential sources for some budget shopping were abundant.

He quickly picked up on the fact that Tucson was loaded with commercial resale shops as well as charity-sponsored ones. Craigslist offered even more choices from private sellers listing garage sales. An ad for a moving sale on Copper Street appeared promising.

Saturday was the big day for weekend garage sales. By Sunday, there would be only leftovers to choose from.

Almost ready to head out on the search, Cary phoned Elizabeth.

There was no answer until the fourth ring, when he heard a familiar cultured voice answer with unfamiliar formality.

"Room A-26, Nurse Ratched speaking."

Cary let out a hoot of laughter. "*Elizabeth!* Is that *you*?"

"Yes, it is I," she replied in mock surprise. "What's wrong? You sound befuddled."

"I had no idea you had such a wicked sense of humor."

"On occasion," she said in a mischievous tone.

"Wow! I've just discovered a new side of you."

"I consider that a compliment, Cary. Wait just a moment, please. I need a sip of water."

When Elizabeth returned to the phone, she asked, "How's your day going? You said you had a lot to do."

"Just getting ready to jump in the truck and go scope out some garage sales and second-hand furniture stores and find a bed for you. Somehow, I don't think you'd be comfortable in a sleeping bag on the floor."

"That's not an experience I've ever had," she remarked dryly, "but I imagine you're correct. Do you enjoy shopping, Cary?"

"Not at all," he conceded. "Some folks consider it entertainment, I guess, but not me. It's a means to an end. My goal is to transform my bachelor-pad into a fit place for you to live. It's not there yet, but I'm making progress."

Elizabeth chuckled. "Cary, dear, you're so kind to want to share your home with me. I'm still awed at your invitation to come and live with you. And I'm absolutely amazed at myself for accepting."

He could picture her smiling as she added, "Is this a sign of senility?"

"What it is, Elizabeth, is wisdom. And courage. It's a sense of adventure that few women would have in a similar situation."

"You mean *at my age*."

"We agreed not to use that nasty three-letter word," he said lightly. "And now I gotta go or there won't be anything left to buy. Talk to you later."

In no time, he was behind the wheel of his red Mazda pickup, his shopping list on the seat beside him. He played radio roulette until he heard something he liked on a country and western station. Cary drummed his fingers on the steering wheel and sang along to "Take Your Time," by Sam Hunt.

On Lee Street, a sign grabbed his attention:

It was obviously homemade, in big kid-font letters on a huge cardboard box placed on the curb. There was another just like it across the street. The effort and enthusiasm in the lettering made Cary smile, and that seemed like a good enough reason to make a change of plans. Forget whatever treasures were waiting elsewhere. He was stopping at this sale first. Cary always preferred to do business with real people.

Cars, SUVs, and a few pickups were already parked on both sides of the street and on the next block as well. A good turnout, and it wasn't yet eight o'clock.

He slowed down and parked behind a Jeep he was following. The new arrivals, including Cary, exited their vehicles and headed en masse toward the house holding the sale. The neighborhood was typical of the 1960s and consisted of one-story houses made of wire-cut brick, each with an attached one-car garage.

Black and yellow caution tape cordoned off the driveway. It looped around a branch of a creosote bush, then down to wind around the mailbox at the end of the driveway. The three-inch barrier tape did its job. It kept the lookers out of the display area until the yard sale's organizers were ready for them.

A blond-haired boy of about nine or ten came out carrying a box of swimming pool noodles that were stacked vertically and longer than he was tall. Cary assumed that the boy was Ethan, and the gray-haired woman wearing glasses, in tan slacks, a flowered top, and a red carpenter's apron, was most likely Grandma.

Grandma looked at her wristwatch—this was not a smart-phone family equipped with digital time devices—and leaned over to speak to Ethan. Whatever she said prompted him to disappear into the house.

Meanwhile, potential buyers, including Cary, milled about, getting as close as possible for a better view of the sale items. They stretched this way and that, jostling for a look at the wares.

Some folks were impatient and not shy about letting everyone know it. One man with a booming voice bellowed, "Open up! I've got five more sales to go to this morning."

Quickly, an older woman in the crowd retorted, "Don't let us keep you."

Peals of laughter rang out, and Cary couldn't help but laugh, too. That wasn't rude, he thought, it was justice—served up hot and instantly by the de facto jury of his peers.

At that moment, Ethan appeared again in the garage. He advanced, right arm behind his back, until he was in the middle of the driveway. Once in position, he brought his arm around and lifted a bugle to his lips and proceeded to play an extremely loud rendition of *Reveille*. The gathered crowd broke into cheers.

The youngster grinned and took a bow to a round of applause.

Grandma snipped here and there, allowing the caution tape to fall to the ground and the crowd rushed in. The sale was on.

Optimism was in the air. Items for sale were almost obscured by the crush of would-be buyers swarming around. Some zeroed in on merchandise that had earlier aroused their interest and snapped it up.

Cary walked past the pots and pans, toys, puzzles, clothing, empty fish bowls and hamster cages, cookbooks, and tools. He had his eye on a certain chair that he wanted to check out. It was a living room armchair with a high back that looked comfortable. He thought it might suit Elizabeth well.

The price tag, safety-pinned to the cushion, was marked $40. He sat down in it and that was all it took for him to make up his mind.

Minutes later, he carried the chair, which was heavier than he expected, across the street and loaded it onto the bed of the Mazda. Cary hadn't tried to bargain or ask for a discount and would have been embarrassed to do so. He had enjoyed the whole experience enormously, which he told both Grandma and Ethan, inspiring smiles all around.

He lauded their organizational skills and commented especially about their "marketing and publicity department that turned out those great signs," which caused Ethan to smile even more as he hopped from one foot to the other with excitement.

Cary couldn't wait to tell Elizabeth about the "production" he had just witnessed. He knew she would have absolutely loved it as much as he had. And he really hoped she would like her new chair.

On to the Copper Street sale he had originally set out for. The prices must have been low and buyer-friendly because none of the items mentioned in the ad remained. So Cary moved on.

His next stop was at a tiny ranch out east off a dirt road. A plank sign identified the spread as "Gabby's." The house was old and rundown. There was a dirt front yard for parking and a hitching post nearby. Around to the side, he saw a barn, a chicken coop, and a corral with a bay horse standing under a drooping desert willow.

The veranda was as wide as the house and filled with all kinds of old furniture. A retired oak church pew was occupied by a large, middle-aged, barrel-chested man outfitted in Levi's, a western-style shirt with snaps instead of buttons, cowboy boots, and a big black cowboy hat. A perky tan Chihuahua sat beside his master.

The dog yipped as Cary walked up the steps to the porch, and only ceased when the man ordered, "Silencio!"

The man didn't speak to Cary or acknowledge him in any way. His attention was focused on a six-pack cooler at his feet. He pulled out a frosty can of Budweiser and popped the top.

The nightstand and chests that had been advertised were still there. One chest was pine and the other walnut, and both had three deep drawers that Elizabeth could access from her wheelchair. Cary liked the pine chest best by far. Its drawers slid in and out effortlessly, like they were on runners of silk. Elizabeth would appreciate that for certain.

He examined the little cherry table and liked it, too. It had clean lines, one drawer and a medium-sized top with plenty of room for a lamp and a water glass or some doodads, although he truly doubted Elizabeth was the doodad type.

The drawer pull was a round wooden knob. Cary pulled the drawer completely out of the stand, observing the great condition of the drawer bottom and the excellent dovetailing on the drawer. Then he wondered . . . he turned the drawer upside down and tried to insert it back into the stand. It went in and fit perfectly—a mark of a fine furniture maker.

Cary smiled and remembered learning that little trick from Mr. Kramer, his high school shop teacher in his freshman year.

Cary realized the owner had been watching him and was making eye contact.

"The pine chest and this little table might work for me. What's your price for both of them?" he asked.

"It's a hundred for the chest and seventy-five for the table," said the owner, not unpleasantly.

Cary nodded. "So, one seventy-five all together?"

Cary ran his hand over the top of the pine chest again, before returning to the dinged-up one that he didn't like at all. It was made of walnut, darkened with age and had multiple gouges and scratches all over.

"How much for this one?" he asked.

"Eighty bucks."

Again, Cary nodded, and moseyed on to other pieces, taking his time.

Two cars drove in. The occupants got out and wandered around without saying much or buying anything. Again, the Chihuahua yipped until told not to, and the man ignored the shoppers and concentrated on another beer.

Meanwhile, Cary bided his time turning chairs upside down to look at the construction, and inspected the stretchers to make sure each one was tight. He even carried an old Sears Roebuck oak kitchen chair out into the sun to see the true color of the wood.

The owner watched him sideways, never looking at him straight on. He seemed to pay no attention to whatever piece Cary was giving a once over.

"You doing okay?" the owner asked, after Cary had been poking around for the better part of an hour.

Cary used his shirt sleeve to wipe the sweat off his forehead as he answered. "Nope, I'm not," he replied.

"What's wrong?" asked the owner, suddenly alert and focused.

"Here's my situation," Cary said, as though he were imparting classified information. "My lady is moving in with me in a few days and I know she'd like that pine chest a whole lot. The problem is that I'm between jobs right now." He stopped talking to let that information settle in.

"So that makes me partial to the walnut chest; but only because of the price," he said. "I really prefer the pine chest."

The owner crimped his lips and let out a deep breath. "Maybe we can work something out here. What about ninety dollars for the pine? With seventy-five for the little stand. That's only a hundred and sixty-five all told."

"Sounds better. Let me see here," Cary said, digging into both pockets of his jeans and pulling out clumps of wadded up cash.

He piled the money in a heap on top of a marble washstand and tried to smooth out the crumpled bills with the side of his hand.

He made little stacks of like denominations, which were mostly singles, a few fives and tens, and one lonesome twenty.

Cary knew from experience that no one likes to be told "take it or leave it." By doing it this way, the seller feels like he's giving you a break. It's a choice he's making. He doesn't feel like you're putting him or his merchandise down.

The owner gave Cary's handling of the money his full attention.

"Gotta fill the tank at the first gas station I see when I get back to town," Cary explained. He picked up the twenty and returned it to his pocket. He glanced over at the owner and received an almost imperceptible, solitary nod.

The rest of the currency on the table lay there until Cary picked it up. He counted aloud. The tens, then the fives and singles.

"That's all I've got—a hundred and fifty-two dollars," Cary said, in a dejected tone.

The owner let out a big breath and threw his hands up in the air. "Oh, hell. It's too hot to stand here and dicker over a few bucks."

With that pronouncement, he took off his black cowboy hat and raked the pile of wrinkled bills into it. He extended his hand toward Cary and declared, "Deal!"

"Thanks, Gabby," Cary said, as they shook hands.

The man chuckled. "No problem, partner, but I'm Gene. The dog's name is Gabby."

Back in the truck again, Cary felt the pressure to go to yet another sale. He decided that he needed to make more progress today.

The next stop on his list was on South Craycroft Road. The advertisement had offered "Miscellaneous household furniture, pictures, and odds and ends. All nice."

He kept looking for the street number listed in the ad, but this was primarily a business district. No, he hadn't made a mistake.

A sign over a business on the west side of the road read "Buddy's Billiards," and displayed the street number he was seeking. It was mid-afternoon, and the parking lot was almost full. Most were older model cars and a few pickups.

Inside, it was a typical pool room. A middle-aged woman, attractive, with a blonde ponytail, was going around with a tray delivering drinks. She passed Cary and smiled. "Hi, be with you in a sec."

And so she was. "You here for pool or lunch?" she asked.

"Neither, actually. I saw an ad about some furniture for sale."

"That's my ad. I'm Blondie," she said and pointed to her hair. "Bet you couldn't guess," she laughed. "I need a few minutes and then I'll show you what I've got for sale. You want something to drink while you wait?"

"No thanks," he said. "Take your time. I'll wait at the bar."

Blondie flashed him a smile. "Won't be long," she said, and went back to her customers.

Just as Cary had guessed after seeing the parked cars, it was an older clientele. He was sure that almost everyone in Buddy's, except for Blondie, was receiving a Social Security benefit every month.

A few minutes later, Blondie tapped Cary on the shoulder. "Follow me," she said.

She led the way through a back room full of billiard and bar supplies and out a rear door to a back parking lot. Just beyond it was a building that might have been a garage or a storage room. Blondie thumbed the combination rotators of the padlock, pulled the locking bar open, then stood aside.

"Whatever you're looking for, I've probably got it," she said.

The building had a musty smell and was stacked with crates, boxes, and household furniture plus some restaurant tables and chairs.

"I'm looking for a bed," Cary said.

"Not a single bed, I bet," Blondie said, as she made eye contact.

Cary shook his head. "Nope. And not a king or queen size, either. No room for one."

"Well, it's your lucky day. I've got a double bed. I think the wood is cherry, but I'm not sure. I'm asking $150 for it, and I'll throw in the mattress and innerspring if you want."

Cary grinned. "I do want," he said. "If you had some new sheets and a blanket, I'd buy those, too. But I better tell you first that I can't give you cash because I spent it all at the last garage sale. Will you take a check? You can trust me that it won't bounce."

"No problem," Blondie replied. "You look honest. How about a hundred for all of it?" she asked, moving closer.

Cary was puzzled. "What happened that I just got a discount without even asking for one?"

"Let me be frank and I hope you're not shocked. Buddy died five years ago . . ."

"I'm sorry."

"Thanks, but don't be. I'm over it. I'm pushing fifty and the only men I ever meet are the ones who come in here to shoot pool—and they're all old enough to be my dad."

Cary sensed what was coming next, but he couldn't be sure.

"You haven't run out the door yet, so you must not be too shocked so far, so I'll go on," she said, laying her palm on Cary's arm. "Life's too damn short to play games. We're both adults and I know I must have about ten years on you, but you're a real attractive guy, and I don't care. I'll be free by seven o'clock. Buy me dinner tonight and let's see how it goes."

Cary looked down for a moment, contemplating how to handle this. He didn't want to offend her. At last, he lifted his head and looked directly into Blondie's eyes.

"Hey, I hear you. And I think it's great that you come right out and say what you want."

"I hear a *but* coming," she muttered.

Cary nodded. "Yep. Here it is, flat out. I'm involved with someone, and my lady is moving in with me next weekend. So . . ."

Blondie laughed. "So! So pay me and take this junk outta here and come back and see me when you've flung your fling with whoever the lucky girl is."

He quickly wrote her a check, which she folded and slid into a pocket. At the door, she stopped and looked back. Cary touched a finger to his forehead and then toward her, as a goodbye salute. Blondie shook her head, smiling, though not so brightly anymore.

"I don't even know your name," she said wistfully.

"I'm Cary." He cocked a sardonic brow. "It's on the check."

She rolled her eyes. "Of course it is. Well, it was good to meet you, Cary. I'll definitely remember you."

• • • ⌐ ⌐ • • •

The parking area at Bogie's was nearly filled, but Cary managed to find a space between two SUVs where he could keep an eye on the truck through the restaurant's windows.

As usual, Jake, the owner, was casually but nicely dressed. For a man in his fifties, he still cut a good figure, and his knife-edged khakis and navy polo shirt—no logo or designer alligator showing—enabled him to blend in with his customers. Only his expression gave away that he was the owner. He had a serious but not unpleasant demeanor. A tiny furrow etched on his forehead stood ready to grow into a frown if things weren't going the way he thought they should.

He perched on the last stool at the end of the bar, his back to the wall, where he regularly kept an eye on things. A glass of diet soda and the local newspaper lay in front of him. He saw Cary approach and nodded. Cary returned the greeting and chose a spot near Jake.

"I saw you drive up," Jake said. "What's all that junk in your truck? You picking up a few extra bucks moving furniture?"

"Guess you haven't heard. My lady's moving in with me next weekend, so I needed to pick up a few things."

"Your *lady?* I had you pegged as a monk or a confirmed bachelor—maybe even a poet. A guy with both feet planted firmly in midair."

Cary laughed. "You're about half right. I'm no monk or poet, but I may be a confirmed dreamer."

"Is this somebody you met at work?" asked Jake. "One of those cute nurses?"

"Her name is Elizabeth, and she's . . ."

"*Elizabeth.*" He repeated the name softly, drawing it out in an approving tone. "That's a nice old-fashioned name."

Cary smiled and nodded. "Yeah, it is. And Elizabeth is a nice—no, she's an absolutely wonderful—old-fashioned girl."

"Congratulations, Cary!" Maria, a server, chimed in.

"I'm happy for you, but now that I'm out of the doghouse with Jake, I got to get back to acting like I work here," she said, heading out with a tray full of orders.

Jake, with one elbow on the bar, turned again to look out the window at Cary's truck.

"Doesn't your girlfriend have anything she's bringing with her? You got a chair . . . and looks like a headboard and some slats for a bed." He paused. "Is that a mattress out there?"

"Yeah, I got a good deal on it," said Cary.

"Do you know these people? The ones where you bought this stuff?"

Cary shook his head. "Never saw them before. Just stopped because of an online ad."

Jake called Maria over. "Maria, check with the kitchen to see what's holding up Cary's order, and bring him whatever he wants to drink. All on the house today," he said, slapping Cary on the back.

"Thanks, Jake," replied Cary, "but I haven't ordered yet. A hot pastrami on rye with mustard and some onion rings sounds good, and some coffee, too."

Jake waved away the thanks with his hand like it was a wand. "It's to celebrate the improvement in your social life," he said, smiling. "By the way, is it okay if I borrow your truck for five minutes?" He scooped Cary's keys up from the bar without waiting for an answer.

Surprised, Cary watched Jake go through the dining room's double doors into the parking lot and head for the Mazda. Jake had always been friendly, and Cary had had a lot of good talks with him, but this was the first time he'd ever offered to comp his meal. Nor had Jake ever asked to borrow his truck.

As promised, a few minutes later, a relish tray arrived. Cary was ravenous. He loaded a cracker with a layer from the cheddar cheese ball covered with roasted almonds. Then he went for the pickled cauliflower, followed by another mega cheese and cracker. He was eyeing the olives and carrot sticks when Maria returned and set his order in front of him.

"There you go," she said. "Enjoy!"

Cary picked up his sandwich and started thinking again about what he wanted to get done before time ran out. The list was long, and he still couldn't quite believe he was fortunate enough to have persuaded Elizabeth to accept his offer to live with him.

He was half-finished eating when Jake returned and sat down beside him. He dropped Cary's keys on the bar and slid them over to him.

"Thanks, Cary. All done."

Cary wondered what Jake meant. What was done? Why did he need to borrow his truck at all? He swiveled to look out the window for his truck. Sure enough, it was in plain view, exactly where he had parked it earlier. But something was different. The truck's payload didn't look nearly so full anymore.

"Jake!" Cary shouted, bolting off the bar stool. "The mattress is gone! What happened to it? What's going on?" His voice rose. Customers turned to stare.

Jake lowered his voice. "Calm down, Cary." He cast his gaze over the dining room. "You'll scare off the paying customers."

But Cary didn't care who overheard. "So you steal my mattress and want to call it even because you've thrown me a sandwich?"

Furious, heat rushed to his face. He left the bar and hurried to the window to get a better view of his pillaged truck. The slats and wooden headboard were visible, and so was the chair, the pine chest and cherry bedside table; but the mattress was definitely no longer on the truck.

Cary returned to the bar as Maria stopped by to see if he needed anything else, but Jake warned her off.

"Sorry, Maria, bad timing. I need to have a word with Cary."

Maria raised her eyebrows but took the hint and departed.

"A *word*?" Cary repeated angrily. "Let's make that an *explanation, Jake. That's what's called for here."

"Come sit down, Cary," Jake said, patting the empty stool beside him. "Finish your lunch. Just relax."

Cary shot Jake a dark look before he obliged. He slid onto the stool, still tense.

"Okay, Jake, what's going on? I don't get it." Cary pushed the plate away, his appetite gone. He concentrated to keep his voice down. He wasn't trying to make a scene, but neither did he care if this discussion morphed into one.

"Question number one: Where's my mattress? It was in the truck when you borrowed it ten minutes ago."

"That ratty mattress that you think so much of is out back behind the restaurant. One of the cooks helped me load it into the dumpster."

"*What?*" said Cary, loud enough that a few patrons turned to look.

"Don't get any ideas about retrieving it, either. We emptied all the wet kitchen garbage on top of it just to make sure you wouldn't drag it out of there."

Cary sat down again. He rested his elbows on the bar and buried his face in his hands. "I can't believe this," he said, his voice muffled. His anger was abating, but not the shock of the missing mattress.

"It's simple," said Jake. "And I'll tell you why. Just don't interrupt me. Okay? Here you are running around trying to get ready for your girlfriend."

Cary corrected him. "Elizabeth!"

"Get ready for Elizabeth but let me ask you this. How old are you and how many beds have you bought in your life?"

"I'm thirty-four and ..." He stopped mid-sentence. After a few seconds, Cary's expression softened. "I guess this is the first. Either the apartments I rented came furnished, or friends would give me one from their attic or somewhere."

"I thought so," Jake said. "No need to feel embarrassed. You've got zilch experience in this department, and you made a mistake. It's no big deal but let me tell you where you went wrong."

He leaned forward, speaking gently. "Cary, the bed itself isn't a problem. It's the mattress that's the problem. You never, ever buy a mattress from strangers, no matter how nice they are or how cheap it is, or even if it's free. You buy a mattress from a store or from a friend. That's it. No exceptions! The reason is simple: *vermin!*"

Cary frowned. "But I looked at the mattress and I didn't see any bugs."

"Cary, bedbugs are nocturnal. In the daytime they hide. You need a flashlight and a magnifying glass. You pull back the seams, look there and under all the buttons if it's a tufted mattress. Bedbugs are tiny and they bite. They live on blood. What a welcome that would be for your girlfriend."

These facts, all new to Cary, were sobering. The thought of Elizabeth sleeping on a mattress infested with bedbugs was too terrible to even contemplate. His self-image as the man who was going to show her the utmost loving care was disintegrating by the minute.

"Jake, I had no clue about any of that," he said in a chastened tone. "I looked for stains and sniffed it for odors, but I thought that the only place you'd run into bedbugs would be in some dumpy fleabag hotel."

"Listen, Cary, here's the deal. I'll ask around. I know a lot of people. I'll find someone—someone I know—who won't try to peddle a pest-ridden mattress, and I'll give you a call."

Cary extended his hand. "Thanks, Jake. I owe you."

The Casita

THE NEXT SATURDAY CAME, and Cary arrived at Fairfield bright and early. Elizabeth had finished breakfast. For the drive to the casita, she wore white ankle-length pants and a blue-and-white-striped top. He greeted her with a kiss on the cheek.

"The van should be arriving in a few minutes," Cary announced. "I have your two suitcases ready. There's a wheelchair, which we now own, on board.

I got a really good deal on it. Only slightly used and very serviceable.

"Also, Bob Jackson, who operates the transport van, gave me a break on the move. He owed me a couple of favors."

"Cary, if I were on a lifeboat, I'd want you to be in charge," said Elizabeth with a smile that lightened his heart—and eased his nerves.

"Thanks, that's nice to hear." He returned the smile. "Oh, and in case you're wondering, I said all my goodbyes here on my final day on the job last Friday."

In a few moments, there was a knock on the door. It was Bob Jackson. Cary introduced the two and within a few minutes Elizabeth was seated securely in her wheelchair inside the van.

It was a short drive to the casita. While Bob Jackson carried in the two suitcases, Cary wheeled Elizabeth along a path on the side of the main house leading to the casita which was situated in the rear. As soon as she caught sight of it, her eyes widened.

"Cary, this is delightful. It's charming!" she exclaimed.

As they neared the front door, Cary caught sight of his landlady, Barb, and her husband, Lee, advancing toward them.

"Here come the neighbors. They want to meet you," he said.

"I'm Barb and this is my husband, Lee," Barb said. "I imagine you've heard Cary talk about his Aunt Joan. Well, her husband Eldon is my brother. We're so glad to see you leave that nursing home. It's quiet here, especially in the casita—it's so far off the street. No one will wake you in the middle of the night."

"I'm so happy to meet you," Elizabeth said in her usual gracious manner.

"Do let us know if you need anything," Barb said. "We're in the house in front, just a few steps away. Now, we should let you two get settled."

Before Cary and Elizabeth entered the casita, she commented, "Awfully nice folks, aren't they. Don't you wish everyone could be like them?"

Elizabeth took a deep breath. She turned her head and looked up at

Cary. He smiled down at her and put his hands on her shoulders.

"Welcome home," he said standing behind her. "The casita and I have both been waiting for you."

Elizabeth, filled with emotion, reached up and squeezed his hand.

"Take me inside, Cary. Please. I can't wait another moment."

As they neared the front door, Elizabeth noticed a ristra of red chili peppers hung on the wall alongside the entrance—a southwestern tradition.

Cary held the screen door open, pushed the wheelchair across the threshold and into the living room. The walls were ochre, rough plastered with mud and bits of straw embedded randomly.

The floors were oxblood-red concrete. A beehive fireplace was located in the corner of the living room. Two casement windows were on the left and built-in bookshelves stood on either side of the fireplace.

"It's such a cozy room," Elizabeth commented. She pointed toward the fireplace. "Is that my new chair?" she asked.

"That's it."

"I love it," she said beaming.

"That's the one I found at the garage sale with the cute kid who played the bugle."

"Yes, I remember. That was the 'Ethan and Grandma' sale that you told me about."

"And now to the kitchen," said Cary. He turned to the right and immediately they were there. An old, wide enamel sink was on one wall with some built-in cabinets on the other.

Elizabeth couldn't quite decide if the kitchen was quaint or just old-fashioned. Whichever, it was certainly from another era. Circa 1940s or earlier was her guess, and that included the old range and refrigerator.

"And now to the bedroom 'wing,'" Cary quipped. He backed up and took Elizabeth down a short hallway, past a bathroom with walls of Talavera Mexican tile, and into the casita's small bedroom.

It held the double bed, made up with white sheets, a yellow and blue coverlet, and several feather pillows.

The cherry nightstand stood beside the bed and the gleaming pine chest stood against the wall. A straight chair completed the room's furnishings.

"I got a second line for my cellphone at a bargain price, so you now have your own phone." He handed her a cellphone which she placed on the nightstand. "I've already got a separate phone number for you, so you can start using it immediately."

Cary went to the bedroom window.

"You'll notice that the window looks out at a thick oleander hedge. It'll stay green all year and also provides some privacy."

He smiled. "As you might have noticed, this is not an upscale neighborhood. Yuppies don't ordinarily settle in places like this. It's just old, plain, and quiet. It's what you might call historic Tucson.

"I'll sleep on the daybed in the living room. It's one more bargain acquisition and it's long enough that my feet don't stick out."

A brass school bell with a wooden handle stood on the nightstand. Pointing to the bell, Cary said, "You can rouse me any time you need me, and I do mean *any time*. There's a lot more to show you, but I imagine you've taken in enough for the morning. Could you go for some lunch on the patio?"

"That sounds wonderful," Elizabeth replied. "Lead the way."

Cary wheeled her out the front door and onto the red brick patio. He stopped at a small outdoor table with matching chairs beneath a large swath of stretched sailcloth that was extended overhead to provide shade.

"It's still mild out here today, but as you know we'll soon be going into our summer weather, and I'm not looking forward to the triple digits," he remarked.

"However, I've already got something to counter that. On those days, I'll switch on the misters, which you haven't seen yet. That's if you'd like to be outdoors reading or whatever you want to be doing.

"In the meantime, I'll go inside and pull lunch together. Most of it is already done and waiting in the fridge. I won't be long. I'm a fast cook."

Cary started inside, then turned back. "And, oh, I almost forgot. I bought today's *New York Times* for you when I was at the grocery store."

Cary laid the newspaper on the table and then departed for the kitchen. He returned a few minutes later bearing two foil-covered plates. After setting down the plates, he laid out folded napkins, flatware, and placemats. Next came stemware and glasses for cold water.

Elizabeth looked down at the covered plates.

"Can I peek?" she asked.

"Not yet. Wait till I bring everything out."

When Cary returned, he brought a salad of greens and tomatoes and other garnishes. Also a basket with slices of bread, rolls, and a butter dish.

"Now you can peek," said Cary.

Elizabeth carefully peeled back the foil from her plate, revealing cold poached salmon with fresh dill, lemon wedges, and mayonnaise on the side.

"Oh, my goodness! This is amazing. I can't believe you did all this."

Cary chuckled. "I didn't. It was Barb. She wanted to do something for your first day here."

"How kind of her. You've been so busy. This was very thoughtful. I must thank her."

Cary stood up from the table. "I almost forgot something. Be right back."

When he returned, he held a bottle of chilled white wine.

He pulled the cork and filled their glasses halfway.

Elizabeth noted the label on the bottle, expressing surprise.

"This is too coincidental. I must have mentioned how much I like this wine."

"Yes, and I also remembered that you didn't want me to buy any more pricey wines, so I chose this dry Mâcon-Villages from France."

Over lunch, Cary pointed to some of the various desert plants in the garden.

"I know you've lived here for a while, so you are likely familiar with many of them," he said. "But there might be a few that you don't know about. Take for instance this night-blooming cereus cactus also known as the Queen of the Night. It blooms only once a year, usually sometime in June or July. And only for one night.

"It's that scraggly-looking stalk right over there." He pointed to an unimpressive-looking plant about three feet in height. "I doubt if we'll get a flower this year because I planted it only the other day. But next year . . . there's a real good possibility. The experience is spectacular. Just one night with maybe only one beautiful flower, and then it's gone."

Momentarily taking her eyes off the cereus cactus, Elizabeth caught sight of a pair of red and black butterflies fluttering above a creosote bush at the edge of the patio.

"Beautiful, aren't they," said Cary. "We have them here on and off throughout the year. And so many different colors. You'll have a chance to watch them when I'm working.

"Oh, I almost forgot. We have a dessert coming. It's frozen chocolate yogurt. You'll like it."

Cary returned shortly with the dessert and served it with the addition of a single vanilla wafer inserted into the yogurt.

"What a treat. Just lovely!" exclaimed Elizabeth. "Where did you learn to do all this?"

"I wish I could take credit," said Cary. "But as you already know, most of this was Barb's doing. The dessert was my contribution."

Tears welled in her eyes, and she began to cry. Cary quickly went to comfort her.

"What is it?" he asked, worried. "Was it something I said?"

"No. No. It's nothing like that. You did nothing wrong. It's about me," she sobbed as her tears continued to flow.

"No one has ever done anything like this for me. Not ever. Not even Arthur. And now, at this time in my life, you come along. I find myself suddenly overwhelmed and I'm not sure I understand it."

As she continued to sob, Cary pulled his chair around next to hers and placed his arm around her shoulders.

"Elizabeth, can you believe me when I tell you that I'm in a similar place?" he asked. "I find myself drawn to you in a way I've never known. It happened so suddenly. There I was walking into your room for the first time. I saw that framed photo of you with your horse and then spoke to you about Steinbeck, and it was done. After that, nothing could have pulled me away."

"Maybe that's it," Elizabeth said with a tremulous smile. "Maybe it was meant to be."

"I'm eager to explore all this with you," Cary said gently. "I'm not afraid of where it might take us. We have time. What would you say to a nap? It's been a busy day for you. I can help you into bed."

Elizabeth offered no resistance. After wheeling her into the bedroom, Cary switched the ceiling fan on to low speed, then lifted her onto the bed. He took care to ensure she was comfortable.

Her heavy eyelids showed that she was on the verge of falling asleep. He kissed her on the cheek as she drifted off.

While Elizabeth napped, Cary further familiarized himself with the work-at-home equipment that had been installed a few days earlier. After a few minutes of tinkering with the various controls, he decided that he had sufficient knowledge to do what was needed.

Within moments, Cary, too, had nodded off in the chair where he was sitting.

Chapter
Six

IT HAD BEEN THREE DAYS since Elizabeth's arrival at the casita.

Cary had returned from his morning run and went into the bedroom to check on her. She was still asleep. Cary leaned over closely and spoke her name.

"Cary, is that you?"

"No. It's George Clooney," he answered.

Elizabeth laughed without opening her eyes. "Tell him to go away. He's too old for me."

"Back to reality. Ready for breakfast?" Cary asked.

Elizabeth nodded. But before Cary could go to the kitchen, he was obliged to perform his nurse's aide responsibilities. Both had acknowledged that every moment they would share together would not all be magical charm.

He needed to assist Elizabeth in the bathroom which he had outfitted with grab bars and other aids.

Later, over breakfast, Elizabeth said, "I have some things I'd like to discuss with you.

"One of those is that I would like to help with our menus. I already have some ideas. I'd like to be in the kitchen, helping where I can. I haven't lost the touch, and it would give me great pleasure to cook for you, albeit my participation might be somewhat restricted.

"Also, I know that we've covered this, but I want to remind you that since Medicaid is no longer paying for my nursing home care, I'll be receiving my Social Security and state pension again. And that means we'll have extra money coming in."

Cary gave an encouraging nod.

"It would be such a luxury to have *The New York Times* delivered every morning," she continued. "While you're busy at work, I could read the newspaper under the lovely sailcloth canopy that you've installed."

"Remember, next week I start a one-week training class," said Cary. "It's online. I get paid for the class, of course, but I've heard that they pack in a lot during those five days. It might cut into the time we can spend together."

Elizabeth reached over and squeezed Cary's hand. "Never you worry. I'm a big girl and I will find plenty to do. What's most important is that I'm here with you."

"We've been so busy that I haven't had a chance to tell you more about the new job," said Cary. "But I think it will work out for us in more ways than I had thought.

"The name of the company is Hollowell Home Warranty Corporation. It's based in Northbrook, Illinois. My immediate supervisor is Ernie d'Alessandro. He's in Missouri."

"It's amazing how the Internet makes all this telecommuting possible," commented Elizabeth.

The week flew by; besides preparing for Cary's new job, the remainder was taken up making changes needed to accommodate Elizabeth's new living situation. Those included change of address forms, subscriptions, prescription refills, banking, grocery shopping, and more.

Each also got the rest they needed for a challenging week ahead. Cary would be required to give his full attention to the online orientation class while also keeping an eye on Elizabeth. Since there would be no webcam focused on Cary—only on the class instructor—and Cary would be using a wireless headset, he could attend to Elizabeth's minor needs without being observed on camera.

On the following Monday, Cary was awakened by his alarm clock before dawn. He peeked in on Elizabeth, who was sleeping soundly.

Because of the time difference, the weeklong orientation class would be starting at 6 a.m. local time in Tucson. He would need to prepare Elizabeth's breakfast and place it in the refrigerator, then help her into her wheelchair when she awoke. He hoped that would coincide with the first break in the class instruction.

"This is a good lesson in time management," he thought. "It must be like this for single moms who have to go to work."

By the time the instructor announced the first break—a fifteen-minute pause—Cary noticed that Elizabeth was awake and patiently waiting for him while reading her book. He wasted no time in helping her with her morning toilette and setting up her breakfast on the patio. All this was a feat in itself.

Moments later, he was back in the virtual class with about sixty seconds to spare.

When the class broke for a one-hour lunch at 10 a.m. (it was noon in Illinois), Cary removed his headset and went to sit alongside Elizabeth.

"How's it going?" he asked. "You've been so patient. I have an hour for lunch. Is it too warm for you out here? Perhaps you're ready for a bathroom call?"

"I'm fine," answered Elizabeth. "I've been enjoying the ambiance, listening and watching the birds coming to your feeder. There's such peace and serenity in this lovely garden."

Cary had their lunch already prepared and waiting in the refrigerator. He had also squeezed lemons from a backyard tree and made lemonade.

When Elizabeth was again seated at the table and they had begun their lunch, Cary said, "I forgot to tell you that you have a choice of several more classical music stations. There are two in Boston, a couple in the U.K., and likely more in Europe. You can stream those on the web."

"That's good to know," replied Elizabeth as she prepared to take a bite out of her tuna salad sandwich. "But throughout the morning, and although I had the radio on and was listening to music, the only thing I could think about was you. Perhaps later, when you're off work, we can talk."

The lunch hour passed quickly, as did the remainder of the working day. Shortly before 3 p.m., the training class adjourned, and Cary went to check on Elizabeth. As he neared her table, he saw Barb approaching.

"Cary, there's a man who says he's from the state who would like to talk with you," said Barb. "Can I show him back here?"

"Sure," replied Cary. "But I wasn't expecting anyone."

Moments later, he caught sight of a middle-aged man with graying temples and rimless glasses approaching from the rear of the main house. He carried a clipboard and wore a short-sleeved, white shirt with a selection of pens in a plastic pocket protector. A laminated photo I.D. hung around his neck.

"Are you Cary Branscombe?" the man asked.

"Yes," Cary answered questioningly.

"I'm Robert Duffield, and I'm with the State of Arizona professional licensing division," he said. "I've got some papers here that I need to serve."

"Can I ask what this is about?" asked Cary. "My CNA license is valid through next year."

"It's not about your CNA license," the man said. "You are being cited for operating a nursing facility without a license."

"That's absurd!" Cary exclaimed. "Does this look like a nursing facility? I have a friend staying with me and she's a guest. You can talk to her. She's right here."

"That's above my pay grade," replied the man. "I'm just here to serve you with these papers." He handed Cary several documents that he had removed from his clipboard. "You can phone the office if you have any questions."

With that, he turned and left. When Cary returned to the outdoor table where Elizabeth sat, he could see by the expression on her face that she knew something was amiss.

"That man said something that upset you," said Elizabeth.

As Cary leafed through the documents, he told Elizabeth about the conversation.

"On the surface, it looks like a case of sour grapes on someone's part," said Cary. "But I'd bet my life it's not coming from Paul. More than likely someone up the ladder in the bureaucratic chain. Someone who didn't appreciate my taking you out of the nursing home. Might have affected his or her performance record."

"So what do we do?" asked Elizabeth.

"I've got someone who knows how to deal with this and will probably enjoy doing it," said Cary. "He likes to take on the establishment. Especially when he believes an injustice is being done."

"I assume you're talking about an attorney," said Elizabeth.

"Right," replied Cary. "His name is Alexander Cargill. He's a young lawyer here in town and heads a nonprofit, Community Legal Services. He goes by Xander. It's pronounced Zander, but I'm sure you know that the X is pronounced like a Z."

She nodded. "Tell me about your friend. And, yes, I knew about the pronunciation of the X."

"Xander is a Stanford law grad, was at the top of his class, but came out here to Tucson because he didn't want to join a big law firm or make a lot of money. Community Legal Services provides representation to low-income clients, often at no cost. They don't get into criminal cases. Those are handled by the Public Defender. He's also in Tucson because his grandmother lived here and there was no one in the family to look after her.

"Xander's father is a federal appeals court judge in Cincinnati. Xander didn't want to be in practice anywhere near there. I met Xander when I first came to Fairfield. His grandmother was a resident there. Xander was up to his ankles in alligators between his professional work and other responsibilities. He's also a volunteer Big Brother and was having a difficult time managing all of those.

"He asked me if I could keep an eye on his grandmother and call him on his cellphone if I had the slightest concern. When his grandmother passed away, he told me I should call if I ever needed his help. So that's what I'm doing now."

Cary scrolled through the contacts on his cellphone and immediately reached Xander. "Okay, yes, yes, I've got it. Can't thank you enough. Yes, I'll be there. Thanks again."

"What did he say?" asked Elizabeth, who had been focused intently on the conversation.

"There'll be a hearing next Friday, and I'll need to appear," Cary said. "The state has obtained an order to show cause and I could be subject to civil penalties. Their filing cites no details beyond its claim that I'm operating a nursing home without a license. Xander says he'll ask the judge to dismiss the case.

"I don't think it will be a problem at work. I'll tell my supervisor that I need a couple of hours off. I'll ask Barb if she can drop in on you during that time, and I'll be available on my cell.

"That's enough of this nuisance for now. Let's talk about dinner and streaming a movie. I'm turning to you for the chef's choice."

"It just happens that I have a recipe for herb-crusted Alaskan cod," said Elizabeth.

"That's great. I love seafood. Never can get enough," said Cary. "I guess I'd better run over to the grocery store and pick up some cod. Anything else we need?"

"No, but I'll need a little help in the kitchen when you get back."

When Cary returned from shopping, the two plunged into their roles as chef and sous chef, and within a short time dinner *alfresco* was served on the patio. As he poured from a chilled bottle of an inexpensive New Zealand Sauvignon blanc, Cary pointed to a single-page printout he had placed near Elizabeth's plate.

"It's a list of movies I think would appeal to us both," he said. "A friend who's a movie buff gave it to me. There are lots of foreign films to choose from.

"I went over the list earlier and chose a movie I believe you'll like," said Cary. "It's Jane Austen's *Emma*. I thought we should start with something light."

"I like anything of Jane Austen's," said Elizabeth, "And I haven't seen the movie. I did read the novel, but that was a long time ago."

• • • ⌐ ⌐ • • •

For Cary's day in court, he wore a tie and jacket. Elizabeth remarked that she had never seen him in anything other than scrubs or casual clothes and that he looked "extra handsome."

It was no more than an hour when Elizabeth's cellphone chimed.

"The case was dismissed," said an effusive Cary. "It was heard by an administrative law judge. The judge looked at the file and asked the attorney representing the state if he had anything to add to the record which wasn't much more than a blank page. When he replied that he didn't and that he would have no objection to a dismissal, the judge ordered the case dismissed.

"Afterward, when we were out in the hall, Xander told me that he could read the attorney's body language. It was telling Xander that when the attorney opened the file, he knew that someone in the state government apparatus had tossed him a 'stinker' and he wanted no part of it.

"Xander said it's unlikely that we'll ever know who was responsible."

Meanwhile, Elizabeth became more assured in her ability to turn out meals from a wheelchair. Cary moved cookware and utensils down from upper shelves to lower positions that Elizabeth could more easily reach.

And so long as the weather held, she could sit under the canopy and read or listen to music while Cary was occupied with his training class.

As soon as the training classes were dismissed each afternoon, the two were reunited and their day began in earnest. Sometimes they went online and took virtual tours of art museums around the world, discussing the history and merits of various paintings. Or they might discuss politics and world events, the environment, climate change or world history. Often, Wikipedia needed to be consulted.

They almost never missed watching the PBS NewsHour or discussing articles of interest they found in *The New York Times*. There were long talks about interpersonal relationships—theirs and others—and sometimes confessions of a sort that they had never shared with anyone else. On occasion, to change their surroundings, they would take a drive to a scenic location and enjoy the beauty of the view.

There always needed to be some time worked in for an afternoon nap for Elizabeth. It was important for her health and to preserve her limited strength.

If they weren't streaming a movie—usually a foreign film—during dinner, they might afterward engage in a game of Scrabble. On other nights, it might be poetry readings. Cary would read some of his favorite Robert Service poems to Elizabeth, and she would regale him with the words of Robert Frost.

At bedtime, Cary continued the practice of giving reflexology treatments which enabled Elizabeth to quickly fall asleep.

Their days were filled with wonderment for each other, and on weekends things got even better. After an extended breakfast, which always included fresh fruit, there would be a surprise pastry or rolls that Cary brought home from a nearby French bakery.

Often Cary would do some gentle exercises with Elizabeth. Afterward, he provided her with a light neck and shoulder massage, in which she delighted.

It wasn't long before Elizabeth proposed that they take some time to share some of their innermost feelings about subjects that are seldom discussed, even between mates.

"I know that we touched on some of these when we spent time together in the garden at the nursing home," said Elizabeth. "But I felt we got only skin deep. Since then, I've had this compelling need to tell you some things that I've never shared with anyone. Not even with Arthur."

"This sounds very important. I'm here to listen whenever you're ready to tell me," replied Cary. His eyes met hers. "I've got some of my own to share with you, but yours come first."

"Well, I'm going to start by referring to a book. I read it when it was first published," said Elizabeth. "It's *The Art of Loving,* by Erich Fromm. Perhaps you've read it."

"I did. Just a couple of years ago," said Cary. "It made quite an impression. The book has sold over a million copies."

"Precisely. But I often wonder what happened to those million readers," said Elizabeth wryly. "I don't seem to have met any of them. At least not any who took what they read seriously. You might recall that in the book Fromm emphasizes that love is something that you must work at every day. What is so often overlooked is making the effort to know your partner. Not just what kind of music or food they prefer. It means getting down deep.

"I've had friends here in Tucson with whom I would have dinner almost weekly—a certain couple in particular—and I realized later that over a period of fifteen years neither the husband nor the wife had ever asked me a single personal question.

"If you had asked me about them, I could have provided you with their life stories. I could have served as their biographer. Because I do ask questions. It's because I'm interested. And I care.

"After Arthur died, a friend fixed me up with a blind date who took me to a symphony concert. During the course of the evening, he asked two questions. That was whether I was retired and where I had worked. Guess who had to keep the conversation going?"

Cary nodded sympathetically. He said he'd often experienced the same personal disconnect.

"In the time I have remaining," Elizabeth continued, "I'd like to share some of those feelings and thoughts with you.

"And in turn, I want to know everything about you. I want to go deep inside your psyche, if you will let me. I want to know where your thoughts take you," she said.

"As you might guess," said Elizabeth, "my mother was neither caring nor altruistic. Not in any way. So from where I acquired a social conscience, I can't say. But it's always been a part of me."

"It's the same for me. Except I know exactly when and where I acquired it," said Cary. "When I was four or five years old and hadn't yet learned to read, I would often beg my grandmother to read to me. One day, she read me a story, *The Little Match Girl*, a Hans Christian Andersen fairy tale. It was about a child who stood outside a restaurant in the freezing cold selling matches. No one was buying her matches, and inside the restaurant diners were feasting on sumptuous dinners, including roast duckling and leg of lamb.

"Through the plate glass window, the starving girl could see the diners. She tried to warm herself by lighting her matches one at a time until they were gone. The next morning, she was found outside frozen to death."

Cary shook his head. "I can't tell you how much that story upset me. I asked my grandmother if that really happened. She said that although it was a fairy tale, sometimes such things occur in real life.

"I didn't know the words *inequality* or *injustice,* but I felt it. It was inhumane. It was unimaginable that they would let a little girl die like that. How could people sit there with a full plate of food in front of them and let that happen?

"That was when I became an activist. At that time, only in spirit. In later years, it got me arrested a few times, but it has brought me a great deal of satisfaction, especially when I feel I've done some good."

"What you've said doesn't surprise me," said Elizabeth. "I wouldn't expect any less of you. But now I must tell you what I've been up to this last week.

"While you were taking your orientation class, I was making some phone calls. Several years ago, I tutored for an organization called The Palo Verde Literacy Volunteers. It's a small, local nonprofit based on the east side with no affiliation to any national organizations. It's nice because everyone knows everybody else.

"When I talked with the coordinator today, I accepted an assignment that starts next Wednesday. What makes this an unusually challenging assignment is that my student speaks no English, only French and her tribal language. She's from the Congo—actually the Democratic Republic of the Congo—and can't read in any language. And that includes French."

"But you speak French."

"Yes," replied Elizabeth. "But before I can teach her to speak and read English, I need to provide her with a basic foundation in French. I was told that she never attended school of any kind and was put to work at an early age. For starters, I will need to teach her the alphabet in French."

"Wow. I can see you like challenges," said Cary. "I assume that she'll be coming here."

"Yes, I've scheduled her for 11 a.m. when you'll be working," said Elizabeth. "Her name is Marie, and she's employed as a hotel maid. Wednesday is her day off."

"Well, feel free to have her either inside or outdoors, whichever suits you best," said Cary. "I'm on wireless equipment, so I can easily adjust. I'm good with these arrangements and I laud you for what you're doing.

"But I know you wanted to talk about things that you've never talked about with anyone before."

Elizabeth turned to face him. "I guess I'm a bit of a coward. First, I tell you how much I need to confess and then I get cold feet." She raised her chin. "I'm going to need you to hold my hand."

"It can't be that bad," he said.

"No, it's not that bad," she said. "But I'm ashamed of what I did and for all these years I've never told anyone."

"You can tell me," Cary replied as he clasped her hand.

"Well, here goes," she said after swallowing hard. "When I was married to Eliot, I was all but certain that he had a male lover.

"As you know, I was devastated and felt trapped in a marriage that should never have been.

"One night when he didn't know I was watching, I saw him take an envelope from his briefcase and slip it into a shoebox that sat on a high shelf in his closet.

"The next day, when he was at work, I took down the shoebox from the shelf, opened it and discovered a bundle of letters. They were all addressed to Eliot at a post office box that I didn't know existed.

"I read all the letters. They were from the man in Provincetown, an artist. All were love letters.

"Did you confront Eliot about them?" asked Cary.

"I couldn't," she said. "It just wasn't in me to do so.

"I felt guilty. I'd never spied on anyone before. I felt so ashamed. It was a terrible feeling."

"Did he ever know that you read the letters?"

"No, he never knew. And it's troubled me all these years."

"You found yourself in an awful position in that marriage with no one to go to," said Cary as he drew her closer to him.

Tearfully, she managed to get out the words, "Now, thank God, I have you. But there's more."

"Go ahead, I'm listening," said Cary.

"This also goes back to my days in Boston, and it's been bothering me for a long time. It may seem minor to others, but for me it's no small thing. You remember, of course, that I was an only child and that I did not know my father, who had moved to Australia before I was born.

"We had a housekeeper named Yolanda living with us for many years. When I was five or six—I can't remember exactly—she gave birth to a daughter. We never knew who the father was, but my mother allowed Yolanda and her baby to remain with us and occupy a space in the servants' quarters. The daughter's name was Margarita, but she went by Margaret in school. We called her 'Meg' at home.

"Meg was very bright and sometimes outshone me despite our age difference. We usually got along well and shared records, books, and magazines.

"But there were times when I felt that my mother showed favoritism to Meg. It made me jealous, and I became angry."

"Then what did you do that was so bad?" asked Cary.

"I was nasty. She was *only* the housekeeper's daughter. I didn't feel that she deserved so much of my mother's attention."

At that moment, Cary's cellphone chimed.

"It's Ernie, my supervisor," he said quickly. "Sorry, this will have to wait."

After a few moments, Cary completed the call and turned to Elizabeth. "No big problem," he said. "They're going to be one agent short tomorrow and Ernie asked if I could start my shift an hour earlier.

"I want to hear about you and Meg, and I don't want to cut you short. So could we reschedule this—and also my own 'confessions'—until we find a good time?"

"Good plan," replied Elizabeth. "It's getting on to the time to be talking about dinner. But thank you for listening." She patted his arm, the fading sunlight turning her hair into a soft white halo. "I feel like some of my burden has been lifted," she said.

Cary was busy working the phone early Wednesday afternoon when Barb appeared with Marie. The new foreign student seemed a bit nervous as she clutched a piece of paper bearing Elizabeth's name and address.

Elizabeth waited beneath the canopy in her wheelchair. Wearing an inviting smile, she beckoned them both over.

Speaking in French, she invited Marie to take a seat beside her.

She thanked Barb for escorting her and then resumed speaking to Marie. She explained to Marie that they would begin all lessons in French for a time and encouraged her to relax.

Cary had prepared a pitcher of fresh lemonade from which Elizabeth poured two glasses, handing one to her student.

The session began with friendly small talk and gradually settled down to teaching Marie the alphabet in French.

Meanwhile, Cary was inside and on the phone with a customer whose air-conditioning wasn't working.

"Have no concerns, Mrs. Dalton," he said. "I've already contacted the folks at A-1 Air Conditioning & Heating. Someone from there should be contacting you within the hour to set up an appointment. The technician will likely be coming from their Greenville location. Hopefully, he can still get to you today.

"Please remember, there is absolutely no cost to you. It's all covered by your Hollowell Home Warranty. We've got your back."

Later, his shift completed, Cary walked outside to where Elizabeth was working with Marie. She caught sight of him and made introductions. Speaking in French, she introduced Cary as her friend, then translated a brief conversation between the two.

Later, after Marie had departed, Elizabeth turned to Cary. "I apologize for the consecutive translation. I would have preferred to do simultaneous translation, but unfortunately my skills have never taken me to that level."

Cary smiled. "I would expect something like that coming from you, the perfectionist that you are."

Elizabeth briefed him on the afternoon's lesson, expressing pleasure and satisfaction with what had been accomplished.

Switching tacks, she ventured, "I assume that in high school you were required to read Dickens' *A Tale of Two Cities*."

"Of course. It made a big impression on me. I thought about what I'd read for years after. It may have been Dickens' best."

"Perhaps you might recall a character to whom we're introduced at almost the beginning, Dr. Alexandre Manette, who after the Revolution, has been released, having been held as a secret prisoner in the Bastille for eighteen years," said Elizabeth. "His release and what follows is referred to in the book as him being 'Recalled to Life.'"

"That's what I was feeling this afternoon when I was working with Marie. I've never told you this, but before you rescued me from the nursing home, I was resigned to spending my final days lying in bed and absorbing book after book until my demise. I want to hold your hands and give you a kiss as an expression of my gratitude that words alone can't convey."

Cary extended his hands, which set into motion fantasies that can only be described as passionate and highly imaginative. In a matter of a few moments, he was again focused on the present.

"There was a moment there when I was with you in a different time and space," said Cary. "It has happened several times in the last few weeks."

"It happens to me, too," said Elizabeth with a knowing smile. "I'm glad to know that it's not only me."

"I'd like to hear more about your experience with Marie today. Did you learn about her background?"

"Indeed I did. This poor girl—she's only nineteen—well, it's a miracle that she ever got here and that she's still alive. She grew up in a village not large enough to have a school. Both her parents died of AIDS when she was six. She was raised by her grandmother. Marie worked in a broom factory so that there would be food on the table."

Cary nodded sympathetically.

"When she was eighteen, her grandmother died, and the other siblings had departed the nest. Determined to seek a better life, she agreed to follow a neighbor girl on a path that would lead them to entry into the European Union.

"They got as far as Libya, where they boarded a dangerously overfilled boat that capsized while crossing the Mediterranean. More than half the passengers lost their lives. Those rescued by the Italian Coast Guard faced deportation, but a church group based in the United States intervened and guaranteed passage and financial support for her and several other survivors.

"We made a lot of progress today. She is very enthusiastic and wants to learn. I hope you don't mind—I've arranged for her to come twice a week. It would be when you're working."

"Hey, no problem," said Cary. "I'm pleased that it's going so well."

"I thought it might be difficult to lay hands on the type of teaching material I need, but I found a source in Montreal," said Elizabeth. "They're shipping it air express, so I'll have it by the time Marie comes for her next lesson.

"There are lots of sources here in the U.S. if you're teaching beginning French in high school or college, but not if you are teaching kindergarten and first grade French." She eyed him teasingly. "By the way, can you tell me which country has the most French speakers?"

He grinned. "I'm sure this has got to be a trick question, so I'll bite. Is it the U.S. or Canada?"

"Good try, but sorry, no, it's the Democratic Republic of the Congo. There are more French speakers in that country than there are in France. The reason is that it was once the Belgian Congo where French was the official language."

Cary glanced at his cellphone and noted the time.

"I have a suggestion," he said. "It's getting on toward five o'clock and it will be a while before dinner. We had to cut short our revelations of our deepest and darkest secrets. Would this be a good time to get back to that?"

"Glad that you mentioned it," Elizabeth replied. "Some of these memories still haunt me and I'll feel better if I can get them off my chest."

"I believe you were focused on Meg when we ended our last session."

A shadow crossed her face. "Yes, and what troubles me most is that I've never been able to get in contact with her and try to make things right."

"Is that because you don't know where she is?"

"Precisely," answered Elizabeth. "In the past, I tried writing letters and wherever I tried, they always came back 'Addressee Unknown' or 'Moved, Left No Forwarding Address.' When the Internet was created, my hopes rose, but still no gold ring. I don't know where she is or even if she's still alive."

"I'd like to give it a try. I once worked as a skip tracer, and my boss told me I was pretty good at it," said Cary.

Her eyebrows lifted. "Cary, if you locate Meg for me, I'll nominate you for the *Légion d'honneur.*" Elizabeth's high spirits suddenly faded. "But frankly, I believe what you're taking on is next to impossible. I've been at this for upwards of twenty years, and I once even hired a private detective. But no luck."

"Okay, tomorrow you'll give me whatever information you have, and I'll take it from there," said Cary. "I can do some searching in between waiting for calls. But now tell me more about what existed at the time."

She paused to gather her thoughts. "Well, I know that my mother was doing all these things to spite me, so most of my anger was directed toward her. And deservedly, I felt. But the crowning blow came when I learned that my mother planned to enroll Meg in Miss Pryce's Armont Hills School, an exclusive boarding school for young ladies in Virginia. It was a college prep and finishing school. And *very* expensive.

"Not that I wanted it for myself. I was in my early twenties at that time and already in college. But I know she did it to hurt me, and I blew up. That incident put an end to my relationship with my mother and it put a chill on my friendship with Meg."

"Understandable," Cary murmured.

"Meg was not keen on attending the school, especially since her mother was employed as a housekeeper, and she tried her level best not to allow it to drive a wedge between us. But I was hotheaded and wanted no part of anyone's apologies or explanations.

"When I left Boston, I had not reestablished contact with Meg, and since then I haven't been able to locate her."

"I can see why you might now have some misgivings," said Cary. "Maybe we can find Meg. I'll certainly give it a good try."

"Thank you. But now, what about your own revelations?" asked Elizabeth. "I've taken up all the time so far."

"To be honest, most of what's on my mind revolves around you and me," he admitted. "A lot was already there to start with, but finding you brought it all out front and center."

"I want to know what it is. All of it." Her voice was firm. "Please don't hold anything back. I want to know."

"Well, I'm uneasy about this, but here goes," said Cary. "I've known about class discrimination since I was a youngster. My grandmother often talked about 'our betters.' My mom confirmed it when I would ask why we couldn't go here or there. In my early teens, I once asked a girl in my class for a date. She had to check with her parents and informed me the next day, obviously embarrassed, that her parents had said no.

"I wanted to know why, so I asked her best friend, who reluctantly informed me that her parents were both snobs and had asked their daughter what my father did for a living. When they learned that my mother was a single mom working as a waitress, that was enough for them."

To his relief, Cary saw no pity in Elizabeth's eyes—just empathy and kindness.

"To say that I was deeply hurt and affected for life would be an understatement. It cut into my feeling of self-worth so deeply that it brought with it a lifelong animosity toward the so-called upper classes."

He picked at a thread on his sleeve. "I realize that class distinction in America is not the same as in England. There, depending on whether you speak the Queen's English, Cockney, or a regional dialect can determine where you go in life.

"But it also applies to *our* relationship in this way. When I met you, you were reading a book with which I identified. I saw the photo of you with your horse, taken when you were in your twenties." His eyes lifted to meet hers. "I was hooked. Infatuated. I saw myself living in that period and wanting to be in your life."

She tilted her head, regarding him silently, allowing him to reveal his feelings.

"But it was approach-avoidance," Cary explained. "I was drawn to you—

and yet at the same time I felt resentful because of your class."

"Still?" she asked softly.

He shook his head negatively. "I've worked my way through that. I no longer have even the slightest reservation about how you feel about me. I love you and I know that you love me. Just being in your presence sometimes sends chills down my spine. The chills are euphoric or perhaps better said, *ecstatic*."

Her eyes filled with emotion. "I know just what you mean, my darling Cary."

"If there's any lingering resentment," he went on, "it would be toward people like your mother, and I know how you feel about your mother and her values.

"There's also a side issue that comes with this. I touched on it a short while ago. It's this. When you reminisce and go back to your life in Boston, my mind shifts gears and I imagine myself there with you. And then I fantasize about what we would have done and said to each other.

"I see us as both young and adventurous. I see us climbing mountains in New Hampshire, rowing a boat on a lake, eating in a funky bistro, or making love on the floor of a cabin in front of the fireplace." He shrugged. "I can't help it. It just comes naturally. I feel we've been cheated. But at the same time, I'm grateful for what we have."

"Do you come back to the present when this happens?" she asked.

"Yes. In fact, I find myself switching back and forth between then and now," he admitted. "I hope you're not shocked or embarrassed."

"Would you be surprised if I told you that this is also where I sometimes find myself with you?" She laughed. "And here I was, too embarrassed to tell you."

"I have something that also falls in the realm of fantasy that I want to tell you," said Elizabeth. "Sometimes when I wake up in the morning, I like to imagine that we are living together in King Arthur's time. That you are Lancelot and I'm Guinevere. I fabricate stories about what we would do and how we would live."

He felt a jolt of surprise—almost akin to déjà vu. "Interesting that you would mention that because when we came to those stories in high school, I sometimes aspired to be Lancelot, but I never shared that with a soul." He took her hand. "I would be honored to be your Lancelot."

They took in each other's image for a long moment.

"And that brings us back to the present," Cary said finally. "I noticed that it's been some time since you've had your hair done—and perhaps you hesitated to ask. But it's been my experience, having worked at Fairfield, that this is very important to a woman. You might remember Ruby Phillips, the hair stylist who came to Fairfield on Tuesdays to do women's hair? She also makes house calls. I believe I can get her to come here."

"Only if I'm allowed to pay," declared Elizabeth firmly.

"Okay. Okay," he replied, throwing his hands up. "You can pay."

"I have a roast in the oven," she said. "It will be ready in about an hour."

"What do you have on the agenda for this evening?" asked Cary.

"Would you like a game of Scrabble after dinner?"

"Sounds great," replied Cary. "You'll probably beat me. I'm sure you're good. I have something for us, too, but it can wait for another night. It's an opera from The Met that we can stream. A pay-per-view. Wagner's *Lohengrin*. Do you know it?"

"Very much so. It's one of my favorites." She beamed at him. "I love the climax when Elsa asks him the forbidden question and he reveals himself as Lohengrin, son of King Parsifal and knight of the Holy Grail. And with that his boat, drawn by a swan, appears on the river and he departs forever."

She smiled teasingly. "Tomorrow evening when we watch the opera and I get teary-eyed, you'll hold me in your arms, won't you?"

"You can count on it," replied Cary.

"Since dinner is yet an hour away, there's also something else I'd like to talk with you about." She squared her shoulders. "Since I've come to stay with you, you have devoted yourself to me, and I can attest that it's something I've never known in my life. I treasure the thought, but at the same time, I must look after your welfare and I'm keenly aware that you've placed your education on hold since I've been with you."

He opened his mouth to speak, but she forged ahead, undeterred. "Sometime in the future when I'm no longer here, you'll need something to keep you going. Something that will give you satisfaction every day. At least until you find that special someone. That something is your education. Although it won't substitute for a soulmate, it will provide you with enough to enable you to continue your life and not give way to drifting."

Cary was deeply moved by her selfless concern for him.

"I can tell you from firsthand experience that every day when you learn something new and every semester when you chalk up more credits, you have this feeling that someone is punching your ticket and you have moved up the ladder toward your goal." She folded her hands. "I feel it's my responsibility to not only encourage you in this direction, but also to help you as much as I can.

"I know that you would like to study at MIT and that you aspire to be a materials engineer. If I don't set you in the right direction to help you get there, then I'm not using this precious time to full advantage."

Cary was momentarily taken aback. "This is another side of you," he said. "You come across like you could be my mother. Add that to serving as my instructor in the humanities, art, history, and foreign languages and as my lover, albeit platonic. You never fail to surprise me. But I feast on it. All of it."

This drew an amused laugh. "Did you believe that I was some kind of timid, meek, unassertive woman?" She waved a hand. "*Au contraire*. I'm more likely the opposite. You might have formed a different impression because of the many years that Arthur occupied my life. I realize now, of course, that I never should have let that happen.

"My friends, who are all gone now, urged me for years to put it to Arthur straight: that he can have only one, either a spouse or a lover. He would have to make a choice. I was almost prepared to do that many times, but I always lost my nerve. But beyond that single issue, I seldom wavered. And yes, I confess to filling all those roles you cited." She paused. "So, beginning tomorrow, I plan to get to work on helping you restart your education."

That evening, as Elizabeth lay in bed after her nightly reflexology treatment, Cary read aloud to her from Wilkie Collins' *The Woman in White*.

"I read this book when I was in college," said Elizabeth. "It's one of my favorites. I believe you'll like it, too."

She had reserved the book from the nearby local public library branch and Cary had picked it up the day before.

"Did you know that Collins was a close friend of Dickens?" she asked. "They often traveled together and collaborated on both drama and fiction. Even more interesting is the fact that Wilkie Collins secretly maintained two families though he never married, and lived independently with each, separated by a distance of only a few miles."

"Really?" Cary asked. "That must have been a lot of work just to keep up such an existence."

She nodded. "He was with Caroline Graves and Martha Rudd, alternating between the two houses for weeks at a time. I often saw my relationship with Arthur in that same light, except that he was never able to stay beyond a few hours.

"There were only a few times in the more than fifty years that this extramarital relationship existed where Arthur and I could spend a full night together. Arthur's best friend, Web McCandless, was a divorcé. He was a tax lawyer, and they did a lot of investments and deals together."

She ran her palm along the coverlet, smoothing it. Her facial expression softened. "On those few occasions when Arthur and I could be closer together, he would book reservations for a conference in Hawaii or Florida or somewhere in the Rockies, depending on the season. It would always be a conference on finance or economics where both Arthur and Web could reasonably explain their interest in attending.

"Web would book a room for himself and his 'girlfriend'—that was me—and Arthur reserved an adjoining room. When the bellhop departed, Web unlocked the adjoining door and I moved into Arthur's room for the duration.

"Although we had the room to ourselves, any time we were in public, I had to stand alongside Web to maintain the guise that I was *his* girlfriend. That included all meals, sightseeing, et cetera.

"If we ran into someone who knew Arthur from back home, he would introduce Web, and Web would introduce me as his girlfriend. He would use only a first name—and not my real name—and then find some reason why we needed to move on. Arthur also used Web as his backup when he would take an extended lunch hour to be with me." She smiled wistfully. "Web was always there for Arthur."

"When Arthur died, had he provided for you in any way?" asked Cary.

"Arthur couldn't name me in his will because I didn't exist," said Elizabeth with a touch of sadness. "But he did set aside an amount from one of his joint deals with Web and left it with him in a trust account should it be needed. It was a modest amount and I used it up in three years to pay uncovered dental and medical bills. He reportedly left a fortune to his wife and children."

"Where did that leave you?"

"I felt like I had nowhere to go," she replied. "I was retired, had no job, very few friends, and certainly no prospects for a relationship. There was not much demand for a single woman in her seventies." She sighed. "I guess I just went into a funk and stayed there. I read a lot of books. They were my companions. I think I just gave up on life."

"Would you believe it if I told you that a few years ago I gave up trying to find a soulmate?" asked Cary. "Instead, I transferred my energy to my work and to different causes I believed in. And then you came into my life."

"But you saw in front of you an eighty-nine-year-old woman. How were you able to square that with the needs of a red-blooded man in his early thirties?" she asked.

"For a brief moment, that thought crossed my mind," Cary said. "But then I realized I'd be unlikely to find another woman like you among the current vintage or anywhere for that matter. I felt that I had this opportunity and that I should act on it. Both of us are defined by a lot more than our ages.

"In my mind, that photo on your nightstand became a fantasy. I began toggling back and forth between the 1940s and the present. The more we talked, the greater my interest became. After those first few days, I was infatuated and had no thought of turning back."

"I sensed that," Elizabeth said. "And I had no inclination to break the spell either. I was enthralled myself. I didn't know how far this could go, but I was eager to see."

"It's late," said Cary as he switched off the overhead light and turned on the lamp on Elizabeth's nightstand. "Tomorrow's a workday for me, so we should get some sleep. Is there anything I can get for you?"

Elizabeth hesitated. "No, thank you," she said softly.

She lay on her right side, on white percale sheets with an eyelet border, her head resting on two down pillows. A candlewick spread covered the bed, and the long-sleeved gown that Elizabeth wore bore a design of tiny pink roses.

Cary bent down and kissed her on her cheek. He stood by the bed and looked down at this lovely woman. He sensed there was something else Elizabeth wanted to say but was censoring herself for some reason.

"What is it?" he asked, in his end-of-the day, quiet voice.

She opened her eyes. "You'll think I'm being silly."

"You're never silly. Talk to me." He sat down on the edge of her bed.

Elizabeth pressed her fingers to her lips for a moment, as though that would keep her thoughts from turning into words, and her words from escaping.

"I was just thinking," she said, and then was silent again.

Cary realized Elizabeth was suddenly shy, and he wanted to know what was so difficult for her to say. It had to be important for her to react in this way. He stroked her cheek with one finger, to let her know he was there, and smoothed her hair gently with his hand. Patience was truly one of his virtues.

Gathering her courage, Elizabeth began again. "I was just thinking . . . that it's been so long . . . since . . . anyone has held me . . . in bed."

Cary felt warmth blossom in his chest. He, too, had longed for physical contact.

"Scoot over a little," he whispered. "Company's coming."

Elizabeth gave him a beautiful smile of welcome and soon she lay nestled in Cary's arms, as close as they could be.

The Rescue

IT STARTED OUT LIKE ANY OTHER Saturday morning in August.

Elizabeth was in her wheelchair under the canopy doing research on her laptop. Cary was cracking the books for the physics course she'd encouraged him to resume.

At about 10 a.m., Cary saw Barb emerge from her house and head toward their casita.

"Cary, I could use your help," she said. "Lee's got a bad back and I need someone to trim a mesquite branch that's growing into our front window."

"Hey, no problem," replied Cary. "I just need access to a ladder and some loppers."

"They're in the garage. I'll lead you to them if this is a good time."

The two headed to the detached garage where he found what he needed. After informing Elizabeth of his plans, Cary headed to the front of the house, carrying the ladder and pruning loppers. Barb pointed to the branch that required trimming and Cary set up his ladder. He had scarcely climbed to the second rung when he apparently roused a colony of Africanized bees.

They came barreling out of their hive in a swarm. Before he could get back on the ground, he had been stung dozens of times.

"Cary, this way!" Barb shouted, as she stood near the front door. She shrieked as the bees attacked her, too.

With hundreds of bees in pursuit, they both darted inside, and Barb slammed the door shut. Only a few bees made it into the house. Cary threw himself on the couch, writhing in agony. Lee phoned 911 while Barb ran to the kitchen, returning with towels soaked in cold water. She applied them to Cary's arms and face until paramedics arrived to transport him to the hospital emergency room.

Meanwhile, two fire trucks and a police patrol cruiser arrived on the scene.

Before anyone could exit the house, they had to wait for firefighters to spray the immediate area with chemical foam to disperse the killer bees.

Despite his blinding pain, Cary asked Barb to call his Aunt Joan and ask her to come and stay with Elizabeth. After reaching Joan, and when it was safe, Barb went to the casita to comfort Elizabeth and tell her what had happened. She assured Elizabeth that Cary's condition, while painful, was not life-threatening.

Later, after a bee expert was summoned, they would learn that the colony of Africanized bees had made its home inside the structure's roof parapet. And because the hive was inside the parapet, the bee expert couldn't transfer the bees to a farm or apiary where they could be commercially productive.

Instead, a cut had to be made in the parapet and the entire colony extinguished. Later, the bee expert estimated the size of the hive and its honeycomb at more than five feet in length. It would have accounted for several thousand bees, he said.

That evening, Cary phoned Elizabeth from the hospital.

"I'm calling to tell you that I'm okay. They're going to keep me here overnight, but likely release me some time tomorrow. I can't wait to get home to you."

"I was so worried when I heard all the sirens. I didn't know what happened," she replied.

"It's okay now. They've given me all kinds of shots and medication. I was asleep for a while, but now they're bringing me something to eat. The doctor said I was stung more than fifty times."

"Oh, you poor man," said Elizabeth. "I can't imagine."

"May I speak to Aunt Joan for a minute?" Cary asked. "I want to thank her for coming so quickly."

Joan was handed the phone and assured Cary that Elizabeth was managing fine, now that she knew he was okay. She told Cary that she would be spending the night with Elizabeth and not to worry.

When the next morning arrived, Lee drove to the hospital to pick up Cary. En route home, Cary said, "I'll bet you weren't in any way aware that you had this monster colony of bees in your roof parapet."

"Heck, if we'd known that, we couldn't have slept," said Lee. "I sure wish there had been another way to make the discovery. Reminded me of my time in the service when we had those battle drills. Everybody really scrambled yesterday when we called for help—fire, police, paramedics, and later the beekeeper. Everybody did their jobs and wasted no time."

On their arrival back at the house, Barb was waiting. She was full of apologies as she walked behind Cary on his way to the casita.

"Barb, you had no way of knowing," said Cary. "I'm glad that the bee expert could get rid of the bees and their hive."

Joan, who spotted them approaching, tapped Elizabeth on her wrist to alert her. A big smile appeared on Elizabeth's face as she reached out from her wheelchair to embrace Cary.

"I missed you and I was so worried," she said. "Joan was wonderful, but you were on my mind constantly."

"I look like I've been in the ring with a heavyweight champ," said Cary, "but they tell me that the swelling will go away in a few days. The good news is that my insurance at work will cover all the medical and hospital expenses. That's one less thing to worry about. Have you had your breakfast?"

"Joan and I made breakfast together," replied Elizabeth. "We had French toast, and I told her about Marie and my tutoring. She seemed quite interested. You're lucky to have her as your aunt."

After Joan had departed, Cary asked, "Is there anything I need to know about—you know, about what may have happened since yesterday?"

"Well, besides worrying, I believe I might have made some headway in my plans for your future."

"What? You've made plans for my future? Maybe you should have asked me first."

"Perhaps you should let me tell you before you judge," Elizabeth countered.

Cary reached over and took her hand. "Forgive me," he said. "Please don't change anything you're doing or the way you do it. Besides my mother, no one in my life has taken the interest that you do. And that's just another reason why I love you."

"You mean no one at all. Only your mother?"

"Well, almost. It was when I was a sophomore in high school in California. That was before my mother died. It was a high school from which few students—even those who graduated—went on to college.

"I had enrolled in an advanced placement course in English literature taught by a Mrs. Kielsmeyer. She was what you might call an erudite individual. That was no surprise, however. She was a Stanford grad with a master's degree and a number of letters after her name.

"She was obviously aware of the pitiful low number of students going on to college at our school and seemed committed to doing something to change it. There were about a dozen students in the class who showed both promise and interest in furthering their education. These students—I was one of them—would meet with her after school, usually in her classroom, and discuss plans for future field trips and that sort of thing.

"She took us everywhere—museums, concerts, live stage theater, the opera. It was my first exposure to the arts.

"Mrs. Kielsmeyer's husband was an orthopedic surgeon. He would often volunteer to drive us students in his car when one vehicle was not enough to transport all of us to our destination. It turned out that he was also an authority on John Steinbeck and served as our guide when we went to the Steinbeck Museum in Salinas."

"Mrs. Kielsmeyer had maintained her connections at Stanford and had success in getting a number of her students placed, some with full scholarships. I was in line for that, but when my mom died, all that vanished and I had to move to Tucson to live with my aunt."

"I'm glad you told me about that," said Elizabeth. "I know now that I'm doing the right thing. You *must* resume your education and reach your goal. I'm going to help to get you there. That's my new mission in life. As a start, I learned by searching online that there's a roadmap for taking you where you want to go. There's nothing complex or mysterious about it.

"You've said you want to get into research and development—R&D— working on new approaches to alternative and renewable energy. For that you'll need to complete your courses at the community college and amass sixty credit hours that you can transfer to a four-year college.

"There you need to complete the next sixty credit hours in what they call 'the upper division' to obtain your baccalaureate degree, and then hope you'll be admitted to a master's program at either the same institution or somewhere else. After that, you can look forward to a doctoral program which can take anywhere from a couple of years up to five years. Without a PhD you can't expect to land a really good position in an R&D lab.

"And from where should you aspire to receive your doctorate degree? From MIT, of course. MIT is and remains number one in the United States for such endeavors."

He smiled at her determination—and at her confidence in him.

"The next question is how do you get there?" Elizabeth said. "Once you're in the upper division, you must maintain close to a 4.0 grade average. When you've earned your bachelor's degree, you must then score high on the Graduate Record Exam, called the GRE, to get admitted into a master's degree program. You'll need to have letters from your professors or instructors recommending you, and you must have a record of volunteering for public service."

"Hey, you've been busy," said Cary.

"I'm not finished yet. There's more to come. I talked earlier this morning with Inez Warren, an old friend I know from my librarian days. She's retired now, but she does volunteer counseling a couple days a month at the library branch near her home.

"I talked with her of my concern about your resuming your education, and she turned out to be very helpful. We had a long conversation. During our talk, she remembered a library patron who shared this tidbit with her. Her patron was a young veterinarian who often came into the branch to research a variety of subjects. Inez at the time was the acting reference librarian.

"It turns out that the two were chatting one day when Inez asked the woman if it had been difficult to gain admission to the veterinarian program at the University of California at Davis from where she had graduated. The vet school at UC-Davis is one of the most prestigious in the U.S.

"The woman smiled and said, 'Interesting that you would ask.' She went on to tell Inez a story that you must hear," said Elizabeth.

"Go ahead. I'm listening," Cary replied.

"This young woman had already completed work on a baccalaureate degree at one of the California state universities. She had taken all the prep courses needed for admission to the vet program and had a 4.0 grade point average. She was among several hundred applicants for admission to the vet school and did not get in on either her first or second try.

"So what did she do, you might ask? She moved to Davis, rented a room in a private home and got a job waiting tables. And when she wasn't working, she volunteered at the vet school cleaning out cages and doing whatever gofer work they had for her.

"Each year when she reapplied and was turned down, she refused to give up. The professors who began to recognize her as a hard-working volunteer encouraged her to keep trying. On her fourth attempt, she was accepted and sailed through with straight A's since she knew just about everything she needed to know by that time."

Elizabeth turned to Cary. "You might need to do something like that someday to get your foot in the door.

"However, what I learned from Inez doesn't end there," said Elizabeth. "I have more news. Inez has a fellow volunteer in her program who's a retired physics professor. He taught for thirty years at Northwestern and was one of the leaders in his field. I checked and found that Northwestern is among the top schools for physics study.

"I asked Inez if this man could help you with counseling or tutoring or perhaps both. She said she wasn't sure but suggested that I phone him. 'He can say yes, and he can say no,' she told me. She provided me with his phone number and added that he doesn't accept payment for his time but asks that any recipient of his tutoring or counseling make a contribution to a local wildlife rescue program—whatever they can afford."

"The man's name is Matthew Eckersley. I phoned him and we had a chat. He immediately offered to help. I explained that you could use some tutoring for your physics course. He was agreeable, and I made an appointment for you. I could see that you were sometimes struggling to fully comprehend what was in the text and I thought this might make things easier to understand."

Cary shook his head in disbelief.

"Elizabeth, you are just too much," he said. "I don't know whether to laugh or cry. I've just never been around anyone like you."

Cary took her hand and kissed it, evoking a smile of satisfaction and pride coming from Elizabeth.

She continued. "Judging from my brief phone conversation with Professor Eckersley, I concluded that he's a very nice man, and I believe he can help you."

Elizabeth glanced at her watch.

"Cary, you need to rest. I'll bet you didn't get much sleep at the hospital," said Elizabeth. "Forgive me for going on and on.

"I made some egg salad this morning. How about an egg salad sandwich, some iced tea, and a dish of your favorite chocolate ice cream? And then a nice nap."

Cary offered no resistance.

• • • ⌐￢ ∟ • • •

Two weeks later, early on a Sunday afternoon, the two decided that they should go on an outing.

"Do you have any special place in mind," asked Cary.

"Well for starters, have you ever been to Kachina Springs Park?" asked Elizabeth.

"No. I've never heard of it."

"Good. It's a little gem of a chapter in Tucson's history, and it attracts very few visitors. It's located far out on the east side and doesn't offer a lot of amenities. So we don't need to be concerned about crowds. We could fix a picnic lunch and be out of here in a half hour. Interested?"

"You bet," replied Cary. "We both can do with a little getaway."

After a half-hour drive, they arrived at the park, where only a few cars were in the parking lot. Cary set up Elizabeth's wheelchair and shortly they were on the way to find a picnic table in the shade. An asphalt-paved walking path facilitated their movement.

"More than a century ago, this was a health spa," said Elizabeth as Cary unpacked the picnic lunch. "When the railroad came to Tucson in the early 1880s, it brought with it individuals who sought the healing waters of the natural warm spring here.

"Of course, there were no automobiles in those days, so disembarking passengers were transported by mule wagons from the railroad station in downtown Tucson some twenty miles over dirt roads to the spa. Often the trip required half a day.

"The spa remained open for about ten years and then closed when the spring began to dry up to where it continued at barely a trickle. It was later a ranch until the land became the park that it is today. Historians believe that about five thousand years ago this site was once home to a Hohokam native tribe."

"How do you know so much about this?" Cary asked.

"When I was in my librarian incarnation, we brought a small group here and I was given responsibility for heading the tour," said Elizabeth. "I suppose I retained a good bit of the details. It tells me that I haven't yet lost my memory for things, and that's a blessing."

"Well, now you've got me interested. As soon as we finish lunch, let's take a stroll."

It wasn't long until the two were back on the path, taking in the sights. They encountered only a few visitors along the way, likely because there were major sports events on TV that afternoon. As they approached a footbridge spanning a dry creek, they heard a feeble whine emanating from a thicket.

"That sounds like an animal in distress!" Elizabeth exclaimed.

"That's what it sounds like to me, too," said Cary. "Let me go check it out."

After applying the brake to Elizabeth's wheelchair, Cary made his way toward the thicket. As he approached, he could hear that the cries came from a small dog or puppy. The animal sounded weak and might have been trapped there for several days.

He surveyed the obstacles to reaching the distressed creature. There were several wild blackberry bushes, all with sharp thorns, and a stand of prickly pear cacti among the blackberry bushes. Also included in the mix was some dreaded cholla, a wild desert cactus bearing tiny sharp spines that evoke fear in every hiker.

"It looks like it's on the ground about ten feet in from the path," Cary reported. "We've got to find a way to get it out of there, but it won't be easy."

He paused. "I'm going to need to get back to the truck and see what I've got because there's no way I can get to this poor thing without some tools and protection.

"I'll be right back. Will you be okay?"

Cary returned with a couple of old blankets, a pair of work gloves and a tire iron. There were no cutting tools of any type.

Without wasting a moment, Cary wrapped himself in one of the blankets for protection from the spines and donned the gloves for the same reason.

"I'll use the tire iron in place of a machete," said Cary. "It will enable me to knock down some of the brush instead of cutting it."

He folded the second blanket and placed it on Elizabeth's lap. "If I can bring the animal out, I'll put it on your lap, and with the blanket you'll have protection from whatever spines might be stuck to it. And I'll give you my gloves. It'll be frightened after all it's been through."

Cary headed back toward the thicket. Using the tire iron, he whacked away at the heavy brush with its sharp thorns. Despite the protection afforded by the blanket and gloves, he nevertheless couldn't avoid getting stabbed by the prickly spines.

Within a few minutes, he returned, his face badly scratched and showing a few cactus spines on his ears. In his arms was a small black and white puppy, who continually whimpered.

Cary carefully set the puppy on Elizabeth's lap, transferred his gloves to her, saying, "Be careful, she's got several sharp spines sticking in her. We'll have to get them out later. She's obviously dehydrated, so we'll need to see if she can drink."

They quickly headed back to the truck where there were some water bottles. Cary opened one and poured a few tablespoonsful into a plastic saucer. With some effort, the puppy lapped up the water.

At that moment, a park ranger happened by. When he saw Cary attending to the puppy, he stopped. "Did you just rescue this puppy?" he asked.

"Yes, we found her in a thicket over there," Cary said, pointing in the direction of the footbridge.

"That pup's lucky," said the ranger grimly. "Yesterday, we found the remains of what was likely its mother and her other puppy. It looked like a coyote or a pack of them made their dinner of those poor animals. There wasn't much left of them.

"There was no collar on the mother, which says that she was probably abandoned by her owner. I'm guessing that she gave birth to the puppies right here in the park and this one was spared by escaping into that thicket. Coyotes stay out of those." He eyed the little dog on Elizabeth's lap. "Are you going to take her to a vet?"

"That's our first stop," replied Cary, as he hurried to pack up and leave.

"I know where there's a 24-hour veterinary clinic and hospital," he told Elizabeth. "It's Sunday and most of the vet clinics are closed."

Within a half hour they were sitting in the waiting room of the McBride Animal Clinic. Outside, the sign read: *We Never Close.*

"Dr. Tran will be seeing your dog in just a few minutes," said the receptionist. "I told her that it's an emergency."

Almost at that moment, Dr. Tran, the on-duty vet, appeared. Eyeing the puppy and her condition, she asked the receptionist to bring a cart used to transport animals within the clinic.

"It will be safer for the dog, and also for us, if we use this to move her to the examining room," said the vet, a young woman. "I want to pull out those spines before we do anything else."

Cary and Elizabeth in her wheelchair followed the vet into an examining room. As the vet used special tweezers to remove the sharp spines, which seemed to be everywhere, Cary told her details of the rescue.

The vet then turned to Cary and said, "I need to tell you that puppies of this tender age require a special diet."

She handed him some stapled sheets of paper which contained instructions for the feeding and care of orphaned puppies. There was much more than either had expected. They would need to purchase a supply of mother's milk replacer along with a feeding bottle and specially designed nipples. Also ample water, which is critical in the early stages; it would be weeks until solid food could be offered.

Orphaned puppies must be fed every two to four hours, and the position in which they are held when fed would reflect later on how well they socialize. There was more, and Cary and Elizabeth would later commit to memory all of the instructions.

Their immediate concern was to drive to one of the chain pet supply stores before closing.

With the puppy now relieved of the spines, she rested comfortably on Elizabeth's lap as they drove to the store. Cary went in with the shopping list as Elizabeth comforted the puppy, stroking her and speaking to her in a soft voice.

In a short while, Cary emerged carrying a couple of large shopping bags and a wicker dog bed.

"I think we have everything we need," he said.

"I gave her frequent water, which she licked from my fingers," said Elizabeth.

When they got home, Cary immediately warmed the replacement milk and placed the remainder in the refrigerator as per the instructions. He attached the nipple and with the puppy in the recommended position on his lap, fed her the portion in tiny amounts.

Elizabeth watched intently.

After Cary put the dog bed on the floor, Elizabeth added a towel to the bed. Cary set a small, shallow dish of clean water on the floor nearby. During the first hour at home, the puppy occasionally whined. But as soon as Elizabeth picked her up and put her on her lap, she settled down.

"And there's one more thing," said Cary. "Our little miss won't be able to sleep with you in your bed for a while. Not until she's housebroken. And we need to give her a name."

"I've already been thinking about that," said Elizabeth with a mysterious smile.

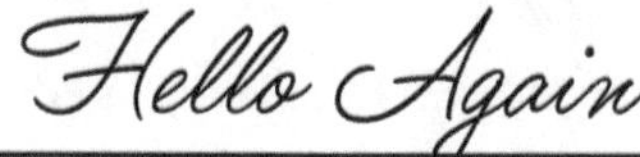

A WEEK PASSED AND THE NEW addition to the household adjusted better than anyone expected. The puppy showed no fear of either Elizabeth or Cary despite her harrowing experience at the park. She seemed comfortable. There was always a full water dish, and she was taken up for bottle feeding every few hours.

Elizabeth worked at her laptop and Cary was taking calls for his work. It was shortly before 2 p.m. when his personal cellphone lit up with a text message. His shift would soon be ending, and he was not working a call at the moment, so he glanced over at the phone, which lay flat on his desk. It showed the sender as Claudia van Voorhees. She was the art appreciation instructor to whom he'd assigned the fictitious name of "Jane" when he told Elizabeth about her.

Why was she contacting him? Had her marriage to the attorney general failed? Cary really didn't need this right now, he thought. He decided to reply after his shift ended, but he wanted to be up front with Elizabeth.

His shift ended, and he immediately went to Elizabeth. "You're not going to believe this," said Cary, "but eighteen months go by, and I don't hear anything from this woman—not that I expected to—but half an hour ago this message pops up."

He showed her the text.

Hi Cary, I'm in Tucson. Must return home tomorrow. Would love to see you. I'm at the Arizona Inn. Please call me. Love, Claudia.

"Okay." Elizabeth paused. "Who is this Claudia?"

"Remember, she's the art appreciation instructor I told you about. Her real name is Claudia van Voorhees." He put the phone in his pocket.

"So what's happening here today?" Elizabeth cocked her head.

"We need to decide how I should handle this," said Cary.

"Why *we*?" asked Elizabeth. "She's *your* friend."

"Because I have no interest in her and haven't since I met you," he replied.

"So how do we sort this out before you answer her?" asked Elizabeth.

"Here's how it is. I want you to know that my commitment to you is unshakeable. You must know that, and I hope that you feel it as well. With Claudia, there can be only two reasons why she wants to see me. The first is that she's back in Tucson for a day and wants to get together. I have no problem with that.

"But I also see a second reason, and it's dangerous. Claudia has a healthy sex drive. She is a passionate woman and may miss what we had. She may see this as an opportunity. Heaven knows what's going on in her marriage. Rest assured, I'm on my guard here."

He crossed his arms. "We need to decide together how I should handle this. To be honest, I'm pretty uncomfortable about it."

"This is something that you must decide for yourself, Cary. I can't decide this for you."

"Since you came into my life, I've hardly thought of her."

Cary leaned toward Elizabeth and took her hand in his. "I don't want there to be any misunderstandings, and right now is the time to make sure that nothing like that happens."

"Meaning exactly what? Were you in love with Claudia?"

Cary dropped his eyes and hesitated as he wrestled with how to respond.

"Claudia did a lot for me. She took me to museums and art galleries and concerts and opera. Lectures and receptions. I was moving in circles and meeting people—artists and others—that I hadn't known existed."

He relaxed as he spoke, remembering the good times they'd had together.

"May I ask . . . if there was passion in your relationship?"

Cary exhaled a deep breath. "There was, and it was fantastic. Gotta be honest with you."

Elizabeth nodded calmly. "Claudia has played a very important role in your life, Cary. You shouldn't feel guilty in acknowledging that. Or for feeling grateful to her."

He couldn't believe what he was hearing. "You want me to see her?" he asked incredulously.

"I want you to do what you want to do." Her voice was tender. "She's obviously been very special in your life."

"I can't believe what you're saying, Elizabeth." He shook his head, confused.

"Cary, please! My life has been all about books and language. Literature. Words used to communicate ideas, thoughts, feelings, beliefs, dreams. Don't try to convince me you haven't understood me."

Cary sat still, staring at someone he thought he knew well, but was taken aback to discover he still had much more to learn about Elizabeth.

"I know the difference between flotsam and jetsam," she said, the words spilling out like a river in a flood. "I know port from starboard. I know the signs of the zodiac and where to find the constellations in the night sky. Shall I list the emperors of Rome? Which century would you like? I know how many *n*'s and *s*'s are in *connoisseur*. The nine Greek muses of antiquity and the realms they reign over are ever-present as I read or hear a symphony or watch yet again Anthony Quinn teaching Alan Bates to dance!"

Cary was stunned. He'd never known this Elizabeth. She covered her mouth with her hand.

"Oh, Cary, I am so sorry. I got carried away. Please forgive me."

He didn't reply.

"You have a strange look about you, Cary. Did I frighten you?"

"You amazed me is what you did," he said, laughing.

"Oh, dear." Elizabeth sighed and finally she laughed, too, but her face had turned red with embarrassment. "Oh, Cary. Dear, wonderful Cary. You are a marvel of a man and a godsend of a companion."

Elizabeth composed herself. "Here's what I suggest. Note the use of 'suggest,' please. Phone Claudia and inform her that you've discussed this with me. Tell her that I would have no objection if you went to see her."

"Are you sure about this?"

"Absolutely! And also invite her here for a brief visit."

A short time later, Cary sat across a table from Claudia in the bar of the Arizona Inn. Both had ordered coffee. Claudia gave Cary her full attention as she listened to him recount how he and Elizabeth had met, become friends, and come to share life together.

"That's quite a story," said Claudia.

Cary shrugged. "If you'd told me I'd be in a relationship with a woman my grandmother's age, I'd have thought you were crazy. But . . ."

"But you are. And you seem to be happy, right?"

Cary nodded. "Yep."

"It's good that you're happy and that you've found someone," said Claudia. "It's just . . ." She leaned in and spoke in a whisper. "It's just that I really miss you, Cary. I miss your humor, your curiosity, your sweetness, and most of all . . . I miss being close to you. I was hoping we could get together, be together, while I'm here."

"I won't lie, Claudia," said Cary. "I've missed you, too, in every way, and you know what I mean. But here's how it is. You and I had a special relationship, but it was pretty complicated. You'll have to admit that."

Claudia nodded sadly.

"Well, there's nothing complicated in my relationship with Elizabeth. I'm committed to her. For as long as . . ."

He cleared his throat. "I guess what I'm trying to say is that she needs me. And I've come to need her, and to love her."

"I respect that, Cary. I wouldn't want to cause you or Elizabeth any hurt. But I promise you that no one—and certainly not Elizabeth—would ever have to know."

Cary put his elbows on the table, then took Claudia's hands in his.

"But I would know. I'd know every minute of every day," said Cary, his voice emotionally charged. "I couldn't do that to Elizabeth. I need to be worthy of her."

Claudia squeezed his hands and slowly nodded her head. "You are an awesome man, Cary Branscombe, do you know that?"

He let go of her hands and waved away her praise as he took a sip of cold coffee.

"Nope. I'm not. I'm just a lucky man is how I see it. I think I've made a real difference in Elizabeth's life—as much as she's made in mine."

The soft buzz of the early cocktail crowd in the bar was the background soundtrack as they each processed what had been said.

Cary had extended Elizabeth's invitation to drop by the casita. He knew that Claudia's curiosity wouldn't allow her to pass up the opportunity. She agreed to follow him in her car and shortly, both vehicles arrived at the casita.

Cary phoned ahead so that Elizabeth could freshen up before they arrived. Seated in her wheelchair outdoors beneath the canopy, she smiled and waved as the two approached.

"Welcome to our casita," said Elizabeth, beckoning Claudia to take a seat. "I've heard so many nice things about you from Cary. He attributes his appreciation of the arts to you."

"Cary was a natural. He came to my class eager to learn. He soaked up everything like a sponge. He's truly amazing," said Claudia. "He speaks very highly of you. Now that I've met you, I'm not surprised. I always knew that Cary would be attracted to a blueblood."

"I'm afraid I can't answer to that," replied Elizabeth coolly. "Where I come from, only the Cabots and the Lodges fit that description."

"Yes, of course," replied Claudia. "Please forgive me."

At that point, Cary felt compelled to enter the conversation and change the subject. "Did you know that Claudia's husband will be launching his campaign for governor next week?" Cary said, addressing Elizabeth.

"That's wonderful," said Elizabeth. She turned to Claudia. "Will you be involved in the campaign?"

"Rogers has asked me to work at his side," Claudia replied. "Help with editing speeches, prepare schedules, line up media interviews."

"It must be very exciting," said Elizabeth.

"Trust me. It will be," said Claudia, glancing at her cellphone. "As a matter of fact, if I don't get back to the Inn—where I've got my laptop—in the next thirty minutes, I'll be in trouble. Rogers will be contacting me with more things to manage for the campaign."

She stood. "You've been very kind to have me over. I wish you both only the best."

Cary got up and escorted Claudia to her car. He returned within a minute or two.

"Whew! Was I glad to see her go," said Cary.

"I commend you on the way you handled it," Elizabeth said. "I, too, am relieved. And I have a question. Did I hear correctly that her husband's first name is Rogers, not Roger?"

"You heard right. Nothing wrong with your hearing," replied Cary. "It's Rogers van Voorhees, and he wants to be governor of New Mexico. He's very ambitious and sees it as a stepping stone to a future race for the White House."

"I suppose I should let you know," said Elizabeth, "but when I saw this unfolding with Claudia, I wanted to tell you that if you had wanted to spend an afternoon or evening with her, I wouldn't object. I'm not unaware that you're a healthy young man and have needs that I can't fulfill."

"This is in character for you, Elizabeth. It's beyond generous. And I love you for it. But I take care of those needs when I'm in the shower," he said.

She blushed, something she wasn't often prone to do. Then she smiled warmly without uttering another word. After a few moments, when both had regained their composure, Cary spoke first.

"Well, getting on to another subject, I need to remind you that we have to come up with a name for our little pup," said Cary. "It's been almost two weeks since we brought her home.

"I've been too busy to think of anything," said Cary. "Do you have some names in mind?"

"Only one. It's Antigone," said Elizabeth. "We could call her Annie. Do you know why I chose that name?"

"I don't. Please tell me."

"In Greek mythology, Antigone was the niece of King Creon who had decreed that one of her brothers who had fallen in battle, Polynices, should not be buried because he fought on the side of the enemy, and that her other brother, Eteocles, who died a hero, should be honored and receive a proper burial.

"Antigone disobeyed the order on threat of death and was brought before her uncle to answer. One of the translations I liked best is this quote explaining her disobedience to Creon: 'You are a mere king. I answer to a higher authority.'"

"Yes, let's go with Antigone," said Cary enthusiastically. "That's a great quote."

"Now we have some planning to do," said Elizabeth. "Your friend Xander is coming for dinner on Friday evening, and I haven't the faintest idea what the menu should be. Do you have any suggestions?"

"I know he loves seafood, so let's focus on that," said Cary. "Outside of the fish counters at the supermarkets, there's Montoya's Seafood Market on Speedway. Whatever they have, it's always fresh. Much of it is brought in from the Sea of Cortez in Mexico.

"What would you think of serving him cabrilla, along with a nice white wine?" asked Cary.

"Cabrilla is perfect," said Elizabeth, "and I know a wine that will pair well with it. Albariño, it's a refreshing white from a winery here in southern Arizona. I've had it a couple of times, and I think that you and your friend will like it, too. Perfect for this hot weather."

She fanned herself with one hand. Sunlight cast dappled patterns through the trees. "I promised to tell you how I came to know something about wine. Well, whatever I know I learned from Arthur. In all those years when we couldn't be seen together in public at a restaurant, we would have lunch or dinner at my apartment. Arthur would always bring the wine. And it was usually an expensive bottle.

"A lecture about the wine accompanied every meal. So I learned a good bit over time. What made it so important to Arthur was that his wife didn't drink—not any kind of alcoholic beverage. And Arthur was a wine connoisseur." She gave a bittersweet smile. "And Arthur didn't want to drink alone."

The upcoming dinner was foremost in Elizabeth's thoughts. Cary had spoken so often and so glowingly about Xander.

"I know I mentioned it before . . ."

Elizabeth interrupted Cary. "Yes, I know, it's Xander pronounced like a Z."

Elizabeth felt that she would be meeting a celebrity. This would be the first friend of Cary's that she would encounter. That, too, kept her spirits high.

Soon Friday evening came and, as arranged, Xander phoned when he arrived and parked on the street in front of the main house. Cary went out to escort him down the path to the casita.

Earlier in the evening, during the dinner prep, Elizabeth had discussed details of the arrangements with Cary. She had explained how for her, preparing a dinner for guests, or even one guest, was a pleasure, not a chore at all. She believed it set the mood for the evening.

When Cary came in with Xander, he assumed a formal pose and said:

"Elizabeth, this man needs no introduction. He's been my role model since we first met at Fairfield. He's saved us from the bureaucrats, he's been an ongoing source of sound advice, and he's done more to help the less fortunate in this community than anyone I know."

Xander was not much older than Cary, and Elizabeth could tell at first glance that he saw himself as "working people" who didn't go to bed at night thinking of his next three-piece suit or how to increase his billable hours.

He wore no tie, and his long-sleeve Tattersall shirt added to that image. He stood about six feet tall, with bright blue eyes behind wire-rimmed glasses and brown hair that needed trimming. His suede shoes were as scuffed as any Elizabeth had seen.

By his appearance alone, one could easily imagine that Xander operated out of a low-rent office with secondhand furniture and an old copier that was always breaking down. It all corroborated what Cary had told her—that Xander's team did work for the poor and disadvantaged who needed legal representation but couldn't afford it.

Cary pulled out a chair for Xander.

"I can't tell you how much I've been looking forward to this evening," Elizabeth said. "Cary speaks of you as if you are Clarence Darrow, Martin Luther King, and Mother Teresa all wrapped up into one."

"I think that Cary exaggerates greatly," replied Xander affably. "But tonight, I'll gladly accept any compliments or tributes. I represented a poor soul in a hearing this afternoon. My client is not well, he's a few years short of sixty, can't work because of a back injury, and is about to get tossed out of a hole by some slumlord for nonpayment of rent.

"The judge castigates me, saying that I'm contributing to the breakdown of the Social Security system and old-fashioned work ethic by filing the man's claim for Social Security disability benefits. Anyway, don't mind me. This is a normal day in the life of a lawyer who represents the poor and disadvantaged."

Directing his comments to Elizabeth, Cary said, "Please, don't get him started on the environmental stuff or we'll never have dinner."

A short bark from the next room made them all turn.

"Oh, that's Annie," said Elizabeth. "She's the orphaned puppy that Cary rescued. We're still feeding her from the bottle. She probably won't approach you. She's still traumatized from a near-death experience. We can share that story with you over dinner."

A moment later, Xander pulled out his cellphone, which he had likely set on vibrate. "Apologies, but I've got to take this," he said. "It's the night nursing supervisor at County General Hospital."

"This is Xander," he answered, stepping away. "Yes, Ms. Spencer, they're my clients. We represented them in a landlord case recently. What are they doing in your hospital? Okay. I got it. Can you put them on? Yes, either one.

"Hello, Mrs. Carberry, this is Xander. You understand how serious this is. If your daughter's appendix is not removed, it could burst and she could die. We're going to ask the judge for an immediate order to proceed with the surgery. Your church will not hold you responsible.

"I've got to get on the phone now with the judge. We can't afford to waste even another minute. This is serious, and I wouldn't lie to you. Trust me. Please let me speak to the nursing supervisor."

Xander waited until the phone was handed back to the nursing supervisor.

"Ms. Spencer, please hold on. Don't go away," said Xander. "I'm going to contact the duty judge and request the order that you'll need. Do you have the papers ready for signature? . . . Excellent.

"Lourdes Estrada is the duty judge tonight and I'm setting us up for a conference call. Please hold on."

Moments later, Xander was in contact with the judge.

"Good evening, your honor. This is Alexander Cargill of Community Legal Services. I have Edna Spencer, the night nursing supervisor at County General Hospital, on the line. We have an emergency involving a minor and we need your assistance.

"Yes, ma'am, it's a life-or-death matter. This nine-year-old girl was brought to the hospital emergency room by her parents a short time ago. We represented them in an unrelated civil matter recently. Their daughter has been diagnosed with severe appendicitis and is in danger of her appendix bursting.

"It's a religious issue. The parents' faith doesn't allow surgery and the parents say they can't authorize it. But they don't want their daughter to die. The ER physician says it could be fatal if the appendix isn't removed.

"Ms. Spencer has the necessary papers filled out and can fax them to you immediately. You can sign using electronic signature."

There came a brief pause.

"Yes, your honor. They are ready to go. A resident was prepared to perform the surgery, but Ms. Spencer asked a surgeon who had just completed an emergency tracheotomy and was about to head home to stay for this, and he's agreed. He's a general surgeon with twenty-five years' experience.

"I should note one more thing, your honor. There's some unsettled law surrounding such emergency court orders . . . Yes, ma'am. I'm on the same page with you."

Immediately, the papers were signed, and the judge rang off.

"It looks like you're good to go, Ms. Spencer," said Xander. "I'll be pulling for the little girl. I'll stop by on my way home. Thanks for everything."

Xander returned the cellphone to his pocket and turned his attention to his hosts.

"The judge knew that there have been lawsuits and appellate rulings on some of these emergency orders," said Xander. "But her words to me were, 'I know that, but in no way am I going to allow this child to die.'

"It's times like this that make whatever inconveniences come with this job all worthwhile." He exhaled a deep breath, eyeing his hosts a bit sheepishly. "But I didn't come here to talk about me. I want to hear all about how you two got together."

"I do want to answer that," replied Elizabeth. "But before I do, Cary told me that you're a seafood lover. We are, too. We can eat right out here on the patio. I believe it's cooled off enough and we have the misters on."

"You're living in paradise here," said Xander. "What else could you want? And right in the heart of Tucson."

Elizabeth nodded in agreement. "We think so, too. But now, I've got a ceviche appetizer I'd like to bring out to get us started."

She wheeled herself back into the tiny kitchen, removed the appetizer from the refrigerator, and placed the three servings on a tray, which Cary carried out to the patio.

Next, he brought out and sliced a fresh baguette.

"Wow. This bread and the white wine play off beautifully against the ceviche," remarked Xander. "You folks really know how to put it on."

"I can't tell you how long we've wanted to do this—to have you over for dinner," said Elizabeth. "We are very much obliged to you for your kindness."

"I don't know if Cary told you how much he did to give our family peace of mind when Grandma was a patient at Fairfield," said Xander. "Oh, and don't let me forget before I leave to give you a form that I brought along. It's a medical power of attorney that Elizabeth will need to fill out and sign if she wants you to have that authority. Without it, if she goes to any hospital here, it would be the doctors who would hold that power should she not be capable of expressing her own wishes."

"Thank you," Elizabeth said.

Xander nodded. "Of course. I can also notarize your signature." He took a sip of wine. "When I was in court the other day representing Cary, I was there on my own time. I didn't want anyone accusing me of using Community Legal Services time to represent a client who might not qualify as low income."

"Do you receive support from the government?" asked Elizabeth.

"We receive our funding from several sources," said Xander. "That includes some from the federal government, but mostly from foundation grants. We are only involved in civil matters. Those who face criminal charges and can't afford their own lawyer are represented by the Office of the Public Defender, a county-funded agency.

"Believe me, there's plenty to keep us busy just handling civil matters. Most of our cases are evictions and other landlord issues. But we also deal with aggressive bill collectors, child support cases, and complaints against state agencies."

Cary heard a timer bell ring in the kitchen.

"That means our dinner's ready," he announced as he rose from his chair.

When he went to the kitchen, Elizabeth began to tell how she and Cary had met.

Cary returned carrying a loaded tray. At each place setting, he set down a plate with the cabrilla along with side dishes of wild rice and pencil-thin baby asparagus.

"It seems all of us are seafood lovers," Xander said. "I can't wait to taste this."

It was as if a starter's pistol at a track meet had sounded. All three immediately lifted their knives and forks.

"I've eaten cabrilla many times before," said Xander, "but never as tasty as this. Is this your own recipe?"

"Partly," replied Elizabeth. "But I got a little help from Chef Google. Actually, I learned while searching that there's a famous chef at a posh Manhattan restaurant who prepares his halibut using a similar recipe. I just combined a little bit of this and a little bit of that."

"And I love this wine," said Xander. "How did you come by this? I've never heard of Albariño."

"It's not a well-known varietal, and it's not expensive," said Elizabeth. "I got a taste of it several years ago. It was wonderfully refreshing. It's produced right here in Arizona. It reminded me of a Mâcon-Villages. But even tastier. I'm glad you like it."

"So please continue with your story," Xander said as he helped himself to more French bread.

"Okay, here it is," said Cary. "You know me, Xander. I've never been able to have long relationships with women I meet. I need food for the soul. I never found it until . . . until I met Elizabeth.

"I couldn't put a name on it. Elizabeth says we share *certain sensibilities*. It's got nothing to do with money or status, but it covers a lot. I guess you could say it's what makes us different from most other people."

"If I'm not overstepping my bounds, might I ask how you deal with the difference in ages?" Xander asked.

"It's okay. It's the same question everyone asks. It's one to which we gave a lot of thought," replied Cary. "I think Elizabeth can answer it best."

"I'm glad that you asked the question," said Elizabeth. "It's a vexing one and the issue is ever-present. We accept the reality that our time together won't be long, so each day is special.

"When we're together, I don't think of myself as aged. I feel in spirit that I'm Cary's age and that we can do everything except activities that require youthful physical stamina and ability."

She twirled her wineglass stem, considering her next words. "We're very much aware that we won't be hiking the Pacific Crest Trail, nor will we be having children or indulging in passionate physical expression.

"But our situation here allows us to share the many significant contributions in the world of literature, the arts, music, and other classics. We also experience the gifts of nature, many of which we have right outside our door.

"Moreover, in the time we've been together, we have managed to explore each other's souls. Cary and I have deep feelings and personal thoughts that we never imagined we could share with anyone."

Elizabeth paused to allow Cary to speak.

"Included in that is a part of our relationship that we rarely talk about with others," Cary said. "Often when I'm with Elizabeth, my image of her shifts back and forth between now and decades ago. I see her when she was twenty-five like she was in the photo of her that was on her nightstand."

"And I can tell when he's doing that, it makes me feel twenty-five," said Elizabeth. She caught Cary's gaze and grinned. "It makes for an interesting day."

Xander sat with both elbows on the table and looked directly at Elizabeth.

"I must tell you that I envy you both," said Xander. "I'm looking at Elizabeth right now and listening to her I can believe she's twenty-five.

"Cary, I believe she's cast a spell over both of us."

Soon it was time for dessert. Cary brought out raspberry tarts and a thermal carafe of coffee.

"Believe me, we don't eat like this every night," Cary said, "but we wanted to make your dinner a special event."

The evening went on and more stories were exchanged.

Around 11 p.m., Xander took another call. "Yes, that's great news. I'm so relieved. Thanks, Ms. Spencer, for letting me know. I'll be on my way home in a few minutes and will stop by the hospital and see the girl's parents. Thanks again for all you do."

He slipped the phone back into his pocket and rose to his feet. "I'll never forget this evening," Xander said with feeling. "You both are role models for me. Whenever I start to believe that a challenge is too great to rise above or that I'll never find the right partner, I'll only need to remind myself of you."

He gave each of them a hug as he said goodnight.

Elizabeth thought she saw tears in Xander's eyes, but couldn't be sure.

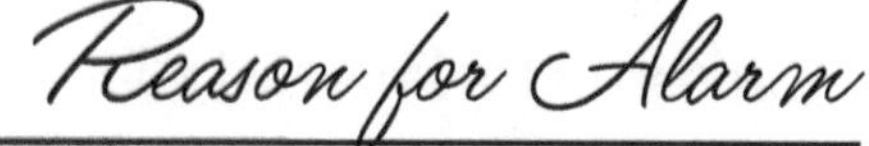

SATURDAY MORNING WOULD NOT be a day to sleep late. Elizabeth had reminded Cary that the tutor she had engaged would be arriving at 10 a.m., and that Marie was coming at 2 p.m.

"You haven't told me much about this man," said Cary as they finished their breakfast of French toast and coffee. "I understand he's a retired professor."

"From what Inez told me, I believe you'll find that he'll be able to answer all your questions and more," said Elizabeth. "I hope he can also provide you with a road map—a guide—to help you make your way into a good graduate program.

"He should be arriving soon. Oh, and we have the dog trainer coming Monday at ten. You'll be working, but Annie and I will be here to receive her."

A half hour later, Professor Emeritus Matthew Eckersley ambled down the path toward the casita, clearly admiring the lush flora and fauna.

Casually attired in Tucson's de rigueur khaki cargo shorts, T-shirt—with the logo of a wildlife rescue facility on its front and a hand-painted likeness of a Gambel's quail on the back—and Birkenstocks, he presented the picture of a laid-back, self-confident individual. He was nicely tanned, stood almost six feet, and had receding gray hair and a pencil mustache.

Cary came out to greet him and escorted him to the patio table.

"Welcome to our casita, Professor Eckersley. We're honored to have you here. I can't tell you how much I appreciate this."

"Please, it's just Matt. Matt will be fine," answered the professor.

"Well, okay then, Matt it is," said Cary.

As Elizabeth wheeled herself out, Cary made the introduction.

"Matt, I'd like you to meet Elizabeth," he said. "It's she who made the arrangements for you to be here."

After a handshake and a warm smile, Elizabeth removed a cover from a waiting tray piled high with almond croissants.

"I'll pour the coffee," said Cary.

Then the two sat down to start work.

For the next two hours, there was continuous conversation combined with the pages of Cary's physics textbook flipping back and forth. He filled more than twenty pages in his notebook.

"Oh my gosh!" exclaimed Cary looking at his cellphone. "Elizabeth said she arranged for you to work with me for an hour."

"Not a problem," replied Matt. "I'm glad I could help. Materials engineering is not an easy field, and solid-state physics isn't for everyone. But I believe you have the stuff to get you there."

"Well, if I do, it will be in no small part due to your help," Cary said. "This morning has been a real eye-opener for me. I want to thank you again. And by the way, Elizabeth and I would like to make a contribution to the wildlife rescue facility where you volunteer."

"Great. I've written the name and directions for getting there," he said, handing him a folded slip of paper. "I volunteer there on Sundays, so you might run into me."

After Matt had departed, Cary offered Elizabeth a glass of freshly-squeezed orange juice.

"I'm still in a daze," he said. "Are you aware of the difference this session has made for me?"

"Of course I am," said Elizabeth. "I wanted to surprise you. Also I didn't want you to choke up prior to meeting Matt. That's why I didn't tell you much about his background."

"What? You mean there's more to him than just being a retired physics professor?"

"Yes, much more," replied Elizabeth. "Professor Eckersley is a Nobel laureate."

Cary gasped.

"Before he retired, he shared the prize with two other scientists, a Brit and a German. It was in connection with their research in particle matter and linear colliders."

She smiled at his astonishment. "Don't ask me to explain it. I came across it on the Internet when I googled him."

She glanced at her watch. "I have Marie coming at two, so perhaps we should talk about lunch plans. Is there anything special that you might like?"

"If we still have any of that tuna salad that you made yesterday, I sure could go for some more of that," Cary replied.

"There is, and it's enough for two," said Elizabeth. "It should be easy to prepare. And I wanted to ask you if you perhaps have any ideas for a Sunday outing tomorrow?" She held up her hand. "But before you answer, I wanted to call your attention to the fact that we have a number of canned items in the pantry that are soon to expire. What would you think of donating those to the Food Bank? It will help to feed hungry people."

"Good idea," replied Cary. "I'm glad you noticed it. Barb volunteers at the Food Bank. I can ask her if she would take along our donation the next time she's scheduled to work."

"Cary, you're such a good person," said Elizabeth, "but I've never had any doubts about that."

"Glad you think so," said Cary. "And about tomorrow, it just happens that I do have an idea. It's apple harvest time down in Willcox. Have you ever been there?"

"No, and I've always wanted to go," replied Elizabeth. "Every time, it was the same old story. Arthur wanted to take me, but he was afraid we'd run into someone he knew."

"The forecast is calling for perfect weather and I'm sure we'll have a good time," said Cary. "I'll volunteer to pick the apples and hand them to you so you can put them in a basket. We can also buy one of their famous pies to take home."

The weekend passed quickly, and on Monday morning, bright and early, the dog trainer arrived at their door. Elizabeth had been left with a favorable impression of her as a result of their brief phone conversation during which Elizabeth had caught an unmistakable British accent.

Elizabeth asked Cary to fill the electric kettle before he logged in to work. She planned to welcome her guest by offering her a choice of coffee or tea before getting down to business.

Two short raps on the wooden screen door were sufficient to set off a barrage of high-pitched barks from the pet crate in the living room.

"Come in!" Elizabeth called out, and a tall woman clad in white shorts, sneakers, and a navy blue polo shirt entered.

True to her accent, she had an even and fair English complexion and carried herself with excellent posture. She wore her mass of long black hair loose with wide bangs that fell below her eyebrows. She swished the hair out of her way with a flick of her head.

"Ms. Gardner?" the woman asked with a smile. She extended her hand and said, "I'm Rayne. We spoke on the phone about your new puppy."

Elizabeth turned her head toward the source of the barking. "You can tell that we have no need of a doorbell here," she said. "And please—call me Elizabeth."

Pleasantries were exchanged and almost simultaneously Cary emerged. He wore his usual "work uniform" as he called it—khaki shorts, a blue chambray shirt with the sleeves rolled up, and leather sandals. His sudden appearance surprised Rayne. She shot a quick glance at Cary.

He gave a nod acknowledging her. "I've got three minutes before I start my shift. Do you need anything, Elizabeth?"

"Cary, your timing is perfect, as always," she replied. "I want you to meet Rayne, the puppy's new trainer. Rayne, this is Cary, my . . . housemate."

Cary suppressed a grin at Elizabeth's new term characterizing their relationship.

Brief chit-chat ensued until Elizabeth said, "Cary, the red tray in the kitchen—it's a bit more than I can manage. Could you bring it out for me, please?"

Cary returned with the tray which held three unmatched earthenware mugs of coffee, paper plates and napkins, and a pie tin lined with a paper doily upon which rested a mound of blueberry scones, still warm from the oven.

Sterling silver teaspoons and spreaders stood in a mug of their own. A small plate of unsalted butter and a half-pint, glass canning jar filled with vibrant-colored apricot jam completed the offerings.

"Oh, my!" exclaimed Rayne, laughing. "I think I've died and gone to Heaven."

Rayne was an attractive woman. The problem, or a potential one, was the lightning-quick flash of interest in Cary that she involuntarily transmitted when their eyes met. He didn't want to hang around a minute longer. Why plant a seed if you don't want it to take root and grow?

Cary bent down and gave Elizabeth a parting kiss on her cheek. He quickly gathered up a couple of scones and his coffee and made a hasty exit to his work.

The two women chatted amiably while enjoying their *kaffeeklatsch*. Rayne explained that she was born in England and came to the United States while working as an *au pair* when she was in her early twenties.

She said she loved the children she had looked after, but when the family eventually returned to England, she had decided to remain in Tucson. She had fallen in love with the desert and the wonderful winter weather.

"Now, let me introduce you to your new student," said Elizabeth as she maneuvered her wheelchair toward the puppy's crate. "This is Annie."

As the two women neared the crate, excited yips of joy began.

"Hello there," Rayne said, as she unlatched the crate, and watched as a black-and-white blur romped joyfully out of the crate and headed straight to her.

"Would you mind if I left you two alone to get acquainted?" Elizabeth asked. "I have a letter to finish that must go into the mail today."

"We'll be fine," Rayne said. "I have a collar and leash with me. I'll be taking her outside to see how she does on a walk."

Rayne began petting the wiggly puppy, who was obviously delighted to have found some freedom and a playmate. Later, after the dog trainer departed on her walk with Annie, Cary stepped out for his morning break. He stopped on the patio to look over Elizabeth's shoulder.

"What are you working on?" he asked.

"I'm checking out curricula at some leading schools for the bachelor's degree in materials engineering," she replied. "You'll have an advantage in knowing what's ahead when you're ready to fill out your applications."

"You do think of everything," said Cary. "This reminds me, do you think you could arrange another session for me with Matt? I still have some questions I'd like to ask him. In this field, you open one door, and it takes you to three more. Now he's got me curious about his research with particle matter and linear colliders."

"I have a hard time understanding any of that," Elizabeth admitted.

"Matt laid it out like this," Cary said, holding up a teaspoon. "You could easily describe this spoon in my hand from what you are seeing. And if you place it under a magnifying glass, you'll see some things you couldn't have seen with the naked eye."

Elizabeth nodded.

"But let's say you decide to look at it under a microscope. Then you would see many things that aren't visible under the magnifying glass. And if you placed it under an electron microscope, then you would see even more."

"What we are doing here is exploring *inner* space, whereas our astronauts and unmanned space vehicles are exploring *outer* space. Scientists, and especially materials engineers, need to know what particles compose the materials they're working with. That holds especially true for those working in cutting-edge research."

"I can imagine," she murmured. "It's all quite fascinating."

"As we probe deeper into inner space in search of answers, equipment such as linear colliders plays an important role in this regard," he continued. "I was reading yesterday about a team that is working to develop a product that, when painted on a surface, can reflect ninety percent of the sun's heat bearing down on that surface. Currently when we coat our roofs here with a white elastomeric, we are reflecting perhaps half that percentage or less.

"If and when this product reaches the market, it could be revolutionary. Imagine how much electrical energy running air conditioners could be saved. This is the kind of research I want to be a part of.

"But what I came out here for was to report some good news. When I checked in with my supervisor this morning, he informed me that corporate had approved me for a raise. My metrics for the last quarter had exceeded the company's standards for its inbound call center reps, and I'll be receiving a dollar-an-hour increase starting next week."

"Congratulations, darling," replied Elizabeth. "Is there anything that you don't do well? You know I'm proud of you. Don't you?"

"It's nice to hear it coming from you," Cary said as he kissed her on the cheek. "But I'd better get back to work or they'll take back my raise."

"I have some news about the dog trainer, but I'll save it for later," Elizabeth said.

Meanwhile, a new tradition had evolved. On Friday nights, dinner wasn't home-cooked, but came from a restaurant. Cary and Elizabeth alternated choosing the eatery, with each selecting their preferences from the restaurant's online menu. Cary handled the pick-up, using an insulated bag to guarantee the food would arrive hot.

They agreed that the weekends should begin in a festive mood, a departure from the daily routine. Splurging on two takeout dinners was their version of a "date night."

On this particular Friday evening, Cary returned with dinner in tow and a small surprise. He found that the table had already been set. An ample green napkin lay beside each white plate.

There was room on the table for the single, long-stemmed red rose that he had brought home for Elizabeth. Removing a narrow, tall vase from the cupboard, he placed the rose in the vase and set it in front of Elizabeth's place setting.

It was then that Cary noticed that a small green cream pitcher in the center of the table was filled with cilantro. Lit votive candles in green glass holders added to the gracious and relaxing atmosphere. He paused in the middle of the kitchen for a moment, taking it all in.

Elizabeth wheeled herself into the kitchen.

"Wow! This is beautiful, Elizabeth. My only complaint is that you're supposed to have the night off."

"I *do* have the night off, dear, but I also try to maintain certain standards."

Cary grinned. "I have noticed that, Elizabeth."

"One simply *must,* Cary. If one begins eating food from plastic containers—or worse yet—from Styrofoam..." She shuddered at the thought. "Then what's next?"

Cary frowned to show Elizabeth that he was thinking hard, trying to find the right answer to her rhetorical question. "Let me guess—the downfall of Western civilization?"

"Something like that," Elizabeth replied, smiling in spite of herself.

Cary proceeded to uncork a dry Vouvray that Elizabeth had chosen. He poured wine into each of the stemmed glasses, carefully placed the bottle on the table so that the label faced Elizabeth, and then sat down to join her.

When Cary was about to pick up his knife and fork, Elizabeth reached across the table and placed her hand on his. "Cary, I adore the rose. Thank you.

"But before we begin, I want to make a toast," she said. *"Con su permiso."*

Cary nodded once and laid down his cutlery. They lifted their glasses.

"Forgive me if this turns out to be a longer than average toast," warned Elizabeth, with a smile.

Speaking softly, and with deep feeling, she began.

"Here's to you, Cary," she said in her soft voice. She spoke slowly and deliberately, enunciating each word and phrase with feeling. "Thank you for the wonderful week you've given me ... for these cozy Friday nights in your very excellent company."

She paused to take a deep breath and glanced away for a second before she continued. "But most of all, Cary, my deepest thanks for ... for truly ... giving me such happiness ... for the opportunity of making a home together."

Cary let his focus rest upon her for several heartbeats. He couldn't take his eyes away. Her face shone with a new radiance, as beautiful as any sunrise or sunset or rainbow he'd ever seen. They touched their glasses together, and Elizabeth sipped from her wineglass, then lifted it toward Cary in tribute. Her fair complexion was dewy from a few errant tears, happy tears though they were.

"Eat, darling," she said to Cary in a lighter tone. "The salad's wilting and the quiche is getting cold."

"Yes, ma'am," he replied with a smile, following her lead.

They began their meal quietly because both of them were savoring the mood rather than the food, but eventually it was Elizabeth who broke the silence.

"It's been a few days, but I haven't had an opportunity to tell you about the puppy's first training session."

"No, and I'm eager to hear," replied Cary taking another bite.

"Well, first let me say that Rayne appears to be a trainer with a magic touch. She was only here for about an hour, but she taught Annie to sit still for her collar and leash to be put on. Then she took her on a meandering walk all around the neighborhood. By the end of the lesson, whenever Rayne halted, Annie would sit at her feet and look up at her."

"Sounds like a good start," he said.

"Yes, it was. Rayne told me that Annie was having fun and totally engaged in the process. It was though they were really communicating with each other. The dog was so focused on what they were doing. Her expression seemed to say: *Are we finished? Or are we resting and then going on? Just let me know.*"

"You never told me that you were a mind reader," said Cary.

"It's a talent I don't often reveal," she replied. "Please tell not a soul or everyone will think I can read *their* minds, too."

They both laughed.

"So you'll have Rayne back for another training session?"

"Most certainly," Elizabeth said.

"Great," said Cary.

She lifted her hand slightly to get Cary's attention. "And there's more news. Not about the dog, but about Rayne."

"You're excited, I can tell. You better tell me before you burst," Cary said.

"Guess what Rayne's hobby is?" asked Elizabeth.

Cary pursed his lips. "Dirt-bike racing?"

"No." Elizabeth feigned exasperation. "She is a genealogist. Immediately, I thought she might help us find Meg."

"Talk to her about it. See if she's interested," he said. "If she's as good at genealogy as she is with training dogs, she'll be a huge help. We can afford her."

"Thank you, Cary."

"Call her tomorrow—promise?"

Elizabeth nodded.

"I've got some news for you, too," said Cary. "I had about forty-five minutes when our system was down today, and I used it to do some research on tracking down Meg. "I went to the census records online and plugged in the address in Boston that you gave me. First thing I learned was that census records only become public after seventy years. Perhaps you and Rayne already knew that, but it came as a surprise to me."

"I remember hearing something about that when I worked at the library," Elizabeth said musingly. "I guess Rayne knows that, being the professional that she is."

Cary nodded. "I found the Ferguson household at 2713 N. Beacon Hill Place. But it was in the 1940 Census, and you must have been about fifteen at the time," said Cary. "There was your mother, Dorothea, you, a Yolanda Alvarez and what appears to be her daughter, Margarita Alvarez."

"Yes," responded Elizabeth. "That's Meg."

"Of course, these are things you already know. Either Rayne or I need to figure out other ways to find Meg. I've googled her so many times that it hurts. There are a few dozen Margarita Alvarezes that show up on any search, but none even come close to a match on her age. She would be about eighty-five if she's still living."

Cary's face softened. "And you should prepare yourself for that. After all, not everyone reaches your longevity."

"Yes, I know," said Elizabeth. "But Meg was healthy. I'm confident that she's still alive and that we'll find her."

Cary nodded. "Fair enough. I've done all the searches under the name Margarita Alvarez, and I'm convinced that we're not going to find her under that name. It may be that she's been married once or twice, and we have no clue as to what those names might be. We need to think outside the box on this one."

"Do you have anything in mind?" Elizabeth asked.

"I can't get into public school records, so we're shut out on that score, but what can you tell me about that private college prep or finishing school that you mentioned a while back? I believe it was something like Miss Parker's or Miss Pryce's."

"It was Miss Pryce's Armont Hills School," replied Elizabeth. "I can't forget it. It hurt me so badly at the time. The school was in a little town near Warrenton, Virginia, but I'm not sure if Meg ever attended."

"It's a lead that we need to chase down," said Cary. "We don't have that many options left."

They clasped hands. It had been a lovely evening. Before Elizabeth went to sleep, she said a prayer that Providence would look after this amazing young man with whom she had dined and who brought such strength and tenderness into her life.

●●● ┌─┐ ●●●

A few days later, Elizabeth awakened with a start. Something wasn't right, and she called Cary immediately.

Cary burst into her room at a run.

"I'm short of breath," she said, gasping. "I don't feel like I'm going to faint, but something isn't right."

Cary's chest constricted with worry. He'd been through this same situation many times at the nursing home and knew what to do—though never before had the crisis involved someone so close to him.

"We're not going to take any chances," he said firmly, reaching for his cellphone. "I'm calling 911. The paramedics will get you into the ER, and you'll be seen right away."

Cary sat on the edge of Elizabeth's bed and comforted her until the paramedics arrived and lifted her onto a gurney. They started her oxygen and a little color returned to her face.

As the emergency vehicle rolled along the city streets, one of the two paramedics received a call from her dispatcher.

"They're telling us that the emergency room at County General is full and that they're temporarily not taking any new admissions," said the paramedic. "We've been diverted to Bowles-Burkhart Memorial. It's a small private hospital here on the east side."

Cary gave a tense nod. "Fine, just hurry."

When they arrived, Elizabeth was wheeled into an uncrowded emergency room where a triage nurse removed her oxygen mask and switched her over to hospital-provided oxygen. Cary had brought along Elizabeth's ID, insurance cards, and other documents and filled out the admitting paperwork.

Meanwhile, a nurse took Elizabeth's vitals and started an IV. After a time, a young doctor wearing a stethoscope around her neck arrived and introduced herself.

"I'm Dr. Miller. I'm the hospitalist here. I'll be taking care of you today," she said as she accessed Elizabeth's chart on her handheld tablet.

"Thank you, doctor," Elizabeth whispered weakly. "Can you tell me what you've found so far?"

"It seems that your numbers are near normal," she replied. "That's fairly common with heart patients. These types of symptoms come and go. But, I'd like to run some tests before we send you home."

Those words alerted Cary. "Doctor, Elizabeth is under the care of Dr.

Geoffrey Rosenfeld, a local cardiologist who is familiar with her case. He may have already done some of the tests that you're considering," he said. "We would like you to consult with him before we go any further."

"I'm familiar with Dr. Rosenfeld. He's a very fine cardiologist, but he's not on our roster of doctors who have privileges to practice here," the doctor replied. "So I'm unable to contact him or confer with him."

"That's unfortunate," replied Cary. "Elizabeth needs the benefit of her full medical team."

He then used his cellphone to contact Dr. Rosenfeld's emergency number. After leaving a message with the answering service, he turned to the doctor.

"I should be hearing back from Dr. Rosenfeld soon," said Cary. "Meanwhile, I would like to place any further treatment or tests on hold."

Appearing flustered, the doctor asked Cary if he was a relative of the patient. Cary reached into a pocket and produced a document which he unfolded and handed to her.

"I have Elizabeth's medical power of attorney, and I'm acting on her behalf," said Cary. "But since she's right here, please feel free to ask her if she approves of my decision."

The doctor let out a huff, obviously not pleased with the way things were going.

"All right," she said with a frown. "You can wait here for your callback. If you need me, I'll be on the floor, and they can page me." With that, she departed.

About twenty minutes later, Dr. Rosenfeld was on the phone.

"Cary, I need the answer to two questions," said the doctor. "They are required to provide this information. Tell them if they don't, your cardiologist will file a complaint with the Board of Medical Examiners. That will get their attention.

"Here are the questions you need to ask: First, what is her blood pressure reading. Second, is there any indication of fluid buildup in her lungs? As soon as you have those answers, call me back on this cell number."

It was about an hour later when Cary again phoned Dr. Rosenfeld.

"It was no more difficult than pulling wisdom teeth," Cary reported dryly. "They were determined not to give me the information, but I was insistent. They finally called an administrator. When I told him that you would contact the Board of Medical Examiners, the administrator caved, and ordered the hospitalist to provide the information. He asked to see my medical power of attorney and practically put it under a magnifying glass.

"Elizabeth's blood pressure was 140 over 75, and the doctor said she saw no indication of any fluid buildup."

"Okay," said Dr. Rosenfeld. "I want you to check her out of the hospital. You don't need their approval to do that. You just tell them you are leaving . . . on my orders. Take her home. You can take a taxi. You don't need an ambulance. She'll be okay.

"I'm leaving my office in about an hour. I have my last appointment coming up here soon. I'll come to your house. I don't want you dragging Elizabeth to the office. She needs to rest. But don't put her in bed unless she asks. Just make her comfortable in her favorite chair or wherever she wants to be. Offer her something light to eat and try to get her to relax. This will likely pass."

An hour later, Dr. Rosenfeld was at their front door and Cary showed him in. Elizabeth was wide awake and seated in her favorite chair. She had taken some tea and toast and was eager to learn what the doctor might tell her.

"Dr. Rosenfeld, it's so kind of you to come here," Elizabeth said. "I didn't know that there were any doctors who still make house calls."

"You're an exception," replied the doctor. "I didn't want you to have to come to the office after what they've already put you through."

"I couldn't figure out why they wanted to do all those tests without first consulting you," Cary said to the doctor.

"It's a money thing," replied Dr. Rosenfeld. "Once some of those private hospitals get their talons into a patient, they'll soak them and their insurance company—or Medicare—for as much as they can get. The hospital where you were taken has a reputation for that sort of thing."

The doctor turned his full attention to Elizabeth, placing his stethoscope in all the necessary places.

"The good news is that no damage has occurred, and Elizabeth can gradually work back into her normal activities," he said. "But you both must remain aware that this is only a reprieve. I'm going to make some adjustments in her meds, but as with any case of congestive heart failure combined with her age, we have to take it from day to day.

"From what I already know, Elizabeth and you have used your time together to maximum advantage, and I admire you both for that." His voice grew gentle. "Please don't let this setback discourage you. Go for whatever your lives allow and have no regrets. I'll be in your corner and do everything I can."

Cary and Elizabeth looked at each other and acknowledged, hands clasped.

"And, Elizabeth, as you know, I'll honor your request for no medical heroics," the doctor continued. "I've got that message loud and clear. So, I'll leave you for now and let you enjoy each other's company. There's no charge for this visit. Call me when you need me."

After the doctor departed, Cary made Elizabeth comfortable in her chair—she insisted that she didn't want to go to bed—and brought her a mug of hot cocoa.

"You've got a winner in Dr. Rosenfeld," said Cary, after he was seated and sipping from his own mug.

"I know. I'm very fortunate," replied Elizabeth. She studied him, seeming to realize that he didn't want to speak any more about her condition. "I, too, would like to get that experience out of my mind and switch to something more optimistic. Anything new in the search for Meg?"

"Well, there is something new, but right now it's not going to get us any closer to Meg," Cary reported. "I learned that Miss Pryce's school closed its doors for good in 1956. It went the way of many of those upper-class private schools. If Meg had gone there, she would have been in the Class of 1946 or 1947."

"But we're not quitting. Have you heard anything from Rayne?"

"She phoned the other day," said Elizabeth. "But nothing so far. She believes, as you do, that if Meg is alive, she's going by a different last name. Rayne checked marriage licenses in Massachusetts going back to the 1940s. Not a trace."

Cary sighed. "Changing the subject, you might remember that my friend Felix Montalvo will be in town over the holidays, and we had talked about having him over for dinner. I wonder if that's still a good idea?"

"The way I'm feeling right now, the answer is yes," replied Elizabeth. "Given the current circumstances, there's no way to say anything for sure. It's still a ways off. If we should need to cancel, then we cancel. From what you've told me about Felix, he sounds like a real character."

"That he is," said Cary. "He's been out of the country for the last five years. You won't be disappointed. And we don't need to prepare a fancy dinner. He would be happy with spaghetti and meatballs, with some toasted garlic bread on the side and lots of beer. He can really put it away. Trust me.

"And speaking of plans, we had talked about a trip to the wildlife refuge where Matt volunteers. We still need to make that donation in his honor."

"I'd be game for it anytime," said Elizabeth.

A 'Do Nothing' Day

Sunday morning, after breakfast, Cary was behind the wheel with Elizabeth sitting beside him in the passenger seat "riding shotgun," as he insisted on calling it. For the outing, Elizabeth wore a gored denim skirt with a white linen tunic, untucked, and a tan leather concho belt. Small antique silver hoop earrings were her only jewelry.

Her wheelchair and a walker were tied down and riding behind them in the truck's bed as they headed east.

The wide, three-lane city streets had given way to a two-lane county road that was lined on both sides by multi-acre ranch properties. Dwellings and barns, though set back from the road, were visible to passersby. The owners had found their dream sites. They lived close enough to town to be only a short drive from their work but far enough away to enjoy what they had come to Tucson for: elbow room, breathing space, privacy, the desert, and the ambiance of the old west.

The weather was unseasonably warm but nowhere near approaching Arizona summer temperatures.

Elizabeth turned to look at Cary. Regarding him from any angle was very pleasant but seeing him in profile was especially rewarding. She liked his high cheekbones, his perfect chin, the crows' feet starting to form at his eyes, and his wavy hair being set alive by the wind entering from the driver's open window.

"Cary, tell me!" she demanded. Elizabeth was not angry, but she was mystified and didn't like being kept in the dark. "I've been so patient, but now you must tell me where we're going and why. Also, you said we would be observing a 'DND' today. What does that mean?"

Cary suddenly pushed down on the brake pedal and extended his right arm and open palm in front of Elizabeth, protecting her from any impact in the event he would need to apply the brakes with even greater pressure.

"Wow! Look at that monster!" he exclaimed, staring straight ahead.

That's when Elizabeth realized what was happening. There was a long snake across the roadway, directly in front of the truck. "Good grief!" she cried out, pushing back in her seat.

"You've never seen a snake before?"

"Not like this one."

"That's a bull snake. Looks like about an eight-footer. Problem is that he's headed north, but he's got to cross this east-west road to do it."

Elizabeth watched, fascinated, as the creature slowly continued undulating its body from one side of the road to the other. All traffic, whatever there was on that county road, had come to a halt. There were no vehicles behind the Mazda, but two westbound cars were waiting for the snake to reach the north berm.

When it finally reached the other side and Cary cruised forward, Elizabeth returned to her questioning. "So, as I was saying—asking—what does 'DND' mean?"

He smiled. "It means 'Do Nothing Day.' I picked it up from some friends in Seattle."

"But dear, we *are* doing something. I'm not sure exactly what yet, but we're in the process . . . are we not?"

Cary nodded. "A do-nothing day means you don't do anything you usually do. For one day, forget your day job if you've got one. Don't do any chores around the house. No laundry, no cooking, no tutoring, no catching up on anything. Do something. But don't do anything you usually do."

Elizabeth smiled. She quickly understood why Cary liked this idea, and she was starting to like it, too. "I see. So you don't take calls, or paint the front door, or . . . plant a hibiscus in the yard where I can see it from the porch. Is that correct?"

Cary stole a glance at Elizabeth, and grinned. "Was that a hint? About a hibiscus?"

Her smile widened. "Yes, it was."

"Done. I'll pick one up tomorrow."

"Thank you."

A few moments passed and then Elizabeth mused aloud, "It seems you take hints very well."

"I try," said Cary.

"Well, then, I suppose I'd better be careful about what I hint at." She glanced toward the peaks of the Rincon Mountains. "I do love being out in the desert like this, but you still haven't told me where we're going on this Do Nothing Day."

"It's a little surprise for you. As you know, Matt volunteers at the Rincon Wildlife Rehab. Evidently, it's run on a shoestring by a woman named Bonnie. They do great work. A couple of vets help by providing pro bono services, and they've got volunteers of all ages. That's where we're headed. I thought you'd like that."

"Oh, Cary, I love it!" Elizabeth said, clasping her hands together under her chin.

"And remember? Matt doesn't accept payment for his tutoring services. Instead, we agreed to make a contribution to the wildlife rehab. I've got a check for Bonnie right here," he said pointing to a white envelope tucked underneath the truck's sun visor.

At that moment, Cary's cellphone sounded. He glanced at the readout before answering. "Hey, Matt. We're on our way. Got held up for a while with some snake traffic crossing the road, but we're only about ten minutes away."

Elizabeth couldn't hear what Matt was saying, but Cary was nodding okay and again pressing down on the brake pedal, but more softly this time. He turned the pickup into a nearby driveway, then backed out and turned the truck around.

"What's that address again?" he asked, speaking into the phone, then added a few uh-huhs. "We've already reversed course. Be there as quick as we can."

Elizabeth couldn't imagine why they were now headed back toward town, but she sensed their trip to the wildlife rehab facility might have just been canceled.

"Cary, what's happening?" she asked.

"Change of plans," Cary replied. "That was Matt. He had planned on giving us a tour of the rehab. But an emergency popped up. Some baby javelinas are trapped at a house in the foothills. Matt and a tech are on the way there now. He wants us to meet him there."

Elizabeth brightened at hearing the news. "Well, this will be better than a tour. We'll get to see an actual rescue."

"Right," responded Cary.

They headed west and not long after picked up Swan Road and soon crossed the dry riverbed of the Rillito. They were in the foothills of the Santa Catalina Mountains.

"Isn't this Flecha Caida?" asked Elizabeth. She was referring to Flecha Caida Ranch Estates, a residential subdivision in an unincorporated area north of the city.

"I sure hope so. That's where Matt said we'd find him."

"Do you know what the name means, Cary?" she asked.

Cary shook his head. "Nope. For years I called it 'Fletcher Coyote' until a patient at the nursing home set me straight," he said, and they both laughed.

"It's Spanish, of course, and translates as 'Fallen Arrow,'" Elizabeth said.

"Hmmm. How do you come to know all these things?"

"Remember, dear, I was a librarian. Librarians are exposed to lots of information over their careers—some of it useful . . . some of it interesting . . . some of it both. And some of it neither."

Cary cut a sharp corner, turned north, and drove uphill into one of the older sections of the tract until he saw a white van bearing the logo of the Rincon Wildlife Rehab parked curbside—except there were no curbs in this area, and no sidewalks either. Only a dirt road flanked by houses on large lots, with mature indigenous mesquite trees, mountain ash, agave cacti, desert willows, and other native species all around. There were giant rocks and boulders everywhere.

A cluster of onlookers was mulling around in a circle staring at the ground. Matt was among them.

Cary parked his truck as near as possible, which wasn't really very close at all, but it was the best spot available. He grabbed a small stepstool from the back of the truck, along with the walker, and helped Elizabeth step down from the Mazda to where she could use the walker.

Matt spotted them and came over immediately.

"What's happening?" Cary asked.

"Let me fill you in," said Matt. "This neighborhood dates back to the 1950s, and it has in-ground, recessed garbage cans. It was innovative at the time.

"Wildlife thrives up here, and the idea was to put the garbage where scavengers couldn't get to it. There are a few hundred houses here that have this type of in-ground set-up. These garbage cans are covered with a heavy hinged lid that the scavengers can't open. It was a great idea, and it works fine . . . until it doesn't."

"Like now," said Cary.

"Exactly," replied Matt. "These baby javelinas you'll see look like they are only two or three weeks old. They're called 'reds.'"

Elizabeth gripped the walker and her expression tightened. Cary became concerned. He knew that she was empathizing with the plight of the babies.

This unplanned glimpse into Matt's volunteer work, although fascinating, posed a danger to Elizabeth due to her heart condition.

"So these babies, these reds, are trapped inside one of those cans?" Elizabeth asked.

Before Matt could answer, an outdoorsy-looking young woman with a ponytail ran up to him. She wore a polo shirt, faded jeans, hiking boots, and a baseball cap.

"There are too many people here," she said to Matt. She spoke rapidly and kept turning her head to look back. "The mother javelina is over there to the left," she said, pointing to a mass of striped agave at the edge of the yard. "She's all riled up and keeps circling around, coming closer and closer to the babies, but gets spooked and then backs off."

"Gotta go," said Matt as he hurried off.

"Cary, did you hear that? There are babies trapped in one of those garbage setups," said Elizabeth.

The anguish showed on her face and in her voice.

"Don't worry. Matt will know what to do," Cary replied reassuringly.

Using her walker, Elizabeth began laboriously advancing up the incline, one small step at a time. The effort was taxing her strength.

Cary's concern grew. "Elizabeth! Stop right there!"

Startled, Elizabeth froze.

In one quick motion, Cary bent down and swept Elizabeth up and into his arms.

"Put your arms around my neck and hold on. I'm not going to let you fall," he said. "And I'm not going to let you miss this either."

Elizabeth's mouth opened in surprise. Cary's sweeping her up off her feet seemed to have left her temporarily speechless. As she was carried onward toward the rescue site, her cheeks flushed with embarrassment. The group of interested neighbors who had gathered to watch the rescue had switched their attention to Elizabeth and Cary.

"Cary," she whispered, "people are staring."

He put his lips near her ear. "It's because you're beautiful," he whispered.

"Oh, shush," Elizabeth said, but smiled nevertheless.

Cary felt her relax in his arms.

Matt saw them approach and waved them over to where he and the young woman volunteer were conferring. Cary carefully set Elizabeth on her feet but kept his arm around her.

Matt laughed. "That was quite an entrance, Elizabeth."

Elizabeth smiled and shrugged as if to convey that she had nothing to do with any of it.

"Take about two steps forward," said Matt. "We're going to make everyone move back in a minute, but I want you to see these baby reds up close while you can."

With Cary on one side and Matt on the other, they helped Elizabeth to inch nearer the edge of the recessed trash barrel. They could look down directly into it and see the two bristly-haired young javelinas, whose coats really did have a red hue.

Frightened, the babies were in constant motion, running in little circles on the barrel's flat bottom. Their tiny hooves clattered loudly, the noise magnified by the acoustics of the steel receptacle.

Against all odds, one or both of the babies kept trying to defy gravity and escape by jumping up against the sides of the can, only to slide back down to the bottom, again and again. Frantic, the babies wanted their mother.

Matt made eye contact with his helper and called out, "Sedona, ask all the neighbors to please leave the yard and go back to the road while we work this out.

"And Cary," he added, "why don't you take Elizabeth back to the truck. She'll be able to see the rest of this pretty well from there. The mama is getting more and more agitated. We need to keep things quiet so she'll calm down while we get her little guys out of that barrel."

So it went. With Elizabeth back in his arms, Cary carried her to the truck and helped her into the passenger seat. He retrieved the abandoned walker from the hillside and returned it and the stepstool to the truck.

He got in behind the wheel, reached into their cooler, and removed two bottles of cold water. After loosening the caps, he handed one to Elizabeth.

"I'm so thirsty," she said, taking a drink. "And it feels so good to sit down again."

"You had a little workout," Cary said.

"Well worth it," replied Elizabeth. "I wouldn't have missed seeing those little javelinas for the world."

They sipped their water and watched. The truck's elevated cab afforded them an excellent view, and they focused on the rescuers as each donned elbow-length, bite-proof padded gloves and protective eyewear.

In gear and ready, with Matt on one side of the barrel and Sedona on the other, on the count of three, they pulled the metal can out of its well and quickly set it on its side.

More noise. The clatter from the metal hitting river rocks on the ground, plus the hooves of the javelinas, as they scrambled out of their prison, made a loud commotion.

With snorts and grunts, the mama came in even closer this time as the babies rushed to her side. She took a sniff at each one and then scurried away toward the brush with the little ones behind her trying to keep up.

"Look at that," said Cary with a laugh. "Freedom!"

Elizabeth leaned forward. "Cary, look! They're out and on their way home with their mother and littermates. I am so relieved," she said with a happy sigh.

With the javelinas' mother in the lead and the little ones following as fast as their little hairy legs could carry them, they rounded the farthest corner of the front yard and disappeared from view.

"Not too bad for a Do Nothing Day, is it?" Cary asked with a grin, pulling another bottle of water out of the cooler. He handed the bottle over, saying only one word: "Drink."

As she drank, she turned to Cary. "Years ago, at our library branch, a gentleman from a wildlife protection group spoke. His subject was the javelina.

"Using a slide projector, he showed us photos of many javelinas. One of the things I learned was that javelinas are peccaries. They are often mistaken for wild pigs. They are not wild pigs or feral hogs. They are distantly related to pigs, but they come from a different family or species." Her lips pursed. "Sadly, they often fall prey to predators such as coyotes or mountain lions."

At that moment another call came in on the cell. It was Matt. He was preparing to depart the rescue site and suggested that Cary follow him back to the wildlife rehab so that Elizabeth could see the facility and the work that went on there.

Cary took no convincing. He wanted Elizabeth to have the tour Matt had promised and looked forward to it himself. He was about to pass on the revised plan to Elizabeth but changed his mind.

Elizabeth, her seatbelt snug, leaned back against the headrest with her eyes closed. Her breathing was soft and steady. The capped water bottle lay in her lap. She was fast asleep.

About twenty minutes later, the truck's roll into the unpaved parking lot of the facility jostled Elizabeth enough to awaken her. Cary watched as she blinked her eyes and stretched.

"Feel okay?" he asked.

"Hmmm, yes, thank you. I had a good nap, and from what I'm seeing . . . is this the wildlife rehab?"

Cary acknowledged, parked the truck, and then switched off the engine. He helped Elizabeth make the transfer to her wheelchair, whereupon the two then headed toward a vintage mobile home that appeared to be the office.

The sign out front read: *Welcome to Rincon Wildlife Rehab.*

The door of the mobile home opened. Matt came down the steps, followed by a woman in her forties clad in jeans and a man's blue work shirt, a visor, and sunglasses. Her hair was more pepper than salt, worn in braids across the top of her head like a tiara. She would look perfectly at home in an open Jeep or on a horse any place in the west.

A younger woman, also in jeans, followed. She was slim and fit and wore her hair in a ponytail.

Matt made quick introductions. Braided Tiara was Bonnie, the middle-aged founder and manager of the operation. Ponytail was a volunteer named Caitlin. Bonnie gave the visitors a gentle handshake and a warm, welcoming smile.

Elizabeth took the opportunity to hand Bonnie the envelope containing the contribution that she and Cary had been waiting to present to her. She explained that Matt had declined a tutoring fee and asked if instead they would make a contribution to the wildlife rehab.

Bonnie accepted the envelope, expressing heartfelt thanks. Then, almost immediately, the group set off on the tour with Matt leading the way.

It was even more of a grassroots operation than Elizabeth had envisioned, cobbled together with building blocks of good intentions and selfless effort.

Matt explained that Bonnie had leased the three-acre plot for one hundred dollars a year for five years. He described the landowner as "a real sweet guy" who cared about the desert creatures as much as Bonnie did. He often volunteered there, and his three busy gas stations in town allowed him to be an angel to the nonprofit wildlife rehab.

As they walked the property, Matt provided a running commentary, aided often by Bonnie. Sedona, who was also present, contributed details and the circumstances surrounding each of the fowl recovering there.

The facility provided the basics for abandoned or injured creatures. There were dozens of pens of different sizes, some with handyman-built cages of wood with hardware store latches and chicken wire.

Canada geese paraded around the grounds, honking and lording it over the smaller birds, all the while looking very regal. Galvanized troughs of different sizes and depths served as makeshift habitats for the many waterfowl.

Matt pointed out various species and especially reveled in the variety of ducks, or "clients" as he called them.

He pointed to brown Rouens, snowy white Pekins, and "the new kids on the block" by which he meant a mated pair of long-necked Indian racers that had recently been brought in.

Elizabeth asked about a multi-colored duck that followed Bonnie everywhere.

"That's a Muscovy duck, and he thinks I'm his mother," Bonnie said with a laugh. "He came here when he was just a few days old and I hand-raised him, so he was psychologically imprinted. Now he's not sure if he's a human that waddles or if I'm a very tall duck."

After about twenty minutes, they came to one of the many troughs where now Sedona was cleaning out and removing excrement deposited by the ducks that sheltered there.

"Yeah, I know it's pretty non-glamorous work," she said looking up at the visitors. "But somebody's gotta do it. And today it's my turn."

"It's getting warm out here," Bonnie said of the unseasonable fall weather.

Wiping sweat from her brow, she suggested, "Why don't we go back to the office and take a break? The evaporative cooler is on in there and I need to cool off. I suppose everyone else does, too."

"Lovely," said Elizabeth, dabbing her face and neck with a handkerchief as they all headed back to where they had begun the tour.

The swamp cooler made the interior of the office very comfortable. Everyone found a place to sit and relax while Sedona poured cups of cold water.

Bonnie bustled around the kitchenette. "We don't do coffee breaks in this weather," she said. "We do ice cream breaks."

Everyone laughed and Matt applauded.

"It's good that we cut the tour short," Cary said to Elizabeth. "I think you really needed to rest and cool down."

"Yeah, I noticed it, too," said Sedona. "I'm a nurse and I work in the ER. You see someone suddenly break out in a sweat, and you have to figure out why and intercede."

Meanwhile, Bonnie gathered plastic bowls from a cupboard and removed a half-gallon of Rocky Road from the freezer. She dipped out generous portions and planted a white plastic spoon in the center of each serving.

Matt could barely wait to begin. He took one mouthful, closed his eyes, and emitted an exaggerated swooning sound.

"Yumm! This is the best ice cream I've tasted in my entire life," he declared. "Just tell me one thing, Bonnie. You run this super rehab facility, and I know you run it on the cheap. How do you explain having such high-quality—deluxe may I say—ice cream?"

Bonnie had been leaning against the kitchen counter as a result of being one chair short. She stopped eating, held her spoon in midair, and brandished it like a weapon.

"What an ingrate, you are, Matt," she said with a frown. "I give you first aid in a dish on a warm day in the desert and you make me defend buying it."

Matt tried to backtrack. "No, no, Bonnie, that's not what I meant."

"Oh, don't go making excuses now," she replied with a sparkle in her eye and a devilish smile. She obviously enjoyed teasing her volunteer.

"My needs and wants are few, but I allow myself one luxury. Translation: I like really good ice cream. But, hey, listen folks, we won't get our work done sitting here, so we're going to have to break this up."

As the group dispersed, Cary said to Elizabeth, "Do you think this might be a good time for us to head home?"

"Yes, it's a perfect time," she replied.

"I'll go get the truck and pull it up close for you," he said. "It will be a few minutes because I need to stop to see Matt. I have a question for him about my physics class."

Cary stood, nodded to Sedona, thanked her for showing them around, and left the office. Only Elizabeth and Sedona remained.

"This has been such an interesting day," Elizabeth said. "And I can't tell you how much I've enjoyed meeting you, Sedona. You've been so gracious. You must come to our little casita and visit us."

"I'd like that," said Sedona. "May I tell you something, Elizabeth?"

"Of course," she replied.

"I think your son is just wonderful," Sedona said. "When I saw him carry you up that hill . . . well, I've never seen anything like that except in the movies."

Elizabeth studied Sedona for a few extra seconds and came to a realization.

"I'm sorry that we made a spectacle of ourselves, but you are right . . . it was a wonderful gesture on Cary's part. I'm not sure I could have made it up there without his assistance."

Sedona smiled and nodded in agreement.

"But, my dear, I must tell you that Cary is not my son."

"Oh. He's not?" asked Sedona, clearly surprised by the revelation.

"No, Cary is a friend. And we share a casita in midtown, not far from the university."

"You're living together?" she asked, her brows lifting.

"My dear, new friend, Sedona. Allow me to elaborate. Cary and I do live in the same dwelling, but it's a bit misleading to use the term 'living together.'"

At this point, Sedona gave Elizabeth her undivided attention.

"Because of our age difference, our relationship might be seen as nontraditional or unusual."

Sedona, her mouth wide open, was now staring unabashedly at Elizabeth.

Elizabeth paused. "Oh, my, I'm afraid I've embarrassed you with my candor."

Her eyes downcast, Sedona shook her head.

"I'm so sorry. I was trying to be as delicate as possible, but also I felt I had to be truthful," said Elizabeth.

"I do appreciate that, Elizabeth. I . . . I just jumped to a conclusion, and it wasn't a correct one. It's my fault for assuming."

"I'm going to be ninety years old on my next birthday, Sedona, and Cary is thirty-four. We enjoy each other's company very much. We've been experiencing this—for lack of a better term—unconventional arrangement for about six months," said Elizabeth.

"I see," said Sedona, trying to hide her disappointment.

Elizabeth smiled and reached over to pat Sedona's hand.

"I think that's great. I really do," replied Sedona.

"You're a lovely young lady, Sedona. I know I've made you uncomfortable, but I hope I haven't burdened you."

Meanwhile, the red Mazda truck rolled up and parked, the motor idling. Cary got out and pulled the stepstool from the truck and placed it by the passenger door.

"Thanks for keeping Elizabeth company, Sedona," said Cary as he gave her a quick hug.

Next, the two women embraced. "You're a lucky woman, Elizabeth," said Sedona as they parted company. Sedona smiled as best she could and waved goodbye, and Elizabeth waved back.

When Friends Count

THE NEXT DAY, after planning her strategy, Elizabeth picked up her cellphone and called Bonnie at the wildlife rehab. After making small talk and again thanking her for the tour and the ice cream, she came to the reason for her call.

"You may remember that I had such an enjoyable conversation with your volunteer, Sedona, and I have some information that might be of interest to her," said Elizabeth. "I don't like to ask for someone's phone number, so I was wondering if I could ask you to contact Sedona and ask her to call me."

Bonnie quickly agreed. Elizabeth would wait to hear from Sedona. Her call came that same evening.

"Oh, Sedona. I'm so glad you called," said Elizabeth. "I've been thinking about you.

"Cary and I have a friend, a lawyer who heads a nonprofit that advocates for the poor and the underserved. He's about your age and I believe you would enjoy meeting him. I decided not to contact him until I talked to you first. What do you think?"

"If he's someone you would recommend, of course I'd be interested," replied Sedona.

"Excellent. I'll contact him and get back to you. Can I reach you on the phone number that's on my caller ID?"

"Yes. Great. Thanks, Elizabeth. I can't wait," said Sedona, unable to hide her excitement.

In the next 24 hours, Elizabeth had talked with Xander, gotten back to Sedona, and learned that the two had set up a date. She now felt free to return to her projects, including an upcoming meeting with Rayne, who said she needed her help with a personal problem.

• • • ⌐￣ L • • •

The kitchen radio awakened Elizabeth just before 7 a.m. Cary always tuned in to KXCI, the local independent station, when he "built breakfast," as he termed it.

"Blue Bayou" drifted in through her partially open bedroom door, and it gave her a good feeling about the day to come. Although she loved everything Mozart, her tastes were eclectic in music as well as in books. Hearing Linda Ronstadt's gifted voice, along with the tempo of the song, gave Elizabeth a charge of energy.

And she would need her get-up-and-go today. It was Wednesday, and she and Rayne had fallen into the habit of getting together regularly for coffee on Wednesday mornings. As a consequence, the middle of every week had come to seem like an unnamed mini holiday to Elizabeth. She loved getting out of the house occasionally and visiting with friends.

Her reverie was interrupted when the phone on her bedside table trilled.

"Hello?"

"Good morning, dearie," said Rayne.

"And a good morning to you, too."

"How are you feeling?"

"Well rested, thank you," responded Elizabeth.

"Lovely. So will we be having our repast 'In' or 'Out' today?"

"Hmmm . . . I think I'd enjoy going out, if you wouldn't mind. Cary is making breakfast, so would lunch be okay? It'll be my treat. After all, you're the chauffeur."

"Great. I'll pick you up around eleven and we'll go wherever the spirit moves us. How does that sound?"

"Wonderful," said Elizabeth with anticipation.

"Bye, love. See you soon."

Rayne arrived on time, and after a brief discussion they agreed that the outdoor patio restaurant at Tohono Chul Park would be perfect.

The place was bustling with the luncheon crowd. Spotting a free table, Rayne immediately rushed over and deposited her shoulder bag and sunglasses on it. Their claim staked, she returned to where Elizabeth waited and maneuvered her wheelchair to the table, which was shaded by a large yellow umbrella.

Menus were waiting, and shortly after the two were settled, a server appeared.

Elizabeth chose the chicken and cheese-stuffed chile relleno. Rayne opted for the tuna salad sandwich with capers and dill. Elizabeth ordered prickly pear iced tea for both.

A cottontail could be seen hopping amid the agaves, aloe vera, oleanders, and bougainvillea growing around the perimeter of the flagstone patio. Small finches of various colors perched a few seconds at a time in a palo verde tree, while a short distance away a red and black vermilion flycatcher fed at one of the bird feeders.

In the time since Elizabeth had engaged Rayne to train Annie, their friendship had developed to a stage where neither felt compelled to talk to fill a silence. Each was content to quietly enjoy the natural desert surroundings.

"So, my dear," asked Elizabeth, "how are things with you? How are all of your four-legged clients?"

"Actually, I have no idea how they are," Rayne answered, looking out through her bangs with a grin. She paused. "I've sold my business."

"What?" The news was a surprise.

"It's true. There's a guy who's just moved to Tucson with a shiny new PhD in psychology, and he plans to specialize as a canine behaviorist or something like that. He made me a fantastic offer," she said, drawing out the word *fantastic*.

"He also wanted to buy my customer list, my business phone number, and my website, which I also sold to him."

"I'm more than surprised," said Elizabeth. "This is definitely news. The joy in your voice says it all. You're happy . . . yes?"

"I'm ecstatic," said Rayne. "It was time. With the dogs it was 'been there and done that.' Time to move on." She rested her elbows on the table. "But I'm still keeping my genealogy research business. I'm not ready to burn all my bridges. At least not yet."

Elizabeth lifted her tall glass of prickly pear iced tea and held it out, which prompted Rayne to do the same. The clink made the congratulations official.

"I'm so happy for you, dear," said Elizabeth.

"I knew you would be. I could hardly wait to tell you, but wanted to do so in person, not on the phone," said Rayne. "And besides, there's something else I need to talk to you about. Something much more complicated."

"And that is?"

Rayne's mood changed instantly, like the sky turning dark before a sudden monsoonal downpour.

"It's about my life," Rayne said, her voice quavering. "In the macro, it's my whole life. It's also my love life, or lack thereof."

Rayne took a deep breath and used both hands to pull back her hair. She closed her eyes, bowing her head for a few seconds.

"I don't know, Elizabeth. Forgive me. I'm just feeling a little lost right now," she said, her voice breaking.

Elizabeth put her fork down, abandoning any interest in the chile relleno on her plate. She did not want to address Rayne's concerns until she could determine whether her friend had recovered enough to be able to listen to whatever help she could offer.

"Talk to me, Rayne. Tell me what's happening . . . inside."

Rayne cleared her throat and pushed away her plate. She tried to pull herself together and looked into the distance for a few moments. Then, with as much poise as she could muster, she continued, although her embarrassment was evident.

Elizabeth's heart went out to her. Whatever could cause this vivacious young woman so much inner turmoil, she could not imagine.

"I'm terribly sorry, Elizabeth," said Rayne. "This is just pathetic. Here I am almost literally crying on your shoulder in a public place. Ridiculous."

Elizabeth reached out and put her hand over Rayne's. "It's nothing of the kind, Rayne," she said. "Please don't be angry with yourself for allowing your emotions to surface. It's quite appropriate. Better to let your feelings come out. Don't suppress them or they'll come back to bite you. Let them out. Let them have air. It will release some of the pent-up tension you're holding. Talking about it—if you can—will help. I promise."

Rayne dabbed the corners of her eyes with her napkin. She took a deep breath. "I think what it is . . . are several things at once."

"Like what? Can you name the things?"

"In about two weeks, I'll have a birthday. The big four-0. Somehow, thirty-nine never seemed very old to me, but forty right now feels like a hundred."

Elizabeth sympathized. She remembered difficult birthdays of her own.

"It also made me realize that I don't have much of a life outside of my business," said Rayne. "The people who hire me become my friends, but when their dogs graduate, so to speak, there go my friends. Of course, each new dog brings new contacts, but it's always starting over."

Rayne looked up. "Oh, Elizabeth, I didn't mean you and Cary. Honest. You two are wonderful and you're keepers."

Elizabeth gave Rayne a smile meant to assure her that she'd taken no offense.

After a moment, Elizabeth beckoned their server and explained that she and her dining companion were in dire need of comfort food, as in *immediately*. He should use his own good judgment as to what that might be after surveying the day's dessert offerings. If he chose pie, Elizabeth told him, he should be sure it arrived à la mode. "And two coffees, please. Fresh and hot."

After the server departed, Elizabeth again focused on Rayne.

"Here's what you must do." She leaned in so that she could speak softly but distinctly while she had Rayne's full attention. "Tomorrow you are to go to the best hair salon in town and get yourself a new hairstyle. Trust the stylist. Tell her or him that you're making a new start at something—you need not say what—but you want a new look. Short, long, whatever they recommend. That's why I want you to go to the best. You need a professional you can count on to deliver."

Rayne appeared to have been caught off guard.

The pie à la mode and coffee arrived.

"And now, Rayne, we owe it to the baker to concentrate on enjoying this wonderful Dutch apple pie à la mode."

Rayne grinned from ear to ear.

"Elizabeth, you are truly the best!" she blurted out.

Brushing aside the compliment, Elizabeth replied, "There's one more thing."

"Yes?" Rayne asked, listening attentively.

"Neither you nor I will speak any more of this until I see you tomorrow. I want you to come to the casita, so I can personally take in what the 'new you' looks like. Your old life is over. A new life is waiting for you. I want you to be aware of that every time you look in the mirror or pass a shop window.

"The change in hairstyle will remind you many times a day that you're off on a new and exciting… fulfilling… course. Seeing yourself will reinforce your awareness and your resolve."

Elizabeth smiled. "Now, dear, please fetch the car while I pay the bill."

• • • ⌐ ⌐ • • •

Elizabeth had not reported to Cary the details of her lunch conversation. When Rayne stopped in the next day, her visit coincided with Cary's midday break. They were nearly finished with their lunch when Rayne arrived.

"Who's that?" asked Cary, squinting into the sun as the well-groomed woman approached.

"Oh my. She did it," Elizabeth said under her breath.

Then the recognition came. "It's Rayne," Cary exclaimed. "Wow!"

Rayne joined Elizabeth and Cary on the patio. She shined as the compliments flew her way. Almost immediately Rayne turned it around, lavishing praise on Elizabeth.

She directed her words to Cary. "It's hard to explain, but it was like she read my mind… and my heart," said Rayne. "And she talked to me like she was a guardian angel on my shoulder."

Elizabeth was embarrassed by the praise and sat quietly.

Rayne couldn't stop talking and thanking Elizabeth. She went on and on about Elizabeth's "gift" and how spot-on her analysis had been.

"Elizabeth, you seem to help everyone you know," Rayne said.

Cary agreed. "She sure does."

"You should be a counselor, Elizabeth, or be one of those advice columnists. You have the gift to do that," said Rayne.

Finally, Elizabeth spoke. "Thank you, dear. That's very kind of you to say."

Soon after, Cary returned to his work, but Elizabeth and Rayne continued to visit. Rayne was more serene after lauding Elizabeth, and Elizabeth was quite relieved to no longer be the center of attention.

"Rayne," she said, "let's go inside and have tea . . . and talk about your future."

"You mean you have more advice?"

"My dear, we're just getting started."

• • • ⌐ ⌐ • • •

That same evening Elizabeth informed Cary that she wanted to start an online advice column and needed his technical know-how to put it together.

"What are you going to call it?" asked Cary.

"I like the name *Ask Guinevere*."

"You don't need to tell me how you came up with the name," said Cary. "Right now, Lancelot here is content to let you handle all the advice giving. I'll take care of the technical stuff. Full speed ahead. You really are cut out for this."

A couple of weeks went by. Thanksgiving came and went. The two had been invited to Aunt Joan's for the turkey dinner with a small gathering of family and friends, all of whom had been briefed so that there would be no awkward or embarrassing questions asked about the couple's age difference.

Meanwhile, Cary's friend, Felix Montalvo, had texted again. He would be arriving in Tucson about a week before Christmas.

As they talked over plans for Felix's visit, Cary glanced at the clock on the microwave. It was approaching eight o'clock.

"It looks like we have time for a game of Scrabble," said Cary. "I know that you win every time, but I still like to play."

"You're on, Mr. Branscombe. And I know you don't want me to let you win. That's why I admire you so much—besides loving you, too."

Cary set up the game board on the kitchen table. When it was over, Elizabeth had won again. This time by an almost-hundred-point margin.

An Adventurer's Tale

A week before Christmas at about seven o'clock, Felix Montalvo showed up at the front door of the casita.

A branch of holly hung from the light sconce outside the door.

Inside a red-and-white-checked table cloth contributed to the bistro-casual atmosphere.

Elizabeth would use her grandmother's Francis I sterling silver flatware without it looking ostentatious. The large Spode plates were sufficiently deep to accommodate the spaghetti and meatballs.

Cary had brought home a baguette that she would turn into garlic toast to be passed around in a basket. She always heated a flat rock in the oven and used it to keep the toast warm. A garden salad tossed with her homemade vinaigrette would be the first course.

What was missing? Oh, yes . . . on that evening, instead of napkins, red terrycloth dish towels would be practical substitutes—and no ironing needed.

Bearded and wearing thick glasses, the six-foot-two Felix immediately enveloped Cary in a man hug.

Felix wore military surplus khaki fatigues with frayed collar and cuffs. His beard and near-shoulder-length hair were streaked with gray.

There was no sign that he had taken care of himself these past years. He carried at least forty pounds more than when Cary had last seen him.

After introducing his friend to Elizabeth, he handed Felix a cold bottle of his favorite Mexican beer. He then asked him where he had been.

"Everywhere. On both sides of the Atlantic. Also in Antarctica," he answered, savoring the imported beer.

"Hey, you remembered," Felix said. "That time out in the desert, if it hadn't been for this *cerveza*, I'd have dried up like a strip of beef jerky."

"How could I forget?" Cary grinned. "Our outfit almost went broke keeping you supplied. But we did save a lot of migrant lives though, didn't we?"

"Yeah. And no sooner had we filled the big drums with fresh water than those vigilante types would push them over and empty them," said Felix. "But we got smart. We set up backup units that followed behind us by an hour and refilled the overturned drums."

"Why, Cary, you never told me about any of this," interjected Elizabeth. "I'm so proud of you. You must have saved many lives."

"Well, you might not feel the same about some other revelations that could come out tonight," said Cary.

"But maybe before Felix goes on, we should serve up dinner," said Cary. "Is the garlic toast ready to come out of the oven?"

"Yes, any moment now," Elizabeth replied. "Just wait for the bell."

"Geez!" exclaimed Felix. "There isn't anything that you forget, Cary."

After Felix had demolished a plate of spaghetti and meatballs and chugged down another beer, the storytelling began.

"Last time I saw you," said Felix, addressing Cary, "you'll remember, I took off in a hurry. Barely had time to pack a knapsack.

"I remember," said Cary.

"My first job after leaving here was as a cook on board a ship that sailed mostly in Antarctic waters. The mission was to disrupt the operations of Japanese whalers. We weren't there alone. Sometimes there were as many as half a dozen other vessels taking part in the disruption of the whaling operations, and all were well equipped for the job. Sponsors saw their money spent on blocking the whalers at every turn.

"The guy I worked for was a one of a kind. His name was Randy Ellsworth from Springfield, Ohio. Retired Navy. Big, tall pipe-smoking fella. Calm, cool, collected. They said he commanded a destroyer escort during the Vietnam War.

"He named his vessel *Leviathan Defender IV.* I guess there had been others by that name in the past. What I didn't know until we set sail was that Captain Ellsworth was among the most feared skippers operating in those waters. The scuttlebutt was that if whalers caught sight of his vessel, they would do a 180-degree turn and head the other way.

"I had heard that Captain Ellsworth received a chunk of money from a wealthy lady in California and had used a portion of it to put into dry dock and pay a goodly sum to have the bow of his vessel reinforced to the point where it was almost as well fortified as an icebreaker's.

"If a whaler thought he could play chicken with Captain Ellsworth, he'd better think again. Ellsworth was prepared to ram him. I have no knowledge that he ever rammed anyone, but I was told there were some close calls.

"He bought a ship's horn that was so loud you could hear it from miles away. It was deafening. That in itself would scare the ... uh, daylights ... pardon me, ma'am ... out of anyone.

"I think I might have worried about all this for a day or two, but then I thought, 'Hey, I'm out on the high seas in international waters where nobody can arrest me, and the ship is carrying more than enough life rafts—these were high quality cork life rafts, not the inflatable kind—and life vests so we wouldn't need to worry if we had to abandon ship.'

"All in all, it was a great experience. I had a generous budget for my commissary, and I fed everyone well. Never had a complaint.

"There was nowhere to go, so we couldn't spend our money. After almost two years at sea, the ship needed repairs, so we put in at Marseilles where there were several large shipyards and dry docks. It was then that I decided to cash in. I spent the next year bumming around Europe. I saw things I'd never seen before."

Felix had again cleaned his plate and was ready for more. Cary noticed and immediately brought him refills of everything.

"Well, here I am blabbing away while this good food is sitting in front of me," said Felix. "Cary, why don't you catch me up on your life while I chow down?

"And Elizabeth . . . that's right, it's Elizabeth, isn't it? . . . I'd like to know how you and Cary met."

Elizabeth obligingly recited details of their meeting, then changed the subject.

"I want you both to know how touched I am to learn of your actions in support of the desert crossers and also those poor whales that cannot defend themselves.

"Your acts of altruism and activism bring back memories of my youth that remain painful to me to this day," said Elizabeth. "And it's something I want to talk about because I sense that you two will understand.

"As a teenager growing up in Boston, I felt a need to help others. I didn't know the word 'altruism.' But I knew that my mother, a domineering sort, didn't have even an ounce of any of that in her soul.

"We had a housekeeper, Yolanda, who volunteered on Sundays at a soup kitchen during the last years of the Depression. It was her only day off.

"I wanted to go with Yolanda and help, too, but my mother forbade me," said Elizabeth. "I wanted to collect in the neighborhood for the March of Dimes when polio was rampant, but again my mother wouldn't hear of it."

"It wasn't until I came to Tucson in the 1950s that I was finally free to do things where I felt I was making a difference. But everything I did then was terribly modest compared to you two," she said.

"But you did *something*, and that's what counts," said Cary. "And now look what you've done to help Marie."

As Felix dug into his food and washed everything down with beer, Cary told of Elizabeth's success in tutoring the young woman from Africa.

Finally, his hunger apparently sated, Felix pushed his plate aside, belched into his napkin, and took the last swallow of yet another bottle of beer.

"Can you stand hearing me talk some more?" Felix asked.

"By all means," replied Elizabeth. "Please go on."

"Well, you know how everyone feels about the Canadian government allowing the slaughter of baby seals, and yet nothing is done to stop it," said Felix. "So I decided to get involved.

"After I returned from Europe, I got a text from a contact in Montreal. He wanted to know if I could take some photos of the upcoming seal hunt. It reaches its peak in February when the pregnant female seals arrive in Canada from their long journey, which begins in Greenland.

"Naturalists believe that it's innate behavior that brings them to the Gulf of St. Lawrence, where mother seals give birth. They deliver their pups while temporarily making their homes on large pieces of pack ice floating in the gulf.

"The pups nurse for only twelve days. After that, they're on their own.

"The hunters are issued permits. They risk their lives by getting out to those ice floes in small boats. There's always a chance that the ice floe will break up."

"It's terrible that the Canadian government permits it," Elizabeth chimed in. "I read that the seal hunters club those little snowy white pups to death. What people will do for money. It's just horrible."

Felix nodded agreement and continued. "I learned that my contact wanted me to do this job because I'm an American and I've done this kind of work before.

"What's not common knowledge is that in order to photograph the baby seals, you need a license issued by the Department of Fisheries and Oceans. Licenses are also required for observers since the government doesn't want protesters or tourists seeing the slaughter. And these licenses are not easy to come by.

"If you're a Canadian and you try to skirt the rules, it's assumed you know the law, and they can throw the book at you when they get you into court. But if you're a foreigner or a tourist—not a protester—you can feign ignorance and the Department of Fisheries officers are more likely to let you go with a warning."

Felix went on to say that after he accepted the assignment, he was put in contact with a man named Thierry in Montreal who instructed him to rent a car and first drive to Boston where he was provided with equipment that included a state-of-the-art camera with a telephoto lens.

"All my expenses were covered. And I volunteered my time. The nonprofit supporting this shoot was well-funded," Felix noted.

Felix told how he was directed to drive to Quebec City where he met a man named Jean-Luc who handed him some maps and instructions in French and English and briefed him on how to photograph the seal killings without getting arrested.

From there he was guided to a "safe house" where a young couple served him dinner and put him up overnight in a guest room.

"There were times when I felt like I was a member of the Maquis—the French Resistance fighters in World War II—or the Underground Railroad in slavery days, where everything was carried out with the utmost precision and secrecy," said Felix.

The next day, he and Jean-Luc began a 30-hour island-hopping car trip that took them to St. John's, Newfoundland.

Jean-Luc had earlier explained that Felix's camera was equipped with a tiny device about the size of a thimble that was capable of transmitting data for a distance of up to a mile. Every five minutes, Felix was to upload everything that he shot—video and still photos—to Jean-Luc who was to be parked in his car about a mile away in a non-restricted zone. Jean-Luc would receive the upload on his cellphone and relay the feed to an unnamed site in Montreal. From there it would be transmitted to the organization's headquarters in San Francisco.

"If I was spotted by Department of Fisheries officers, I was to yank off the transmission device and toss it into the woods. Well, this is exactly what happened about an hour after I began shooting," said Felix.

"I had set up in a blind just off the road where the hunters on the ice floe couldn't see me, but my camera caught their actions sharp and clear.

"When an officer in an SUV pulled up and asked to see my papers, I pleaded no knowledge of being required to have a special license. I identified myself as a freelance photographer from the U.S., saying it was my first trip to Canada.

"The officer cited the law, warning me that I could be arrested for violation. After examining my equipment, he removed the cartridge containing the photos and video from my camera and said he was confiscating everything I had shot. He added that he was giving me a break by not also taking my equipment.

"I thanked the officer and assured him that I would be leaving the area immediately. He apparently had taken no notice that there had been a special attachment to the camera.

"Once I was clear of the restricted area, I phoned Jean-Luc. We agreed to meet at the nearest gas station, which lay about six miles away."

After that, the two returned to Quebec where they parted company, said Felix. Driving on, Felix held his breath until he had safely crossed the border and was back in the U.S. He had brought with him an Oregon license plate that he had bought at a scrap yard and switched it to his rental car after leaving

Newfoundland.

When he got back to Boston and turned in his photo equipment, he decided to stay around for a few days and visit some old friends, he said.

"But that didn't last long. After a day or two, I received a text from a headhunter in New York making me an offer. There was a sous chef position on a yacht docked in Palm Beach.

"The man who was to have filled that slot had to cancel. The vessel was scheduled to leave Palm Beach the next afternoon to reposition on the French Riviera. They would wire me a ticket leaving Boston on the red-eye that evening and would have a car waiting for me at the airport in Florida.

"The headhunter went on to say that my salary would be $2,500 a week plus overtime and a full benefits package. I would have my own quarters below decks.

"I stopped him to explain that I wasn't an haute cuisine chef and that my experience was limited to serving as a cook on board working vessels."

Felix was told that was no problem since he would be assisting a French chef holding a Michelin star. They needed someone who spoke French and had worked at sea. He would need to feed the crew on the way over. The owner would fly to St. Tropez on occasions, but wanted the yacht to be there stocked and waiting.

"I learned en route that the owner was a 38-year-old self-made billion-aire. He had finished high school and then started designing video games. He sold his company to one of the giants in the industry for $2.5 billion and retired.

"That gig lasted three years, and now I'm back in Tucson with more money in my bank account than I've ever had in my life," he said.

"Look, I've talked enough." He pulled his chair closer to the table. "Believe it or not, I could go for one more serving of that great spaghetti and meatballs. The garlic toast, too. And if there's any beer left, I'd love to have another one."

Obligingly, Cary headed back to the big pot of spaghetti and began refilling Felix's plate. Elizabeth had taken Cary at his word and prepared more than enough.

Meanwhile, Elizabeth engaged Felix in conversation. "Cary hadn't told me that you're fluent in French," she said.

"Yeah, my mother was French—from the provinces—and she spoke to me only in French so that I would pick it up," he replied.

Speaking in French, Elizabeth informed Felix that she had been given private French lessons as a young girl and minored in French literature in college.

"When I graduated, I aspired to work at the United Nations," said Elizabeth, "but you can guess where those plans went."

Despite her frustrations, Elizabeth said she remained undaunted and had always considered French to be her second language.

"Interesting that you should say that," said Felix.

Then switching to French, he said he felt like a different person when speaking French. "It's not me. It's not regular old Felix."

At that moment, Cary returned with another heaping plate of spaghetti and meatballs together with garlic toast and another beer.

"This is gonna do it for me," Felix declared, patting his stomach "You don't know how long I've been hankering for this. On the yacht you would never see this kind of food.

"When I finish this, I need to let you folks go to bed." he said looking in Elizabeth's direction. "Anyway, it's been a great evening. You sure it's okay if I sleep on that couch over there?"

After taking his last swallow of beer, Felix walked a few feet to the living room and kicked off his shoes. He plopped down on Cary's daybed, pulled a blanket over himself, and immediately fell asleep.

Meanwhile, after some kitchen cleanup and helping Elizabeth get ready for bed, Cary went to a closet, pulled out a sleeping bag and rolled it out on the floor near the fireplace. In a few moments, he, too, was fast asleep.

The next morning, Cary brewed a pot of coffee and set out Danish pastries for Felix.

Shortly thereafter, following a warm handshake and a bear hug, Felix reminded Cary that he would return to help him put up some extra kitchen shelves so that Elizabeth could more easily reach them. She struggled at times to take out dishes that were out of her reach from the wheelchair, but had never complained.

"As soon as your landlady gives you permission, let me know, and I'll be back," Felix promised, with a wave. "Thanks for the hospitality. That's a great lady you have there, Cary."

The Eco-Warrior

Cʜʀɪsᴛᴍᴀs ᴡᴇᴇᴋ ᴡᴀs ᴀ ʙᴜsʏ ᴏɴᴇ. Cary would be off work for the holiday, but he still had five days ahead of him answering calls for Hollowell Home Warranty.

As he worked his shifts, Elizabeth made preparations for Christmas dinner. They had invited Matt, her tutoring student Marie, Cary's former boss Paul Giroux and his wife, Marcella, and Xander and Sedona. Others would be out of town and sent regrets.

The challenge was how to accommodate everyone inside the casita.

The hosts brainstormed a solution that involved temporarily moving some furniture, including Cary's daybed.

Cary got an okay from Jake to borrow a couple of his restaurant tables and some chairs for a few hours on Christmas Day when Bogie's would be closed.

While Cary handled the logistics, Elizabeth took charge of the menu, preparing a lengthy shopping list for what would ultimately turn out to be a dinner worthy of note. Since Christmas fell on a Sunday, most of the fresh ingredients would need to be bought on Saturday.

She had chosen a Napa Valley chardonnay to accompany the Pacific sea scallops appetizer, and a Château Léoville Barton to complement the crown pork roast. Cary would toss the fresh garden salad.

Despite the demand these preparations imposed on her strength, Elizabeth felt exhilarated. Being a hostess was an experience she had longed for these many years and been denied. Now, although a bit late in her life, it was all coming together for her.

Christmas arrived on a cool, sunny day. The guests were on time and all were in good spirits. Elizabeth had orchestrated everything to perfection.

The hum of pleasant conversation and laughter began almost immediately. Marie discovered that Matt spoke French, having spent time as a lecturer at the Sorbonne. Paul Giroux also put forth an effort, having learned some of the language from his French-Canadian grandparents.

Meanwhile, Xander and Sedona couldn't take their eyes off each other.

When dinner toasts were in progress, Xander announced with obvious pride that he and Sedona were engaged to be married. Everyone hooted and cheered as they raised their glasses to toast the new couple.

The postprandial discussions continued into the evening. When it was over and Cary, assisted by Xander, came back from returning the tables and chairs, he learned from Elizabeth that Paul had recruited Marie to work at the nursing home.

She would give notice to her current employer and begin training to be a Certified Nursing Assistant with tuition expenses paid while on full salary.

Before the two went to sleep that night, both expressing a feeling of accomplishment and personal satisfaction, Cary sat on Elizabeth's bed and said, "Elizabeth, you've outdone yourself."

Elizabeth smiled and sighed. "I admit I'm a little tired," she said. "But I enjoyed every minute of it."

The next day at breakfast, Cary asked Elizabeth if she had received any requests for advice on her *Ask Guinevere* blog.

"Nothing so far," she replied. "But I'm not giving up. Rayne has a friend who knows Ella Vee Tisdale. She has a blog, *Help! Ella Vee*, that has more than a hundred thousand subscribers along with at least that many Twitter followers. Rayne is going to see if her friend can get me a mention."

"Sounds great," Cary said. "I'm sure it would take off if you could just get some exposure."

The following Saturday morning, Cary and Felix were busily engaged in the casita's tiny kitchen. Not surprisingly, Felix was a jack-of-all-trades and carried tools of almost every description on his truck.

Cary had received approval from Barb to install some open low shelving easy for Elizabeth to access. With Felix working and at the same time supervising, the job was getting done quickly. After almost two hours and a few beers, the work was completed.

Elizabeth was delighted and asked Felix to stay for lunch. She had prepared sandwiches on sourdough. After some small talk, Felix cleared his throat and addressed Elizabeth directly.

"I told Cary on the phone that I wanted to share an episode in Cary's life with you," he said. "And he told me I could go ahead. That you had no secrets between you."

"Cary told you the truth," she replied. "In these last months, there's very little that we haven't shared about our lives. However, as I'm given to understand, this one promises to be an eye-opener."

Felix nodded. "Well, you know that Cary volunteered his time to work with us putting out water for immigrants crossing the desert."

"Yes, he's told me about that and how he was almost arrested by the Border Patrol," she said.

"Well, that's only where the story begins," said Felix. "There were some of us who wanted to do more . . . take it to the next level. And that meant really crossing the line.

"There were some mining companies that wanted to explore potential sites in the Coronado National Forest. One of those locations was in the Santa Rita Mountains immediately south of here. I'm sure you know where I'm talking about. There's still a lot of controversy and protests going on in that area as we speak.

"At the time, many of us were inspired by Edward Abbey, and if you've been around here for a while, you'll remember that he was a real hell-raiser. He was a role model for activists, and before he died, he wrote several books on protecting the environment.

"His mantra was to do what you have to do to protect the environment.

"I decided to start an Edward Abbey Brigade of eco-warriors. It was somewhat like the Lincoln Brigade made up of Americans who fought on the side of the loyalists in the Spanish Civil War. Hemingway was among those.

"So I recruited about a dozen men, including Cary, who were willing to stick their necks out.

"It was a secret society, structured so that if one or two members got arrested, they would have no knowledge of the names of the other members and would not be able to pass such info on to the authorities. I based this on what I read about secret societies and brotherhoods in 18th and 19th century Italy.

"There the names of the members were known only to the president and the secretary.

"My list of member names was safely hidden on the cloud. I had it set up so if anyone found the location on the Internet, the document was programmed to self-destruct.

"We all chose a *nom de guerre*. Mine was Control, named after a lead character who headed MI6 in a John le Carré spy novel.

"Would you like to guess what name Cary chose?"

Elizabeth wasted no time in replying. Breaking into a smile, she answered, "Lancelot."

"You know your man," said Felix. "And in my opinion, he lives up to the name."

He cleared his throat, apparently replaying the event in his mind with a degree of pleasure. "It was on our third mission, and it was in mid-May as I recall. The winter was past, and it was already beginning to warm up. We had targeted one of the mining companies' exploratory projects. It was in the Santa Ritas. This time it was to disable bulldozers, backhoes, and other equipment belonging to the private contractor who was hired by the mining company to clear a stand of native mesquite trees that stood in the way of the project.

"It was about three in the morning, and we were dropped off by our transportation man just outside the chain link fence that had been installed to protect the equipment. There were six of us and we all wore black outfits and black ski masks.

"We were equipped with bolt cutters and wasted no time in cutting an opening in the chain link fence. Once inside the protected area we set about wreaking damage to all the heavy equipment and before leaving, we poured sugar into all of the fuel tanks.

"We encountered no problems with the getaway, but the next day and the day after it was 'hold onto your hat.' Local television news and the front pages of most of the state's newspapers reported how numerous projects had been vandalized the night before, and that authorities vowed to arrest those responsible.

"It was just coincidental, but we had no way to know that other eco-defense groups had also executed missions that same night.

"By the next day, Tucson was crawling with federal agents—FBI, ATF, Homeland Security, U.S. Marshals, Border Patrol—anyone they could muster.

I quickly decided that the six of us needed to make ourselves scarce. And without delay.

"The remainder of our cadre would be okay. They weren't on the mission and their names wouldn't be known to law enforcement.

"I already had several scenarios in mind should something like this occur, and fleeing wasn't one of them. We needed to stay in the area where we couldn't be discovered and lay low. But I first needed to consult one of our cadre—an expert in this particular area. That person was known to our team as Gray Feather.

"Gray Feather is not a Native American, but he's a student of Indian lore and especially knowledgeable when it comes to tribal history in Arizona.

"I hurried to a pay telephone. I didn't want to use my own cellphone in case it was being tapped. I reached Gray Feather and after a less-than-five-minute consult, we decided we could avoid arrest by hiding in the Cochise Stronghold east of here.

"You may have heard of this landmark, but not many are familiar with its history.

"Cochise, for whom our neighboring county here is named, was the chief of the Chiricahua Apache tribe. That tribe numbered no more than a thousand at any one time, and of those only a couple hundred were warriors.

"Cochise succeeded in holding off and eluding Union and Mexican forces for almost a decade before signing a peace treaty.

"The Cochise Stronghold is in the Dragoon Mountains which lie inside what is now the Coronado National Forest. The entire mountain range is only fifteen miles long, but the part that makes up the stronghold is an area of about two or three miles of granite peaks and giant boulders. There are many narrow ravines, sheer cliffs, and deep crevices within its borders.

"Cochise is buried somewhere in the stronghold, but nobody knows exactly where. Secrecy was his last dying wish.

"Anyone can enter the stronghold, but the unfamiliar will soon find themselves in a labyrinth from which return is something more than a challenge.

"In summer months, you'll encounter extreme heat and find little water. Even those who've had survival training will find it's no picnic. I had water purifiers for every man, and that's what got us by when we were able to find even brackish water. Thankfully for us, we had Gray Feather who knew the right places to locate water.

"By prearrangement, our driver picked each of us up in his van after midnight. To cover our tracks, we had told our significant others or landlords that we were taking a week off to go to Puerto Peñasco, a popular beach resort in Mexico on the Sea of Cortez, also known to Arizonans as Rocky Point.

"It was 3 a.m. when the van arrived near a state campground not far from the stronghold. Our driver had shut off his headlights and we quietly slipped out of the van and were led by Gray Feather onto a footpath that would take us deep inside the rock formations.

"We all had the flashlights which came equipped with our cellphones, but once inside, out of concern that we might be spotted, Gray Feather asked us to switch them off and wait until daybreak when he would take us deeper inside.

Gray Feather had brought along a pair of night vision goggles and led us to a sheltered location where we could nap until daylight.

"I'm convinced to this day that without Gray Feather we would not have survived. During those thirteen days, we rarely made a fire for fear of detection.

"Food was also a factor. We had carried in with us some packets akin to military field rations, but even by allowing ourselves small amounts each day, they didn't last beyond a week. Fortunately, Gray Feather managed to find us water almost daily, but it took some time to purify.

"Nights were cold, and days were hot, but we managed. We had to maintain radio silence, so we couldn't use our cellphones. A couple of us had tiny portable radios and could sometimes pick up news.

"It was on a very hot day that one among our party spotted a migratory Canada goose that had apparently got separated from the flock and was trapped in the canyon. It was immediately captured and prepared by Gray Feather for a rotisserie entrée that evening and fed to our ravenous band. It was the only time during the thirteen days that I remember going to sleep on a full stomach.

"On a couple of occasions, we had barbecued rattlesnake for dinner, but there's not much meat on those babies, so it really wasn't more than an appetizer.

"Early in the morning on the thirteenth day, I decided that Gray Feather and I would slip out, walk past the campground looking like tourists, and make our way to a nearby convenience market and use the pay telephone to make a call to our transportation contact.

"I had been monitoring the news on the radio and was under the impression that the furor over the vandalism had died down. I knew that there had been some arrests among a couple of the other eco-defense groups that had struck around the same time we did, but lately there was nothing being reported.

"Our transportation man agreed with my assessment, so we arranged a pickup for 3 a.m. the next day. I asked him to bring food and a supply of water.

"All went according to plan. On the return trip to Tucson, we rehydrated and stuffed ourselves with whatever there was to eat.

"As we neared Tucson, we agreed that it would be a good idea upon our return to ask if anyone had come by to see us or ask about us and then decide whether it was safe to remain. No one reported such an inquiry, so we all felt fairly secure."

Turning to Cary, Felix said, "I don't believe I ever asked you how things went for you after we returned."

As Cary prepared to answer, one could see by the expression on

Elizabeth's face that she was agog at what she had heard.

"I was already living here in the casita at that time. When Barb—that's my landlady—asked if I had had a good time in Rocky Point, I smiled and answered *yes*," replied Cary.

Then, turning to Elizabeth, Felix continued, "I want you to know that your Cary here was a stalwart during that experience. He's one of those guys I'd want to have with me if I were on a life raft somewhere out in the Pacific."

Felix let out a sigh. "As for me, it wasn't long before I pulled up stakes and decided it would be best for me to take some time far away from here.

"Now, it's been five years, and the statute of limitations has run on any federal charges. Same goes for the State of Arizona."

He grinned. "I'm glad I had a chance to share this part of Cary's life with you. It's an experience I won't forget. But I'm going to have to say goodbye now. My daughter is waiting for me."

He rose to his feet. "She's buying a blueberry farm in Oregon, and she wants me to join her and her husband and the grandkids there. I decided to make her a gift of the money that I saved up these last five years so that she can buy the property without need of financing.

"We're driving up there tomorrow to sign the papers. You'll have to come and visit us."

"You are one of the most fascinating guests we've had here since I've been with Cary and I'm so glad I've come to know you," said Elizabeth warmly. "And thank you so much for helping Cary with the shelves."

Felix leaned over and gave Elizabeth a gentle embrace followed by a long hug for Cary. After he'd left, and the two were seated outside under the canopy, Elizabeth turned to Cary.

"I'm still trying to take all this in. I don't know how you could have kept all this bottled up."

"I just wasn't sure how you would take it," he replied.

"That was five years ago. In your future, you'll have resources available in the lab to help you reach your goal of protecting the environment," said Elizabeth. "In the meantime, put sugar in your coffee, not in anyone's gas tank."

···⌐￢···

A few weeks passed, and both Cary and Rayne again reported coming up dry in their search for Meg.

Cary decided to pursue a new course. Rather than continue to search for Meg, which had proven futile up to this point, he decided to do an online records search on Elizabeth, but not under her maiden name of Ferguson or Gardner. Instead, this time he would focus his search on Elizabeth Grayson, her married name.

"Why a name I haven't used in more than fifty years?" she asked. "And why search under *my* name when you're looking for Meg?"

Cary shrugged. "I've exhausted all the other avenues. We need to try something new. Something outside the box."

Elizabeth didn't object when Cary said he would go online and order a public records search of the name Elizabeth Grayson. He said he believed it would be worth the modest cost.

What he subsequently discovered shocked even the seemingly unflappable Cary Branscombe.

It was later that day when Cary burst into the kitchen where Elizabeth was removing a roast chicken from the oven. He could barely contain himself.

"You're not going to believe this," he whooped, almost out of breath. "But the State of Massachusetts is holding a large sum in its Unclaimed Property Division for the widow of Eliot Grayson."

Elizabeth's delicate brows arched. "Impossible. I left Massachusetts penniless.

"Yes, but there are some things you didn't know at the time."

"Such as? As you already know, my mother disowned me."

Cary nodded slowly. "But your husband didn't disown you."

"That's right." She frowned. "When he died, there was no money. I had to pay his bills."

"You told me that," said Cary. "However, when I ran the public records search under the name Elizabeth Grayson, what pops up but a listing on the site of the Unclaimed Property Division, Treasurer, Commonwealth of Massachusetts."

Cary leaned across the table. "I did a double take. Because right next to your name is the amount of the unclaimed property—$161,000."

Elizabeth's mouth dropped open. She seemed bewildered.

"I immediately phoned the Unclaimed Property Division and got lucky. I spoke with a very nice woman who was able to tell me that the unclaimed amount originated in Barnstable County and that if I needed more information about the origin, I'd need to speak with officials there. She added that the folks in her office could help when you're ready to file a claim."

"Barnstable County is on Cape Cod," said Elizabeth, her heart pounding. "Provincetown is in Barnstable County and that's where Eliot would go on weekends. He was on his way home from Provincetown when he died in that accident."

"Of course, I remember. But I'm not finished," said Cary. "I made a call to the office of the County Treasurer and Tax Collector in the town of Barnstable. That's the county seat. They told me that I was contacting the right office, but they could furnish only limited information over the phone. Apparently, the unclaimed funds originated from some property in Provincetown that was later sold at auction by the county.

"I asked how I could get details. The woman I spoke with said that she wasn't permitted to make a recommendation, but suggested that in a situation like this, with us living thousands of miles away, it would make sense to hire an attorney practicing in the area.

"So I got back online and pulled up a list of attorneys in Barnstable

County. I knew we'd want someone with many years of experience and who won't charge you an arm and a leg."

She nodded agreement. "And?"

Cary smiled. "I found our man on the first call. His name is Ellis McCleary. This guy has got to be in his eighties.

"I caught him just before he was ready to leave his office in Provincetown and had time to brief him with what little information I had gathered. He said he'd begin checking tomorrow and get back to me.

"I asked him if he would need an advance deposit, and he declined, saying I sounded like an honest man.

"You know, this is like waiting for the outcome of a mystery movie," Cary remarked.

"How do you think I feel?" asked Elizabeth, beholding him with admiration. "I can't wait until you hear back from Mr. McCleary."

Unclaimed Funds

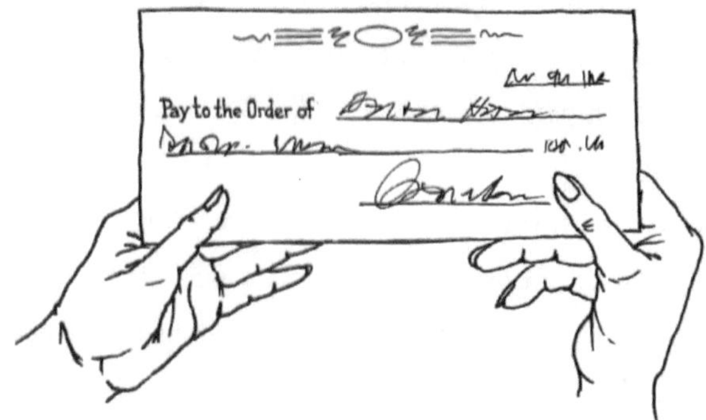

EARLY THE NEXT AFTERNOON, Cary had ended a busy shift and was finishing a bowl of New England clam chowder—perhaps not a coincidence—when his cellphone chimed. Ellis McCleary, the lawyer in Provincetown was on the line. He said he had news to share.

"I've been on the phone most of the day," said the lawyer, "and I believe I've got the story down. It's a whopper."

For the next forty-five minutes, Cary jotted down notes. When he had hung up, he turned to Elizabeth. "This is better than fiction.

"Now I can explain everything, right down to the last detail," he said.

"Please Cary, don't keep me in suspense," she pleaded. "Tell me what you've learned."

"To start with, your late husband, Eliot Grayson, owned a cottage in Provincetown that you didn't know about," said Cary. "And that cottage was occupied by a man named Martin Fletcher, a local artist who painted seascapes."

"Yes, that was the name of my husband's lover," exclaimed Elizabeth. "He's the man who wrote the love letters that I found."

"That's right," said Cary. "Fletcher used the cottage as a gallery, and he also lived there, which I'm told isn't uncommon for artists working there. When Eliot went to Provincetown on weekends to visit, that's where he most likely stayed."

Cary studied his notes. "Now according to old Ellis, when Martin Fletcher learned that Eliot had been killed in the crash, he did what he should have done and attempted to contact you. But by then, you had already left for Tucson. He got back his letter stamped 'Moved, No Forwarding Address.'

"Unable to reach you, Martin Fletcher didn't know what to do. Instead of consulting a lawyer, he called on a real estate agent he knew. The real estate agent advised him to remain where he was and simply pay the property tax bill each year when it came due, and no one would be the wiser.

"For the next forty years, Martin Fletcher continued to pay the property tax each year until his death in 1990. At that point, his niece, Annabelle, who's also an artist and had been displaying her work in the gallery, remained in the cottage, and continued to make the annual tax payment.

"That went on for another fifteen years until 2005 when things came to an abrupt end for Annabelle. What happened was that a neighboring property owner sold his place, and it was bought by a couple who intended to open a seafood restaurant and bar in that location. Although the property was zoned for commercial use, the new owners needed a liquor license, which required approval of the neighbors.

"So what happened was that the applicants—the husband and wife—came around to Annabelle to ask her approval. Although she had no objection, Annabelle immediately realized that she couldn't sign their application form because she wasn't the legal owner of the cottage. She panicked.

"Thinking quickly, she said she needed a day or two to make a decision. After they left, she contacted an attorney.

"The attorney advised her that if she forged Eliot's signature on the neighbor's application, she could face criminal charges. He told her if she wished, she could tell the applicants that Eliot was currently unreachable, but that she as the tenant would write on their application that she had no objection to the issuance of a liquor license.

"The couple was pacified, but when their application was submitted a red flag went up.

"There was an inquiry by the county attorney's office, and it was discovered that Eliot Grayson had been dead for more than fifty years.

"Although no charges were brought, the property was placed for auction, and the proceeds sent to the Unclaimed Property Division of the Treasurer's Office.

"No surprise—the successful bidder at the auction sale was Annabelle Fletcher, who with the assistance of a local mortgage broker, obtained a loan and was able to take title and remain in the cottage. She still lives there today.

"The auction sale brought in $161,000 which remains among billions of dollars in the Unclaimed Property Division coffers. I learned that the Commonwealth of Massachusetts, unlike other states, does not take possession of unclaimed funds after a certain number of years. Instead, they remain as unclaimed funds in perpetuity. So you have no deadline worries to be concerned about."

"So what do I need to do to claim the funds?" Elizabeth asked.

"I'll have to get back to McCleary and give him an okay to proceed on your behalf," replied Cary.

Cary again consulted his notepad. "He's going to need copies of your marriage license, Eliot's death certificate, proof that you were Eliot Grayson's wife at the time of his death, and documents showing that Elizabeth Grayson legally changed her name to Elizabeth Gardner and likely several more documents.

"McCleary can help round up whatever paperwork exists in Massachusetts, and we'll need to pull together whatever is needed from Arizona. Having talked with McCleary, I have the impression that his fee will be reasonable as there's no litigation involved here. It's just a matter of jumping through the legal hoops."

"While we're waiting for all this to come together, let me show you one of the emails I received today," said Elizabeth. "You know about that Tweet that Ella Vee sent out to her blog followers. Well, it really got results. While all the responses I've received so far aren't ones where I can help, there are a few where I believe I *can* help."

She wheeled over to a table and picked up a computer printout. "Here's one of those that I've finished. I'm going to post it on my *Ask Guinevere* blog tomorrow. I'd like you to take a look and tell me what you think."

Dear Guinevere,

Much like you, I am also the older woman in a December-May involvement. "Ken" is my junior by twenty-two years. He is a wonderful man, and I have no regrets about having entered into this relationship almost five years ago.

Ken is changing his place of employment soon, and this has me concerned. We'll be living in the same city, but he'll be with a new company. Even now when we are outside of our circle of friends, people we meet for the first time often stare.

I can't handle it. I become very self-conscious and just pray that no one says to me something like, "It's so nice to meet Ken's mother."

I truly want to avoid these awkward situations, and I'm writing to ask you for a solution.

If I color my hair to cover some of the gray, I think it would make me appear younger. At the same time, if Ken would agree to add some flecks of gray to his temples, he would look a little older. Then, at least visually, we would appear to be closer in age and more likely to be perceived as a couple.

(signed) *Not* Ken's mother

Guinevere reply:

Dear Not Ken's Mother,

I sympathize with your problem more than you might expect. Recently, a new acquaintance who meant to deliver a compliment was effusive as she told me how wonderful she found "my son." Of course, she meant my life partner, Lancelot. The young woman was quite embarrassed, and I daresay disappointed. These are among the uncomfortable moments that you and I, and others in the December-May relationship category encounter.

It's Ken's feelings and opinions that should concern you.

In good marriages or relationships, partners consult each other before making such decisions.

You and Ken also might want to consider the time and expense each of you would incur on a regular basis, whether you go to a colorist at a salon or do it yourself at home.

If either or both of you decide to go ahead and add more color to your life (sorry, but I couldn't resist), remember that this decision is a reversible one, should you change your minds.

Best of luck,

Guinevere

• • • ⌐──┐ • • •

Several weeks passed. It was a Friday afternoon when Cary, who had finished his shift, emerged from the casita and approached Elizabeth. She was sitting outdoors beneath the canopy, working at her laptop.

"I just got off the phone with McCleary. It's a done deal!" exclaimed Cary. "The Massachusetts Treasurer's Office has signed off on your claim. Everything's in order and they'll be wiring the funds into your checking account on Monday."

"That's wonderful," Elizabeth said.

"McCleary's a prince. His total fee comes to $2,200." Cary sank into a chair next to her. "I must have thanked him a dozen times. I told him you would be writing to him shortly to thank him personally. I would never have dreamed . . ."

A few days later, Elizabeth informed Cary that the $161,000 had arrived, and she had instructed her bank to add Cary's name to her account.

"When I'm gone, I want you to have these funds for your education," she told Cary firmly. "You will have scholarships and work-study, and when you make your way into graduate school, you'll likely get a teaching assistantship or lab assistantship for which you'll be paid. But that won't cover everything.

"I don't want you to be burdened by student loans that you'll be paying off for the rest of your life. This money will be there to fill in those gaps when you need it."

Cary frowned and opened his mouth to object, but Elizabeth pressed a finger to his lips.

"No. Don't say anything," she said. "There's no way I can ever repay you for all that you've done for me. And those of us who share the kind of feelings that we have for each other don't think in such terms anyway."

Cary, filled with emotion, swallowed hard. "I don't care about the money," he said. "I just wanted to see you have what's rightfully yours. But it means the world to me that you're thinking of my future . . . my education. What did I ever do to deserve you?"

They didn't speak. They just held hands and together watched a gray cottontail skirt around the edge of the brick patio.

Eureka!

ANOTHER WEEK WENT BY. Cary redoubled his efforts to locate Meg. He had the feeling that time was running out and he was desperate to make this search bear fruit, if only for Elizabeth's sake. If he succeeded, it would be the ultimate gift.

He went back over his notes on where his search had taken him. Until now, every time it had brought him to a dead end. But today he was both inspired and determined.

What about that prep school for girls that Meg might have attended? That's assuming Elizabeth's mother had had her way. He had not fully pursued that thread, he thought.

Cary had learned earlier that Miss Pryce's closed its doors in 1956, but if Meg *had* attended the school, it would have been prior to then. He realized he might have been missing a major clue.

Elizabeth was five years older than Meg, which meant that Meg would have been born in or around 1930. And if she attended the school, it would have been in 1946 or 1947.

He decided it was worth another try.

During his lunch break, Cary went online and located the Virginia town that had given the private school its name, Armont Hills. He checked to see if the town had a public library. It did and he phoned. His call was answered by a female voice.

"How can I help you?"

"I'm trying to locate a long-lost relative of my wife's," replied Cary. "And I believe that the relative attended Miss Pryce's Armont Hills School sometime back in the 1940s. I know that the school closed for good in 1956, but I'm hoping to get in contact with someone from the school who knows where the records are stored. I thought I might get a start by talking with the town historian." He paused. "That is, if there is such a person."

"Well, you're talking with her," the woman replied dryly. "I'm Melissa Saalwaechter, the town librarian. I'm also the town historian. How can I help?"

Maybe his luck was finally turning. "I sure hope you can," he replied. "My name is Cary Branscombe, and I'm calling from Tucson, Arizona. Although Miss Pryce's closed many years ago, I'm wondering if anyone kept the school's records and if they might be intact somewhere."

"There's a chance that I can help, Mr. Branscombe. Alma Frisby worked in the registrar's office after she graduated from high school and was promoted to the position of registrar during the school's last years. She's in her eighties now and doesn't get around very much. However, she was in the library recently and I had a nice chat with her. I can give you her phone number if you like."

"Absolutely. I can't thank you enough," he said.

Moments later, Cary entered Alma Frisby's phone number and his call was answered.

"Yes, this is Alma," replied the voice on the other end. "You say that Melissa Saalwaechter put you in contact with me? I don't know how much I can help. You know the school closed in 1956. I was just barely old enough to vote then. Lucky for me, after they closed, I found a job in the office at our local high school. But I've been retired for almost twenty years."

"Might you happen to know if the school's records are stored anywhere?" asked Cary.

"The records were kept in the basement of the old office building on campus for a while," said Alma. "But when the property was sold, all the buildings were torn down, and the new owners built one of those mini-shopping malls there. I heard that the records were shredded and carted off."

"That's too bad," said Cary. "I was hoping to find a clue that might take me to the person I'm looking for. I do want to thank you for taking your time to talk with me, Ms. Frisby." He paused. "One last question. Do you know if they still have class reunions for Miss Pryce's students?"

"I'm glad you asked," she replied. "Yes, they do. But because there are so few graduates still attending the reunions, in some cases the reunion commit-tees combine two or three years into just a single reunion. Sometimes they invite me because I'm one of the few staff members or faculty who's still living."

"This is very helpful to know," said Cary. "The person I'm looking for would have been in the Class of either 1946 or 1947."

"I can give you the name of the woman who coordinates the reunions for those years," she said. "It's Gwen Eversole and she lives in Charlottesville, but I don't have a phone number."

"No problem, I can find it online," said Cary. "Anyway, I can't thank you enough. You have made a lady, who's almost ninety, very happy. I'll get busy on this right now. And thanks again."

Within a few minutes, using an online search, Cary found his target. The woman was listed under "Desmond and Gwen Eversole" at what appeared, following a Zillow search, to be an upscale address in Charlottesville, Virginia.

He entered the phone number on his cellphone. After several rings, it went to voice mail.

Cary left a detailed message and awaited a return call.

Early the next morning when he was preparing breakfast, his cellphone chimed. It was Gwen Eversole.

Following an exchange of pleasantries, Ms. Eversole said, "I must tell you, Mr. Branscombe, that nowadays with so many of our classmates gone, I rarely get inquiries such as yours. But if you'll give me the name of the student that your friend is trying to locate, I'll do my best to help you find her."

Cary turned the flame off underneath his scrambled eggs and hurried to find his notes. "Thank you so much. It's very kind of you to take your time to help me. To the best of our knowledge, the individual in question was in the Class of either 1946 or 1947. At the time, her first name might have been Margarita or Margaret. Her friends called her Meg. About her last name, we're really not sure."

Cary flipped the pages of his notes. "The name on her birth certificate was Alvarez, but she didn't use that name. She grew up in an economically privileged environment in Boston."

After a long moment of silence, Ms. Eversole responded.

"I have a feeling I know who you're talking about. I believe this young lady was in the Class of 1946. Does the name Margaret Ferguson ring any kind of a bell for you?"

When he heard those words, Cary was so stunned that he almost dropped the phone. It was as if he had just unearthed the Rosetta Stone or broken the Enigma Code.

"Mr. Branscombe?"

Cary pulled himself together. "You did say Ferguson? Did I get that right?"

"Yes, I did. Is that some sort of a clue?" Ms. Eversole asked in bewilderment.

"Yes, ma'am. It certainly is," he replied. "What you just told me has solved a sixty-year-old mystery. You see, Margaret's aunt was Dorothea Ferguson, who hailed from an old Boston family. It was she who not only provided the tuition to enable Margaret to attend the school but chose Miss Pryce's herself and virtually insisted that Margaret go there and nowhere else."

"It's all coming together for me now," said Ms. Eversole with obvious increased interest. "It's been sort of a mystery for me, too—but for other reasons.

"Margaret was noticeably different from the other girls. Although she was among the brightest in our class when it came to scholarship, most of the other girls seemed to have a sense that 'she wasn't one of us,' if you know what I mean.

"They didn't include her in their extracurricular activities and, of course, that made her standoffish. My friend, Cynthia Curtis—bless her heart, she's gone now—and I were the only ones who tried to let Margaret know that not everyone in the school was a snob. We tried to include her in our activities, and sometimes she would join us.

"After graduation, I coordinated a class reunion every ten years. Margaret didn't attend the first one in 1956, but she remained in contact by filling out a simple form that I would mail out periodically.

"However, she attended the twentieth reunion in 1966 with her husband. Unfortunately, it proved an embarrassment for us all."

"What happened?" asked Cary, now sitting on the edge of his seat.

"It was a disaster in every respect," replied Ms. Eversole. "After it was over, I broke down and cried. My husband, Desmond, bless his heart, was there to console me. If he hadn't been there, I don't know what I would have done.

"Mind you, this was 1966, not 1866. We had had John Kennedy and Martin Luther King by that time. Desmond had been asked by Lyndon Johnson to serve on the Board of Governors of the Federal Reserve. We all had an obligation to conduct ourselves in a civilized manner.

"Well, that didn't happen. Margaret showed up with her husband, a tall and very engaging African American gentleman. Never mind that he was a professor on the faculty at MIT, an advisor to NASA, and one of the nation's leading mathematicians. Almost all our attendees and their husbands froze the couple out. They didn't greet or speak to them and generally went out of their way to avoid them.

"Desmond and I were appalled, as were Cynthia and her husband. We immediately went out of our way to make them feel welcome, which drew stares in our direction and unkind looks.

"I remember a conversation I had with Errol, Margaret's husband. We conversed a good deal of the time in French. His last name, I recall, was St. Laurent. The same name as the famous French fashion designer, Yves St. Laurent. I should add that I was a French major in college.

"He told me how his family emigrated from the Caribbean island of Martinique, a French possession, first to Montreal and then to a small town in Maine. It was Calais, which had a sizable French-speaking population.

"We chatted for a good while. I asked him about his work for NASA and he said that he assisted with plans for future space flights in the specialty area of orbital mechanics. When I asked what that was, he explained that when a rocket is launched you don't simply point it in the direction where you want it to travel. Instead, the rocket must be directed to a point in outer space, and from there it can be placed into an orbital position and make its way to the targeted planet. A lot of higher math is needed to calculate just exactly how that's done."

She paused for breath. "After the reunion, I received a lovely note from Margaret thanking me for my kindness. That was the last I heard from her."

By this time, Cary had taken several pages of notes and was thinking what Elizabeth's reaction would be when he told her all he had learned.

"I'm going to have to prepare my friend for this," said Cary. "It might be too much for her to take in in one day. Elizabeth will be turning ninety in a few months." He tapped his pen on his notepad. "Might you happen to have Margaret's last known address?"

"Oh yes. I still keep neat and tidy files, even at my age," replied Ms.

Eversole. "I have it right here, the last address for Margaret St. Laurent. It's 1342 N. Westerbrook Lane, Belmont, MA 02478. Let's hope that they are both living and in good health. And if you or your friend, Elizabeth, are in contact with Margaret, please convey my warmest regards."

"I, too, am hopeful, and you can rest assured that I will not only pass along your regards to Margaret, but I'll let both her and Elizabeth know how your help has been indispensable," said Cary. "Thank you so very much. And I know you'll be hearing from Elizabeth."

What now? Cary asked himself.

Rather than immediately break the news to Elizabeth, he decided to perform a Google search to determine whether Margaret St. Laurent was still living. In a few moments, he found the answer. Errol St. Laurent, age 87, and his wife, Margaret, 85, resided at the Belmont, Massachusetts, address where they had apparently been living for the last fifty years. A landline number for them was also listed.

Cary stared at the number, his heart pounding. He had to decide whether to attempt a phone call before informing Elizabeth.

He would simply introduce himself as Elizabeth's friend. There was nothing to gain by delaying, he thought, so he proceeded to make the call.

Meg answered the phone on the third ring. Her surprise was evident though she immediately began asking question after question, most of which Cary was prepared to answer.

She said that she had been trying for years to locate Elizabeth without success.

Cary explained that Elizabeth had legally changed her last name which made finding her online almost impossible.

He said that because of Elizabeth's advanced years and fragile health he would like to first brief her himself and in stages. After that, a telephone call would be a first step.

Both agreed that such was a reasonable plan, and that Cary would be back in contact with her within the next couple of days.

When Cary ended the call and walked outside where Elizabeth had been reading a book and saw that she had dozed off, he decided not to disturb her but wait until she awakened on her own.

He went back to his computer and prepared to start the second half of his shift. Later, when he saw that she was awake and stretching her arms, he went to the kitchen and prepared coffee.

"What have you been up to while I slept, my darling?" she asked as Cary set her coffee cup onto a saucer. "But before you answer, let me show you what I've been working on. Unless you see something that needs correcting, I'm ready to post it to the web."

"I'm on my 15-minute break, but let me see what you've done," Cary said.

She handed him a few pages of hard copy, which he read aloud.

Dear Guinevere,

I read these advice columns regularly, but never in a million years could I have imagined I would be writing to you asking for advice for myself. However, because you specialize in couples with a significant age gap, I am turning to you for help.

Six months ago, I met Jim (not his real name), who is forty-five, and I thought I was the luckiest sixty-year-old woman alive. Right from the start, he was very attentive and always a gentleman. We have similar tastes in many areas and are of the same religious background. I had been widowed for three years, and I was very lonely.

It's wonderful to see Jim across the breakfast table every morning instead of an empty chair. He moved in a few weeks after we met and rented out his condo. He contributes to our household expenses and often goes grocery shopping for which he won't let me pay.

My late husband and I had paid off our mortgage years ago, and I own this house free and clear. So far, so good.

Lately, though, Jim has been paying close attention to the real estate sales in our neighborhood and talks about the skyrocketing prices and what my house would likely bring if it were on the market. He says this house is too big for just the two of us and insists that it would be better if I sold my house and we moved into his condo.

He says that "we" could use most of the windfall from the sale of my house to invest in the stock market as well as afford to travel whenever we wanted.

I've told him that the negative points of selling my house are several: no longer would I have my wonderful neighbors, many of whom have become my very dear and closest friends. Also, I would have to give up most of my furniture—many antique family pieces--if we were to downsize to a condo.

Jim has a good job, but a modest salary. By contrast, I'm in management and earn about twice as much as Jim.

I've always lived below my means and never flaunted my good fortune. Neither Jim, my friends, nor any of my neighbors have any idea of my financial status.

I should mention that I have an adult son and daughter living nearby and both have cautioned me.

I want to believe that Jim has my best interests at heart. The things I've told you, however, leave me with doubts.

I need help to sort this out. I'm counting on you, Guinevere.

With all my thanks,

Trusting (with Reservations)

Dear Trusting (with Reservations),

You express your concerns very well. All "December ladies" must remember the advantage our age gives us. We know the world now and have a hard-earned understanding of the people in it. To deny that is a mistake.

There are red flags flying just about everywhere.

It's very clear that you do not want to sell your house or to commingle your funds or assets. You may not have yet decided whether or not you wish to pursue this relationship, even if on other terms.

Whatever you decide, I would advise you to consult an attorney. He or she can walk you through the steps you need to take to protect your assets.

If you wish to scale down this relationship or bring it to a close, you should rethink your current housing arrangement. The longer you share living space with him in your home, the more difficult it will be to ask him to move out. If you like, you could do this in increments to avoid confrontation. First by informing him that you met with your family lawyer and found that you cannot sell your house because in your will you are leaving it to your children.

Also, you might tell him that you are in no way ready for marriage and that you might never be.

Be out front that your desire for travel isn't anywhere near what his appetite is and that you want to spend more time with your children and your grandchildren.

Wait a day or two to allow that to sink in. Hopefully, in that time he will realize that there's nothing there for him and he will be in a frame of mind to end at least the live-in part of the relationship.

If that doesn't happen, then move on to Part Two in which you inform him that a number of repairs and renovations that have been put off will need to be done in the next few weeks and that you will be staying with one of your children during that time. Further, that your son will be staying in your house as a security measure.

At that point, he will surely get the hint.

With all my best wishes,

Guinevere

"Good answer," said Cary. "If I were in her shoes, I'd send this guy packing.

"I just came out to check on you. I'm back on duty in just a couple of minutes. I'll be off at three o'clock, and I've got some interesting things to report," said Cary as he headed back toward the casita.

When his workday ended, Cary returned to Elizabeth who was now seated at the kitchen table stirring milk into her coffee.

"Before we get any deeper into *Ask Guinevere*, let me brief you with the latest on the search for Meg," said Cary. I've got news."

"What kind of news?" asked Elizabeth. Her eyes widened.

"I've found her," said Cary.

"You've found her? Is she alive? Did you talk with her? Where is she? Will I be able to talk with her? When?"

Cary took Elizabeth's hand, held it firmly to calm her, and said, "The answer to all your questions is 'yes.' I've spoken with her, and we'll need a day or two to set things up. She seems very nice.

"Right now, though, my concern is to keep you from getting too excited and raising your blood pressure. You will be talking with her soon, I promise you. And I believe a visit can be arranged.

"But for right now, let's try to relax and talk about dinner. I'll fix a nice salad and we can watch a movie. I've got a couple of discs we can choose from . . ."

"Cary, you don't understand. This is huge! I can't think about food or movies. You've found Meg, and she's alive," said Elizabeth sobbing. "I've prayed for this day for years, for decades, and had almost lost hope. Next to finding you, this has got to be the happiest day of my life," she added.

Cary beamed and kissed Elizabeth on her cheek.

"I want to hear every detail. Is she married? Where does she live? What did she sound like on the phone? Tell me everything. Don't leave anything out."

"Okay. Okay. First of all, she's been married for many years to a professor who's retired from MIT. They have a daughter and grown grandchildren. Meg cried when I told her that you had been looking for her. She seemed just as happy to be found as you were to find her. She can't wait to see you. Said she'd call their travel agent tomorrow and start the ball rolling to come out here for a visit."

For the next hour, Cary obligingly poured out every minute detail of his successful search, including his conversations with everyone he had spoken with that day.

Elizabeth listened intently, her eyes closed and both hands crossed over her heart.

When she had heard everything, Cary prepared a late-night dinner of cheese omelets. After that, Elizabeth was ready for Cary to read her to sleep.

A day passed. Cary had made arrangements that enabled Elizabeth and Meg to speak briefly via phone.

Their first conversation consisted primarily of each expressing their feelings of frustration they had experienced in their attempts to locate each other and their joy in now being reunited. Elizabeth told Meg that she was finding it difficult to follow Cary's advice that they should save all the details and questions until they would be together in a couple of weeks.

Meg agreed and assured Elizabeth that she wouldn't leave Tucson until every noteworthy experience had been shared and every question had been answered.

Meg said that her daughter, Andrea, would accompany her on the visit. Cary would handle the hotel reservations and rental car. Mother and daughter would stay at the Arizona Inn.

That seemed to pacify Elizabeth and she was able to turn to Cary and begin making arrangements for the visit. Menus were prepared down to the last detail, wines chosen and desserts to be baked. Perhaps also some sightseeing could be worked in.

Elizabeth was almost giddy as the time drew near to Meg's arrival. Meanwhile, to keep her emotions under control, she focused on her *Ask Guinevere* advice column, which was pulling in more readers by the day.

Reunion

The big day arrived, and Cary was on hand at Tucson International Airport to meet the guests. He held a handmade sign: *Welcome Meg and Andrea.*

At this point, Meg knew few details of Elizabeth's relationship with Cary other than that he was a friend. Cary guided them to the rental car counter where he provided them with hand-drawn maps and directions showing how to get to the Arizona Inn and to their casita.

By the time they arrived at the Inn, it would be midafternoon. They had agreed that following a long flight, including a connection in Dallas, the travelers should rest and get a good night's sleep. They would drive to the casita the next day.

On the following morning, which was a Saturday, mother and daughter arrived at the casita. Elizabeth could barely contain herself.

As they made the walk between the front house and the casita, Cary came to greet them. Meg walked with a cane and was stooped over, not unusual considering that she was eighty-five. Her daughter, Andrea, was by her side. It was clear, however, that Meg wished no assistance and wanted all to know that she was quite capable of managing by herself, thank you.

Wearing his brightest smile, Cary declared, "Welcome to our home. Elizabeth can't wait to see you."

The "our home" part clearly came as news to Meg. Her eyes widened, but she simply nodded and smiled back. "And I can't wait to see Elizabeth," she replied.

Elizabeth, seated in her wheelchair on the patio, got her first glimpse of Meg in more than a half-century. The tears flowed as Elizabeth let her emotions overcome her sense of decorum.

Meg, tastefully dressed for the occasion, wore a peach linen pantsuit and Ferragamo leather pumps with a sensible heel, both fashionable and appropriate for a woman who navigated with a cane. A silk ivory-hued blouse matched the color of her hair, which she wore short but stylish with side-swept bangs.

Elizabeth recognized some similarities at once. She, Meg, and Andrea shared similar facial features, including an aquiline nose, but very attractive. It made her stop for a moment, but she was too excited to dwell on it.

Andrea was outfitted much like her mother, though her suit was of a more casual cut and in an eggshell hue.

Elizabeth smiled and waved to them.

As Meg approached, Elizabeth reached up from her wheelchair with outstretched arms. For several moments, tears and emotions made it impossible for either of them to speak.

When the embrace finally ended, Cary beckoned the women to take seats at the outdoor table and passed around a box of tissues.

"I had prayed that I would see this day come," exclaimed a still-sobbing Elizabeth. "You can't imagine what this means to me—all of us being together like this."

"You are not alone," replied Meg, still dabbing her eyes. "With each passing year, I would realize that there was less chance. Perhaps we both hung on just to make this day happen.

"Where should we start?" asked Elizabeth. "But first I think I should ask you to introduce this lovely young woman seated beside you."

"Well, I still like to think of Andrea as my little girl, but Andrea recently retired from her teaching position at Georgetown where she was a law professor," said Meg.

"I can empathize with Mom," said Andrea. "I have two children who are both married, and they're still my 'little ones.' They never grow up in our eyes."

"Who would like some coffee or iced tea?" asked Cary. "We'll be having lunch soon. But it's a beautiful day and I believe we'll all be very comfortable out here.

"You can't imagine how good it feels to be getting out of Boston at this time," said Meg. "It's late March and at home we're still getting Nor'easters. But first, Elizabeth, you must tell me why I couldn't find you all these years. I even hired a private detective agency and they, too, struck out."

Elizabeth explained how she had legally changed her name after leaving Boston and begun a new life, making it impossible for anyone to track her down. She also recounted the many frustrating years she spent as "the other woman," always believing that Arthur would end his unsatisfying marriage and be free to marry her.

When she reached the point where Arthur had passed away and began telling about her slow decline and how she could no longer manage on her own, she paused.

Cary returned with iced tea for everyone. As the guests sipped their drinks, Cary and Elizabeth pointed out the different cacti and desert plantings. At that moment, their attention was drawn to a red and black butterfly.

"I've never seen a more beautiful butterfly," exclaimed Andrea.

"It's called a Red Admiral," said Elizabeth. "They are common to this area, and we see them often around our patio."

Meanwhile, Elizabeth resumed telling her story. She recounted how the two had met on her first day as a patient at Fairfield. She said she had felt an instant affinity, one that quickly deepened as the days passed. There were afternoons in the garden discussing books and poetry, picnic lunches, and sharing life stories.

"Before I met Cary, there was no one and nothing left in my life to look forward to. My health was at rock bottom, and I felt like the nursing home was the final stop—the last one before the cemetery. But Cary changed all that. My twilight years are turning out to be the best of my life."

Meg reached over and patted Elizabeth's hand. "I'm so happy for you, Elizabeth. You truly deserve it. And it's obvious you two belong together."

"When I told my friends at Fairfield that I planned to leave and move in with Cary, one asked—not very delicately, I might add—if Cary might be more interested in my money than in me." She shook her head. "I had to laugh because almost everyone there was on Medicaid.

"And better yet, as far as our financial picture is concerned, I'm now receiving both my Social Security and my state pension. I had to surrender those to Medicaid when they began paying my nursing home bill. And Cary, by working from home, can keep an eye on me and at the same time earn a living. We have no worries.

"But enough of me. I can't wait to learn all about where *you've* been and what *you've* done these last sixty-some-odd years. First, though, we need to have lunch. I'll bet you all are starved."

"Whatever you have planned will work for us," Meg replied affably. "What's important is that we can be together and share so much of where our lives have taken us."

"If you'll excuse me . . ." At that, Elizabeth wheeled herself out of the patio and headed toward the kitchen.

After she had departed, Cary slowly shook his head. "She's just amazing. I try to keep her from overdoing, but I can't hold her down. She asked me to build her some low shelves in the kitchen so that she can reach everything she needs. She wants to be independent."

Shortly, Elizabeth emerged from the kitchen and said to Cary, "Darling, the seafood crepes are waiting for you on the counter. They'll take only a few minutes to heat and can be served after the vichyssoise. The Albariño is chilling in the refrigerator."

"I'm on it," Cary said, and headed back to the kitchen.

Elizabeth explained, "There are a few things that I can't do and one of those is managing at the stove. It's just too high for me to reach without either risking an accident or burning the food. But I've taught Cary a few things about cooking that he'll be able to use in the future. Lucky for me when I say he's a quick learner."

Presently, the vichyssoise was served followed by the seafood crepes. Alongside came green salads and a cutting board bearing a freshly baked French baguette. A plate containing pats of sweet Irish butter was placed alongside. On a nearby smaller table was an ice bucket that kept the white wine chilled.

As the lunch drew to a close and Elizabeth served her homemade blueberry cobbler for dessert, the focus turned to Meg.

"The last time I saw you," said Elizabeth, "was after you returned from a trip to Europe that Mother had arranged. That occasion was very brief because my relationship with my mother had turned from bad to worse."

"Yes, and I remember that it ended in a spat," said Meg. "After that, I don't remember your having any further contact with Dorothea."

Elizabeth shifted her position. "I should add that I've never had any regrets about the breakup," she said. "Also I want you to know that I was keenly aware that you had to walk a fine line when it came to my mother. Your mom, Yolanda, was in her employ, and you couldn't afford to risk offending Dorothea."

"It goes far beyond that," said Meg. "And as things unfold here this afternoon, you'll have an even better understanding of what all lay behind this.

"But before I get into that, let me tell you a little bit about my family.

"We have two grandkids. There's Nicole. She and her husband, Max, live in Noumea. It's the capital city of New Caledonia, a French island possession in the Pacific.

"Both are very independent and have turned their backs on corporate America. They raise shrimp which they supply to the island's many restaurants; they operate a small art gallery where Nicole displays her paintings and Max his sculptures, and they also guide tour groups during the tourist season.

"Our other grandchild is Kyle. He and his husband Hillel—he's an Israeli—live in the Florida Keys on Islamorada. Both are IT experts, and they telecommute—you know, work from home. Sometimes they work when they're out on their boat.

"And I don't believe I mentioned Andrea's husband, Brian. Like Andrea, he's also retired. His career was with the Justice Department in Washington. Now he likes to spend his time working in the garden and volunteering.

"I met Errol in my junior year at UMass. Dorothea had wanted me to go to Williams or Wellesley and I had the grades to get in. But at the time, money was tight. Actually, I was pleased that I didn't have to go to one of those Ivy

League schools. I managed quite well at UMass.

"I often remind myself that if I had gone to another college, I never would have met Errol. If that had happened, my lovely daughter and her children might not be here either."

"I like that way of looking at fate," responded Elizabeth. "Because if things had gone differently for me many years ago, I might not now be with the love of my life and holding his hand."

Cary blushed at Elizabeth's comment but didn't seem to mind.

"When Errol and I began dating, we faced some huge challenges," said Meg. "I was living at home. Mama was still with Dorothea, and I knew that if Dorothea found out that I was in a relationship with an African American, she would be furious.

"So we had to do everything in secret. I lied to Dorothea and told her that I was going on weekend trips to the Cape with some girls I met in class. Because there were very few places where Errol and I could go in Boston and be unnoticed, we would drive to Maine, where Errol's family lived.

"Errol's parents were very supportive of our relationship, but there were a couple of female cousins who asked him point blank why he couldn't find a woman of his own race.

"Finding acceptance was very difficult. It wasn't until Errol had received his master's degree in mathematics that we began to search for another place to live.

"We had heard a lot about the San Francisco Bay Area and its liberal and progressive culture. So Errol began scouting for teaching opportunities at the community colleges there.

"I decided I would need a story that Dorothea would buy, although I knew that she wouldn't be happy with any proposal or plan that would take me away from her.

"I told her that I had a great opportunity to see a part of America that I've never seen before along with some good job possibilities, and that at the same time I wouldn't be alone.

"I lied again and said that two girls I knew from college were moving to San Francisco and that we would be sharing an apartment. If I found that I didn't like it, I could always come directly home.

"Dorothea made me promise that I would phone every week and write to both her and Mama in between.

"So with that decided, Errol and I packed up his car and headed west.

"When we arrived in San Francisco, we quickly discovered that what we had heard was true. Living there as a mixed-race couple was not a problem. It seemed like no one paid much attention to us. The same also held true for gay couples.

"While we were there, the California Legislature passed the Unruh Civil Rights Act, which prohibited almost all forms of discrimination. After that, we could travel to other parts of the Golden State for weekend getaways with a much greater sense of freedom.

"We rented a small bungalow in the Richmond District. It didn't hurt that the landlady was a staff attorney for the ACLU. She made us feel welcome.

"We installed two telephone lines—a line for the house that either of us could answer and a second line that was in my name and that only I would answer . . . in case it was Dorothea calling. We asked the phone company for a red phone to remind Errol which one not to pick up.

"We loved the neighborhood. People of all races and ethnicities lived there. There were mom and pop restaurants offering every conceivable foreign cuisine.

"Were you able to find work?" Elizabeth asked.

"Strangely enough, I got a job the first day I started looking," said Meg. "And Errol landed a part-time teaching position across the bay in Hayward the first week.

"Such jobs like where I was hired can take an interesting turn, let me tell you. The ad in the newspaper said this company was seeking an expediter. No experience necessary. It turns out that the job was with a large commercial electrical contractor in the city. The company headquarters was located in an industrial section, but its projects were spread out all around the Bay Area.

"These are not the folks you call if you need to have a new electrical panel installed in your house. They contract to put in electrical systems in mega-projects such as manufacturing plants, hospitals, schools, and government buildings when they are under construction. The contracts often ran in the millions of dollars.

"When they hired me, this company was experiencing unacceptable delays in receiving needed equipment and supplies for its projects, and they decided that they needed a full-time person to ride herd on their supply orders. That was going to be me.

"You can imagine how my knees were shaking during the interview. It was with one of the company vice presidents, and he was using words that weren't in my vocabulary. Technical stuff.

"When I reminded him that I was inexperienced, he reassured me, saying 'I can tell from just this brief interview that you are up to it. You can do it.' He went on to say that the company was suffering unnecessary losses because of lost workdays caused by the shipping delays. He said that the CEO was determined to stop the flow of red ink.

"He asked me if I could start the next day and said he would assign an employee familiar with the work to brief me.

"I showed up early the next morning and by day's end I was sailing. I guess I was meant for that position. It seemed I had a knack for learning who to call at each of our suppliers. I treated them with great respect, but I was persistent. I always apologized for calling to check on our pending orders because I often found that I had to phone every day for a week or more to keep them on track.

"I routinely sent thank-you notes when the deliveries arrived on time. Meanwhile, I gave the slowpokes drop-dead dates that were as much as a week in advance of the dates when we actually needed the supplies.

"Although the starting pay was low, within a few weeks I received a substantial raise and another increase a short time later.

"Lost workdays no longer existed and the company's CEO could not have been more pleased. And this, of course, reflected well on the vice president who had hired me.

"One morning, not long after receiving another pay raise, the vice president called me into his office.

"'Meg,'" he said, "'I'm on the spot today. One of our project managers called me an hour ago and said he's quitting effective immediately. He was not happy here and is taking another job in the L.A. area.'

"The vice president went on to say that he had eight electricians from the union hiring hall on the job working on an electrical system for a new hospital being built near Fremont, a suburb south of the city. The foreman assigned to the project was in dire need of updated budget figures and supply delivery dates. These would have been provided by the project manager who had just quit.

"Before I go further, I should tell you that traditionally every job that is contracted requires assignment of an onsite foreman and a project manager. The project manager needs to be good with figures and know how to order supplies and get them to the job on time. These positions are traditionally assigned to men.

"I knew where this was leading. 'Yes,' I said. 'If you need me to do this job, I'll do it.'

"Overnight my salary doubled. The next day, I was driven out to the job by the vice president and introduced to Jeb, the foreman assigned to the project.

"In that business, you can expect to be exposed to some rednecks, and Jeb was no exception. He looked me over as if he had X-ray vision.

"'Never seen a girl to be put in this job,'" Jeb grumbled. "'But we need to keep this project moving, so we'll go along with whatever the boss says.

"'You can reach me on my work phone. It's over there in the shack,' he said to me. With that he walked away.

"I wondered what his reaction would have been if he'd known I was married to an African American.

"For the next several weeks I worked from the office. A messenger took paperwork back and forth between the office and the work site. I did my job and Jeb did his.

"I hope I'm not boring you with all this," said Meg. "Please tell me if I am."

"This is fascinating," replied Elizabeth. "Please go on. I want to know what happened."

"After that first assignment, there were others to follow, and it was then that things really got interesting. I'd never been challenged like this before. Often, I took my work home with me.

"Errol, meanwhile, had been accepted into a PhD program at the University of California at Berkeley and was commuting across the bay two to three times a week.

"One evening when I was working at home and Errol was cracking the books, he paused at the dining room table and asked me to explain what I was doing.

"As you can imagine, Errol is both curious and a quick study and after about twenty minutes of scrutinizing a particular job's financials, he asked me some very pointed questions about the expenditures. Such as 'Why are you paying so much for this when you can buy in larger quantities without waste, and save a bundle?'

"Errol's suggestions were always very specific. He said that makes them more valuable to the recipient, and he was right.

"I would pass these suggestions on to the vice president who would come back with words of praise and sometimes another hefty bonus check.

"I kept that job, and when Andrea came along, I arranged to work at home much of the time and hired a nanny on those days when I had to go into the office.

"After Errol received his PhD, he was immediately hired to teach at one of the state universities in the area. That was good, but what really made it for him was when he got a contract consulting for the National Advisory Committee for Aeronautics, soon to become NASA.

"Once he had established his reputation with NASA, major colleges and universities took notice of him. One of those was MIT.

"At the time, several events of major consequence occurred. Errol was being interviewed at MIT, and I was being offered a promotion and another pay raise at work which I knew I couldn't accept because we were on the verge of moving back to Boston.

"Added to that was that Dorothea had been diagnosed with pancreatic cancer several months before and her time was short. I made three trips to see her in the space of a couple of months.

"On my third trip, she died while I was at her bedside at Mass. General.

"There was no funeral, as she had outlived most of her friends. As I'd mentioned, money had been tight, but there was enough left to cover her final expenses. Errol and I also took some money from our savings to take care of any shortfalls.

"Dorothea left me the house, and when Errol received official notice of his hiring at MIT, we moved back to Boston and into the house. That was good because Mama could never have managed there alone.

"For the first couple of years it was okay, but Errol wanted us to have a house that we could really call our own. He had his eye on a place in Belmont that was on an acre and surrounded by large trees, with lots of lawn and a very comfortable guest cottage.

"Rather than sell Dorothea's house, we kept it and rented it to a corporation whose president would reside there. That was almost fifty years ago, and six presidents have lived there. We still own it. It's put Andrea and our two grandkids through college and grad school.

"After we moved to our house in Belmont, Mama was with us for almost eight years. She enjoyed cooking for us and was at our dinner table almost every evening. She also enjoyed her privacy in the cottage. Of course, she doted on Andrea and taught her to speak Spanish at an early age as she did me. It came to serve her well in her career as she was qualified to be sent to Inter-American conferences and the like."

At that point, Meg's whole demeanor changed. She appeared tense.

"Now, I have something very personal that you need to know. It was a great shock to me, and I'm sure it will be to you, too.

"When Mama lay dying of heart failure—we had known that she had a weak heart—it ran in her family—she made a deathbed confession.

"She told me that she was not my mother. Dorothea was my mother. A love child some may call it."

Elizabeth gasped, and Cary went to her side.

"Mama had sworn to Dorothea that she would never reveal her secret. But Mama said she was torn between keeping her word to Dorothea and leaving this world without me knowing the truth.

"And she wanted you to know, too, Elizabeth. We're half-sisters.

"Remember, Elizabeth, when you were five years old, your mother and Mama went on a trip to the Cape, and you were left with your grandmother to care for you.

"They were gone for almost six months and returned with a newborn child in Mama's arms. Of course, that was me.

"The cover story given to the family was that Mama had had a brief affair with a married man and was pregnant with his child. Because marriage was not a possibility and abortion was a crime, a decision was made that Dorothea would accompany Mama to a maternity home in Brewster.

"Dorothea told those around her that Mama had been a trusted employee and she felt she should be forgiven her indiscretion. Besides, she said, she could never find a replacement with Mama's loyalty, skills, and ability.

"While I could understand this rationale, what didn't make sense was that Dorothea would be away the entire time that Mama was at the home for unwed mothers.

"My suspicions were confirmed by what Mama told me when she was on her deathbed.

"The truth was that it was Dorothea who was pregnant and that it was Dorothea who hatched this scheme to save her reputation.

"Mama agreed to go along with it out of loyalty to Dorothea.

"While the days passed and they were waiting in Brewster for the birth, Dorothea confided in Mama and told her the whole story.

"It was 1930, and Dorothea had been invited to a reception at the home of one of Boston's first families. The honored guest was the British ambassador. Among those in his entourage was a naval officer serving as a military attaché at the embassy in Washington.

"Both had had a couple of glasses of champagne, after which the naval officer invited Dorothea for dinner at a nearby restaurant. The evening ended in the officer's hotel room.

"Before they knew it, the evening was over. Dorothea returned home and the officer was back on duty at his post in the embassy.

"It was a brief encounter and subsequently put out of mind. That was until Dorothea discovered that she was pregnant.

"Mama said that while they were waiting in Brewster, Dorothea told her that she had later looked up the naval officer in *Burke's Peerage* and learned that he was the son of a baronet. His father sat in the Lords.

"Dorothea never attempted to contact the officer because she was certain he was married. Years later, during World War II, she told Mama that she had read in *The New York Times* that the officer had perished in a historic battle when British naval vessels encountered their German counterparts in the Strait of Denmark between Greenland and Iceland.

"One of the British vessels, the battlecruiser HMS *Hood,* was sunk by the German battleship *Bismarck,* and almost the entire crew of 1,400 went down with the ship, including the officer, whose name was listed among those lost. There were only three survivors.

"When Mama and Dorothea returned home with me in Mama's arms, Mama had in her possession a birth certificate bearing her name as the natural mother. She told us that had been arranged by Dorothea's lawyer, who apparently had managed to bribe both the midwife who delivered me and the local official who was instrumental in the issuance of the document.

"I suppose this all goes to explain why Dorothea favored me over you; why she was intent on seeing me receive a fine education and even going to the extent of making me change my name to Ferguson on the pretext that it would make it easier for me to be accepted at Miss Pryce's.

"I also believe that it was her way of getting back at you, as she considered you a disobedient child. She could be very vindictive."

At that point, Elizabeth spoke up. "Yes, it was always a bitter relationship."

"Mama seemed so relieved that she had told me the truth," said Meg. "I assured her that despite what she had told me, she would always be my mama and I knew that she loved me. She died that night in her sleep.

"That's the whole story. I've been waiting for years to share it with you, Elizabeth, but I couldn't find you."

Elizabeth and Meg clasped hands and shed tears.

"Whew! What a story," said Cary.

"I always felt there was something more behind this," said Elizabeth. "But I never could quite put my finger on it. Dorothea asking you to call her Auntie—now it all makes sense." She gave a heavy sigh. "But worst of all, and what I've felt so guilty about all these years, is the way I took out my frustrations on you. Can you ever forgive me?"

"You need feel no guilt," Meg replied firmly. "It was Dorothea who created this situation and it gave her satisfaction to see you upset. After all, no one defied Dorothea, and you had to pay the price for your independence."

They all sat there for a moment without speaking.

"I have a suggestion," Cary said. "This has been intense, especially for Elizabeth. What do you say we all take a break? Elizabeth could use a nap, and we'll get back together for dinner.

"Do you like Mexican? We have a Mexican restaurant nearby that has the best tacos and enchiladas in town. I'll get takeout and we can eat right here on the patio.

"We'd like to see your family photos. We could look at them after dinner."

Meg and Andrea quickly agreed to the plan.

Returning in the early evening, Cary welcomed them back with Margaritas and tortilla chips and salsa served on the patio. He kept the entree warm in the oven.

After a few moments, Cary rose. "You've got to see this," he said, pointing to the sky. "This is one of our more spectacular sunsets. Come over here, you'll have a better view. And bring your cellphones so you can take pictures."

Cary guided Elizabeth to an ideal viewing position and the others followed. The sun was quickly traveling west and taking the daylight with it. Left behind, low on the horizon, was a vibrant band of yellow like a candle flame, and above it a swath of orange and pink. And above that, the sky was baby blue, forming a breathtaking symphony of color.

The group bore silent witness to Mother Nature's magnificent work as the sky changed rapidly. The colors became more intense until it was time for them to disappear. They faded away gradually. And then they were gone.

All returned to the table and enjoyed their Mexican dinner. Later, they went indoors, sharing photos on their cellphones, and telling stories that had waited for years to be shared.

The next day Cary drove all four in Meg's rental car on a sightseeing tour of Tucson, which included a tram ride in Sabino Canyon and a drive through the Saguaro National Monument.

Meg and Andrea departed for home the following day with tearful goodbyes. To ease Elizabeth's heavy heart, Cary had arranged for weekly Zoom get-togethers for Meg and Elizabeth.

And now Elizabeth knew. The whole story; all the details. Late, perhaps, but she knew.

Chapter
Eighteen

The Interview

____

Elizabeth's ninetieth birthday approached.

The invitations had gone out, all hand-inscribed by Elizabeth, of course.

There would be no gifts, please, but contributions to the Rincon Wildlife Rescue Center would be gratefully appreciated. Due to limited space, guests were invited to "drop in" between 2 and 5 p.m. so that all could be accommodated.

It was on a Sunday and the weather was perfect. There were decorations, including balloons and colorful crepe paper streamers. A punch bowl was on the round patio table and a large sheet cake that Cary had ordered lay on a nearby table.

Xander and Sedona, now husband and wife, were the first to arrive, followed by Marie and then Rayne.

Soon came Aunt Joan and her husband, Eldon. Also, Paul Giroux and his wife, Marcella.

Felix Montalvo was still in town, and he brought his daughter, Caitlin.

Also Matt, Dr. Rosenfeld, Barb and her husband, Lee.

Everyone was in a festive mood, and it turned out that there were more reasons to celebrate.

It was made known that Sedona was expecting a child and that Marie had completed her training for her CNA license and was now active and receiving full-time pay for that position.

Elizabeth felt a great sense of accomplishment when she looked upon all the individuals she and Cary had brought together.

The birthday party went on for much longer than expected. It was almost 9 p.m. when the last guest departed, after which Cary and Elizabeth were able to kick back and review the event over coffee and the mini-sandwiches that remained.

•••┌─┐•••

It was a couple of weeks later, on a Saturday afternoon, when Cary's phone chimed.

"Hello. Is this Cary Branscombe I'm speaking with?" asked a female voice.

"May I ask who's calling?" he replied.

"This is Mackenna Farnsworth. I'm calling from Bangor, Maine." She paused. "I hope I'm not calling at a bad time."

"No, it's fine. What's this about?"

"I'm a freelance writer. Your name was given to me by a friend of Rayne Carmichael."

"If it's about Elizabeth and me, I'm pretty sure that the answer is going to be no," answered Cary. "But if you'd like to tell me what you have in mind, I'll run it by Elizabeth."

"Wow! I like that from the start," exclaimed the freelancer. "From what I've picked up third hand, you and Elizabeth have a great story. I know that there are writers better than I who are in the national spotlight and would like to do this story. But I believe I have something I can offer both of you that they probably can't."

"I'm listening," said Cary, not hiding the skepticism in his voice.

"First, I would be writing this piece for *The New England Sketch*," she said. "We're not very well known outside of the northeast, but here in New England we rank right behind *The New Yorker* in readership. We have a circulation of about half a million.

"As I mentioned, I'm a freelancer, not an employee of the magazine. I can make my own decisions right up until the time I put a manuscript into the hands of my editor. Why do I point this out? Because I am able to hold this story in confidence and not submit it for publication during Elizabeth's lifetime, if that would be her wish."

Cary sat back in his chair. "Go on."

"For one, my editor wouldn't know about it because I'm not going to tell him. And if he did know about it, I'm not going to provide him with my copy because I don't submit to pressure. I have an income. I teach English lit at Cardell College near here. I'm tenured and I don't depend on earnings from my freelance work.

"Am I known for keeping my word?" she continued. "Check me out."

Cary couldn't help but smile. "Fair enough."

"If you'd give me your email address, I'll reduce all this to writing and I'll send you my cellphone number, home address, and a list of references and some links to a few write-ups that were done about my work. Also, I'm an activist and I support some social causes that aren't always popular."

Cary could relate to that. "Not a problem," he said.

"Okay, I'll say goodbye for now and hope that I hear from you."

With that, the call ended. Cary rose from his chair on the patio where he had been engrossed in a textbook and headed for the kitchen. There, Elizabeth was leafing through a French cookbook.

"Who was that?" she asked, looking up.

"Well, it seems inquiring minds want to know," he replied in an amused tone. "It was a call from a freelancer working for *The New England Sketch*. Ever hear of it?"

"Yes, of course. Dorothea subscribed to that magazine for years," said Elizabeth.

"The woman who called is an English professor at a college in Maine. She freelances on the side. Heard about us from a friend of Rayne's," said Cary. "Doesn't take long for the word to get around. I told her I'd talk to you. That the decision would be yours."

He leaned against the kitchen counter. "She said that if you agreed to be interviewed, the story would not see print during your lifetime if that is what you'd want."

Shaking her head in disbelief, Elizabeth took a deep breath. "Do you have any thoughts on this, Cary?"

"Let's look at this as if it were a business decision or a political decision and take it step by step," replied Cary. "Or better yet, let's say this is a question that was sent to Guinevere."

"Yes, let's do that," said Elizabeth, looking relieved. "Why don't you be Guinevere for the moment?"

"I'll do that, but again the final decision will be yours," said Cary.

She nodded.

"All right, so I'm now Guinevere responding to Elizabeth G.'s request for advice," said Cary, momentarily adopting a falsetto voice.

"The way I see it is that you need to ask yourself several key questions. The first one is 'Do I want others outside of my friends and family to know about this either now or after I'm gone?'

"If the answer is 'No,' stop right there. There's no need to go further.

"If your answer is 'Yes,' then you need to choose between 'While living' and 'After I've departed.'

"Next, you must ask, 'Can I trust this freelancer to keep her word should I decide that I don't want the story published in my lifetime?'

"And finally, 'Are there others that I need to consult because their names would be mentioned in the story?'"

His voice returned to normal. "Okay, Guinevere has spoken. Now let me hear from you."

"You do manage to get to the point, Cary," remarked Elizabeth. "I must tell you that I'm torn about deciding on an answer to the first question. In one sense, I want to keep my life private. And yours, too.

"But I would like older women who are living under circumstances like I was to know that it's not over until the curtain comes down, and that there's always that chance of finding happiness and fulfillment.

"So I'd say my answer is 'Yes' provided that we can verify somehow that this writer can be held to her word and also that Meg would be okay with this." She paused. "And perhaps most important, are you okay with this?"

"When we began this conversation, I said that it's your decision, and if you're good with it, so am I," replied Cary.

"I'll phone Meg tomorrow," Elizabeth said.

The next morning, Elizabeth was on the phone.

"I can't see this as a problem," said Meg after Elizabeth had briefed her. "My family has known about this since Mama told us. And that's been almost fifty years. All of our friends, bridge partners—you name it—have all known. I can't think of anyone close to us who doesn't already know.

"As for newcomers, I can't imagine that our newspaper carrier will stop bringing us the paper if he reads about this in *The Sketch*. I suppose as a courtesy I should run this by Andrea although I'm sure she'll have no problem with it," said Meg.

"That's awfully kind of you," replied Elizabeth. "And there's one more thing. Cary would like to check on the reputation of this writer, but he has no New England contacts. Would you or Errol know someone in journalism whom you could ask about her? Her name is Mackenna Farnsworth, and she's an English professor at Cardell College near Bangor, Maine."

Meg thought for a moment, then replied. "My bridge partner, Alice, has a son who's an editor at *The Boston Globe* and possibly can make some inquiries on our behalf.

"But tell me, my dear, how are you feeling? I hope you're not overdoing. And please tell Cary how much I enjoyed meeting him. He's everything you said and more."

After the phone call, Elizabeth brought Cary up to date, then went on with her daily routine, including reading her email, often bringing with it new relationship questions for Guinevere to resolve for her followers.

Later the next day, Meg called to report that Andrea had given the proposal her blessing and that Alice's son had spoken to a fellow editor at a newspaper in Maine where Mackenna had once worked as a reporter.

"The editor had only good things to say about her," said Meg. "He went on to recall that Mackenna served on the newspaper's staff until she was hired to join the English department faculty at Cardell.

"In the two years that she worked on the newspaper, she received a number of statewide awards, plus an honorable mention in a national journalism competition.

"But get this," said Meg, "while she was at the paper, she went to jail for contempt of court for refusing to name a whistleblower who provided her with information about a local corruption investigation. The judge subsequently ordered her released after serving almost a week in custody.

"I believe that says something about her integrity. And the editor told Alice's son that if she had one flaw it was that she would not breach journalistic ethics under any circumstances."

After thanking Meg for her help, Elizabeth turned to brief Cary.

"I guess that means that we follow up with Mackenna," said Elizabeth. "Would you like to phone her and ask what the next step is?"

"Yes, I suppose we need to know whether the interview will be here in person or over the Internet on Zoom or one of those other face-to-face sites," said Cary.

The next morning Cary phoned Mackenna but couldn't reach her. He left a message on her voicemail. She returned his call within an hour.

"I'm on my lunch break," she said. "I teach a class in about forty minutes, but I can talk now. Has Elizabeth made a decision?"

"Yes," replied Cary. "But it's based on the condition that you don't submit the story to anyone until . . ."

"Of course. That's what I promised and that's what I'll do," said Mackenna. "Oh, and I got a call yesterday from an editor at the newspaper where I worked before coming here to Cardell," she added. "He said someone had phoned to ask about me."

"That's right," said Cary. "It was the son of a friend of Elizabeth's sister in Boston who's an editor at *The Globe*.

"We're ready to do the interview," said Cary. "Will you be doing a virtual or do you want to do it in person?"

"I much prefer doing this in person," Mackenna said. "I have a long weekend off starting next Friday. Would that work for you and Elizabeth?"

"Anytime. Let us know when you're coming."

"Good. I'll get online right away and see what's available for next Friday," she said. "You won't need to do anything. I'll get a room at one of those airport hotels and rent a car. All I'll need is your address. I'll email you once I've booked a flight."

Cary was impressed by the woman's professionalism. He went to report to Elizabeth.

"I think this is now a done deal," he said. "This woman is no amateur. She seems to know what she's doing."

It wasn't long before he received Mackenna's email. She would be arriving early in the evening on Friday and would come to the casita on Saturday morning.

When they were finishing dinner on Friday evening, Mackenna called to let them know that she had arrived in Tucson and would be at their casita the following day.

Appearing punctually at 10 a.m. with a canvas carry-all bag slung over her shoulder, Mackenna stood just under six feet in her Birkenstocks. Outfitted for the Tucson summer heat, she was clad in khaki cargo shorts and a sleeveless powder blue turtleneck.

Her caramel blond hair was pulled back into a single braid, giving her an athletic appearance, likely someone who ran every morning when the birds were just waking up. She had an aura of wholesomeness about her and looked to be in her mid-thirties.

"Hello. I'm so happy to meet you," said Elizabeth as Cary pulled out a patio chair for Mackenna, and then took a seat next to Elizabeth.

"Do you mind if we get started?" she asked. "I've got to be back in the classroom on Tuesday, so I just have today and tomorrow."

"Of course," replied Elizabeth. "Please begin as soon as you're ready."

"Are you okay with me recording this interview?" Mackenna asked. "I take notes, but I don't do shorthand and I often need to go back and play the recording."

"That's fine," said Elizabeth. "Neither of us has ever sat for an interview, so you might need to guide us."

"Basically, the three of us are going to have a chat. So just relax while we get to know one another. Okay? I'll start with some easy questions."

She readied her pen and reporter's notebook. "How did you two meet? Elizabeth, why don't you go first."

After each shared their first-meeting stories, Mackenna asked them to pause for a few moments whereupon she then asked Cary to tell her about his background—that being his experiences from the time he was a youngster until the time he met Elizabeth.

"This may seem long, drawn out and unnecessary," said Mackenna, "but in order to write about you as a whole person I need to know who you are. And your life didn't start the day you went to work at the nursing home nor Elizabeth's when she arrived there. I want to know where you've been and what you've done up until now."

Cary took a deep breath and then began, starting as a five-year-old in California. His account went on for about forty-five minutes at which point Elizabeth politely interrupted and announced. "If you would excuse me for a few minutes, I'll bring out some fresh lemonade that was made this morning. You must be parched."

She wheeled herself into the kitchen as Cary followed, returning shortly with a pitcher of lemonade and three glasses partially filled with ice cubes.

"This is so thoughtful of you," said Mackenna. "Is this made from your own lemons?" she eyed the large lemon tree in the yard as she sipped from the glass.

"Yes," answered Elizabeth. "But they were squeezed and the juice frozen a few months ago when we had a bumper crop."

"Again, I apologize for taking you through all this background," said Mackenna. "But believe me, it's so essential to the overall story."

Cary resumed and about a half hour later concluded by bringing Mackenna up to the current moment.

Elizabeth was expecting to be interviewed next, but Mackenna seemed sensitive to the fact that the morning session had been tiring for Elizabeth.

"I'm going to suggest that we take a nice, long lunch break so you'll both have time to rest," suggested Mackenna. "I can come back at around three o'clock."

"Oh, that's kind of you," said Elizabeth. "But I've prepared a lovely tarragon chicken salad for our lunch."

"Tell you what," said Mackenna. "I was given the name of a Mexican restaurant on the south side where President Clinton reportedly dined when he was in Tucson. My friends tell me I should not miss it. I'll take myself to lunch there and we can enjoy the chicken salad later for dinner. I don't want to miss that either."

"Excellent idea," declared Cary. "Why don't you go and enjoy the Mexican cuisine now? I'll fix a little something for us and Elizabeth can have a nap. That way we'll be ready when you come back."

"A deal," she replied, packing up her recorder and notebook and heading out toward the street.

After preparing a sandwich and iced tea for Elizabeth, Cary helped her to bed and removed her shoes.

"Why does that always feel so good?" she asked.

She dozed off almost immediately.

Cary pulled out one of his college texts and intended to study but went the way of Elizabeth and was soon asleep on his daybed with Annie tucked in beside him.

When Mackenna returned, they gathered on the shaded patio. Elizabeth resumed telling her story. Afterward, Mackenna was ready with a list of questions. The first one was for Cary.

"What were your thoughts that afternoon when Elizabeth first came into your life?" she asked.

"I'll be honest," he answered. "Something clicked in me almost instantly. I had that brief conversation with her about Steinbeck. I saw her photo on the nightstand. I was literally starved for that kind of companionship. I fell in love with her then and there.

Mackenna turned and glanced quickly at Elizabeth. The effect of Cary's remarks was evident. There were tears in Elizabeth's eyes and a beautiful glow about her. She appeared deeply moved.

Cary continued. "There was nothing for me to think over. It was done. For several years or more—I don't know exactly how long—I had been hoping to find a woman with who I could do more than hike the Grand Canyon or take to bed. I wanted to share all the things you've heard us tell you about, and I couldn't find such a woman.

"Now I'd finally found her. If she was eighty-nine or twenty-nine, it didn't matter. I wouldn't be lonely anymore. Even if it was only for a few months or a year or more. We spoke the same language."

Mackenna turned to Elizabeth. "Okay, now I'm going to ask you the same question."

"My response was different," she said, dabbing her tears with a white handkerchief. "The thought of a relationship never entered my mind. Of course, I was impressed that an attendant would take such an interest in me, and I could see that he was well read for a man of his age. But I just attributed the attention he was giving me to the fact that he was a very kind and considerate individual.

"Also, I suppose that at that moment I was still in a state of feeling sorry for myself.

"But things began to change a few days later when Cary came in early, on his own time, to take me into the garden and read poetry to me. I did consider this quite unusual, and it caused me to indulge myself in deep thought after I returned to my room.

"I liked this man, and I thought that if I were back in Boston and twenty-five again and had met him then, I would be immediately smitten.

"But since that wasn't the case, I began searching my mind for a reason why a young man like Cary would take such an interest in a relic like me.

"He couldn't be after my money, I thought to myself, because he must have known that I was a Medicaid patient. So what was it?

"I was ambivalent about allowing this to continue. Although I was soaking up every moment that I was with him, at the same time I was concerned about what people would say or if perhaps I was making a fool of myself.

"When I finally sorted it out, I came to the conclusion that, first, I didn't have a long time remaining on this earth, and second, what would I have to lose by taking a chance on happiness?

"As you now know, I found it well worth taking that risk.

"However, let me add that when Cary asked me to live with him, I was completely caught off guard. But even then, it came to make sense. He could no longer work at Fairfield because of his involvement with me, and if he were to work somewhere else, I would rarely be able to see him.

"So it turned out that he had put forth a very practical plan. And with him able to land a work-from-home job; it's been ideal.

"Since then, we've never looked back. And I've never been happier or more fulfilled. I love this man with all my heart and soul.

"And you can put this in your story, too. If I were his age today, I wouldn't be able to keep my hands off him."

Mackenna briefly broke into a smile upon hearing the last comment, then regained her composure and continued with her questions.

"I'd like to ask you, Elizabeth, if you often think about your mortality and how you deal with this issue."

"I take it one day at a time," she replied. "I'm not focused on it as a regular thing. I go about my daily work, which keeps me very busy, and Cary and I take lots of time-outs to enjoy sunsets, the garden, movies—or just being with each other.

"When I do think about it, I don't envision a hereafter where we might meet again someday. Instead, I know in my heart that what we feel for each other now will continue to exist, but in a different form. It will be out there somewhere in the universe in time and space—alive and powerful. It's the kind of love that will last forever."

It was immediately obvious that Elizabeth's answer to her question had touched the interviewer. Before reaching for her water glass, Mackenna sat for a moment without moving. After taking a few sips, she cleared her throat and said, "You should know that your words are strikingly descriptive of your deepest feelings."

Makenna paused. "I'm glad that this interview is recorded because when I write this up, I want to make sure that every word you've just said is printed exactly as you said it. It's beautiful and something that should be shared. If for no other reason because it's so rare."

She then turned to Cary. "And what about you? I'm sure you've given this some thought, too."

Cary stroked his chin, concentrating on what he was about to say. "I know that our time together is short. I try not to let that interfere with our day-to-day lives. I know that Elizabeth doesn't have the same energy that she had when we started out here almost a year ago. I know that someday I'm going to lose her, and I'll be devastated."

It was quiet on the patio. Cary looked up to see two Red Admiral butterflies flitting about.

He hesitated, gathering himself. "When that day comes, I know I won't want to stay here," he said. "Too many memories. We've talked about this, and I'll probably pack up and take the dog and we'll head east to Massachusetts.

"Elizabeth's sister, Meg, has offered me the use of their guest cottage. I'll get a night job and enroll in day classes and throw myself into my studies. That will allow me less time to grieve over what I've lost."

Mackenna flipped back through the pages of her notebook, then looked up at Elizabeth and Cary.

"I'm surprised," she said. "But it looks like we've just about reached the end of the interview. Things moved much faster than I'd expected. It seemed that you were so comfortable telling me your stories that everything just flowed. So this might be a good time to ask each of you if there's anything you'd like to say that I might have missed or just anything at all?"

Cary went first. "The way I look at it, we're all once young and some of us live to be old. We're the same person. At the time I met her, Elizabeth was the same person she was in the photo on her nightstand. I was drawn to this woman who was aged but more mature and wiser.

"Besides," he added, "where does one find a woman of my age today who reads *The New York Times* and *The New Yorker* and appreciates art, classical music, and candlelight dinners?

"And there's one more thing. Since my mother died, no one has ever asked me any personal questions until Elizabeth came into my life. None. No one. And I'm not exaggerating.

"As a CNA, everyone wanted to tell me all about their lives and their problems. I listened and I empathized. But it never worked the other way around. I was surrounded by people, but I was lonely.

"It's different now. If I've had a bad dream or have had a difficult time on the phone with a frustrated customer, Elizabeth wants to know. She wants to know everything about what's going on inside me, and I want to know about her. It's a deep satisfaction that many people living on this planet have never or will never experience.

"That gives you an idea as to how important these basic essentials are to me."

"Yes, they are so important, and they are all too often overlooked," replied Mackenna.

Elizabeth looked up at the digital clock. It was nearing 6 p.m. The sky had been clouding over and at that moment it began to drizzle, turning quickly into a downpour. Bolts of lightning flashed, followed by sequential loud rolls of thunder. The wind picked up and they hurried inside.

"This is our monsoon season," said Elizabeth. "We wait for these rains all year.

"Before this downpour began, I wanted to say that there was nothing I wish to add to what I've already said. So perhaps we may be finished.

"And it looks like dinner will be indoors tonight. Is everyone hungry?" asked Elizabeth.

"We have the chicken salad in the fridge, and we have a loaf of whole wheat sesame from Barrio Bread," said Elizabeth. "And then there's a bottle of

Mâcon Villages that's been chilled."

"That sounds wonderful," said Mackenna.

Cary nodded in agreement.

"I've been thinking that since we finished a day earlier than anticipated and you don't fly out till Monday, perhaps you might let us show you Sabino Canyon tomorrow," said Elizabeth. "It's Tucson's crown jewel, and there's a tram tour available. That way, I wouldn't have to do any walking, which I can't do anyway.

"It's a mini Grand Canyon, visitors often say. And since it's getting pretty warm now, we would need to take the first tour which departs at 9 a.m. We could have breakfast when we return home."

"Sounds great," said Mackenna. "Count me in."

•••⌐⌐•••

The day after Mackenna departed, the two were having coffee and sweet rolls. Cary had just finished the first couple of hours of his shift.

As he sipped his coffee, Cary rested his elbows on the table and looked directly at Elizabeth.

"I haven't wanted to ask," he said, "but I've noticed changes in you."

"It's true," replied Elizabeth. "I hoped you wouldn't notice. I don't have as much energy as I had just a week or two ago, and my breathing has become more difficult.

"Today things are a little better, however, and I'll just take it and be content. I don't want to waste this precious time trying to find something in medicine that doesn't exist." She squeezed his hand. "I want to spend this time with you."

"Whatever you decide, you have my support," said Cary.

"Thank you. And now do you want to know what makes this day special?" asked Elizabeth.

"Is it something I should know?" replied Cary.

"It's our first anniversary of committing our lives to each other," said

Elizabeth.

"And I have something to commemorate the occasion." She reached over, slid open a drawer, and handed Cary an envelope.

He immediately opened it. Inside was a single sheet of paper which he unfolded. Elegantly inscribed in her calligraphy was a description of what lay in her heart.

Dearest Cary,

I come empty-handed on this special day,

But I come with a heart full of love.

And unlike the Greeks or the Magi, I arrive sans gifts.

No present could be worthy enough.

I quarrel with the characterization "First Anniversary" because

In my heart I feel we have been together for what seems a lifetime.

You are the gift, my darling—my knight in shining armor.

With a smile and a lively spark in your beautiful, sea-foam green eyes.

Thank you for making these amazing 365 days interesting, meaningful, and gentle.

Thank you for your love, kindness and patience.

Thank you for being quick to understand, quick to forgive, and quick to do what is noble in every instance.

You are my hero, my role model, my partner, my mate, and above all,

My Beloved.

With tears in his eyes, Cary gently embraced Elizabeth and tenderly kissed her cheek. Neither spoke for a while. Then Cary went to the kitchen and returned with two glasses of champagne.

The silence wasn't broken as Cary read the tribute again, then looked into Elizabeth's eyes and said, "Thank you. You don't know what this means to me."

"It means everything," he said.

The Queen of the Night

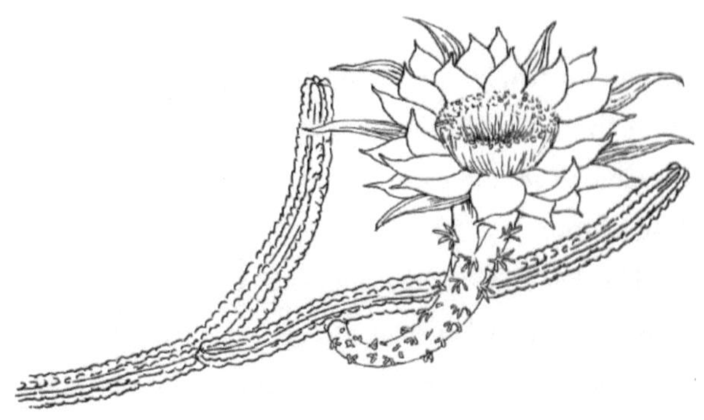

ON A WEEKDAY MORNING IN JUNE, Elizabeth awakened and discovered that she lacked the energy to get out of bed. Her breathing was labored.

She eyed the school bell on her nightstand that she had never needed. Today was different. Elizabeth clanged the bell three times. Immediately, Cary was at her bedside.

"Cary, I don't feel my usual self," she said in a voice just above a whisper.

"I'm afraid it's my heart."

Cary tensed. "I'm calling Dr. Rosenfeld right now," he said as he pulled his cellphone from his pocket.

He walked to another part of the casita where he had better reception and returned a few moments later.

"I got the doctor himself," said Cary. "He's coming over on his lunch hour. In the meantime, he said to use oxygen from your cylinder and if it gets worse to call 911.

"If you'd feel better staying in bed, I can bring you something light, or if you'd prefer to be upright, I can take you outside under the canopy and switch on the ceiling fan and misters. Can I make you a nice cup of green tea?"

"I'll take your kind offer darling. I'd like to be out on the patio." She reached for Cary's hand. "And yes, the tea, please."

When the noon hour arrived, Dr. Rosenfeld was there, medical bag in hand, and found Elizabeth sitting upright on a chaise lounge beneath the canopy.

After examining her, he closed his bag and paused.

"Elizabeth, I wish I could give you better news," he said. "This is what we all hoped we wouldn't see for a long time, but sometimes nature doesn't seem to pay much attention."

He patted her hand. "Continue taking the medication that I prescribed. It won't do much to counter what we're seeing, but it's all we have.

"You've made it clear to me that you don't want any heroics, that you don't want to be in a hospital or nursing home and that you want to spend your remaining time here with Cary. I have a copy of your advance directives on file in my office.

"Meanwhile, I'm going to place you in hospice care. A nurse will be arriving before the end of the day. She is authorized to administer palliative care medications for purposes of comfort, and she'll stop by every day or more often if needed.

"I'll also order a portable oxygen concentrator that will be installed later today. That allows you to manufacture your own oxygen."

Elizabeth nodded. "Thank you, doctor."

"Of course. I'll be available on call, and the hospice nurse can get in touch with me at any time." He looked regretful. "I wish there were more I could do."

After the doctor departed, Cary wrapped his arms around Elizabeth and held her. His shoulders shook as he wept.

"Darling, let's look at this as the most wonderful year of our lives," she said, trying to keep her voice from breaking.

As she wiped tears from her eyes, Elizabeth looked at Cary. "A thought crossed my mind just now and I'm not sure if I should be asking this," she ventured. "But I want us to be married. Even if it's only for a day or a week. Perhaps there's not enough time. I don't know."

Cary managed a smile. "If you hadn't suggested it, I would have," he responded. "There is enough time."

He kissed her cheek. "I would like nothing better than for you to be my wife. It would mean a lot to me."

••• ⌐_ •••

Cary phoned Xander, who immediately offered a solution. "Don't worry, we can have the ceremony at your casita early this evening," he said. "I'm on good terms with a justice of the peace, who is authorized by law to perform weddings. If I call her now, I believe I can get her for this evening.

"The more difficult part is getting the marriage license. There is a provision for applicants who can't appear in person, but there are a lot of hoops to jump through.

"I can take care of those, but some of it will have to be done after the ceremony. I'll bring a form with me this evening that both you and Elizabeth can sign. I'm a notary so I can take care of that end."

"Got it," Cary said. "What else?"

"You'll need to line up a couple of witnesses. If you don't hear from me, expect me at 7 p.m. with the justice of the peace. It will still be light at that time, and we can do this outdoors." His voice softened. "Tell Elizabeth to please hang in there. We'll have you married before sunset."

Cary cleared his throat. "I can't thank you enough."

He hung up and briefed Elizabeth. A short while later, a technician arrived to install the oxygen equipment, followed by the hospice nurse. Her name was Katie. She was middle-aged, clearly professional and competent, with a compassionate manner. Her presence had an immediate calming effect on Elizabeth.

Cary seized the moment to excuse himself and walked to the main house, where he found Barb at home. She quickly offered to serve as a witness and also volunteered her husband, Lee, who wasn't home at the time.

"Do you have wedding rings for the ceremony?" she asked.

"I wish we did," answered Cary, "but all this just happened an hour ago."

"Tell you what," said Barb. "Why don't you and Elizabeth use our wedding rings? We can certainly be without them for a while, and it wouldn't be a real wedding without the rings."

Again, Cary felt blessed to be surrounded by such kind and caring people.

"Barb, you and Lee have been so good to us these many months," said Cary. "I don't know how I could ever repay you."

"You know the saying, Cary. 'What goes around comes around,'" she replied. "Now you need to get back to Elizabeth. We'll be there at seven."

In the meantime, Katie, the hospice nurse, had made Elizabeth more comfortable, providing her with a soft nasal cannula connected to tubing that delivered oxygen from the portable concentrator.

Elizabeth insisted that she be properly attired for her own wedding. While Cary was at Barb's, Elizabeth had an inspiration. She asked Katie to call Fairfield and get Nadine, the CNA, on the phone. Once connected, she told

Nadine of her dilemma.

"I know just the place, Ms. Gardner. It's a resale shop near here. No worries. We'll have you outfitted, and you'll be pleased," Nadine promised.

Around 6 p.m., a surprised Cary tapped on the bedroom door. "Nadine from the nursing home is here. Did you call for her?"

Elizabeth brightened. "Yes. Please show her in."

A few minutes later, Barb stopped in briefly to deliver a bridal bouquet that she had crafted using fresh flowers from her garden.

Just before seven, Xander arrived with the justice of the peace.

The participants and witnesses were all wearing their Sunday best. The bride, outfitted in an elegant, pearl-colored satin dress with long chiffon sleeves, managed a radiant smile despite her condition. Also present was Nadine who was beaming with satisfaction.

"I'd like to introduce to you Justice of the Peace Dolores Marquez," said Xander, turning toward the woman in the black judicial robe.

"Thank you for coming on such short notice," said Elizabeth in a weak voice.

As introductions were made, Cary whispered into Xander's ear, "When and how do I pay her?"

"Don't worry," replied Xander. "I've got it. It's our wedding gift to you."

Within moments the ceremony was under way. The judge led them in their vows. When the time came for the wedding rings, Cary reached into his pocket and produced the two borrowed gold bands, slipping one onto Elizabeth's finger and handing the other one to Elizabeth. She in turn placed the ring on his finger.

Both were misty-eyed when the judge reached the closing words, "With the powers vested in me by the State of Arizona, I now pronounce you man and wife."

Cary bent down and kissed Elizabeth. The witnesses broke into light applause and the ceremony concluded. All present were aware that Elizabeth was very weak, and they remained only a short time to congratulate the newlyweds.

"I'll get all the paperwork taken care of and I'll phone, or text you if I have any questions," Xander told Cary. "In the meantime, call me if you need me."

"Xander, you are the best friend I've ever had," responded Cary.

After the others had departed, only the hospice nurse remained.

"I'll stay here as long as you need me," she said to Cary. "Afterward, I'll be on call. You can reach me any time, day or night, and I'll be here to help. Just call me on this number." She handed him a business card.

Cary wheeled Elizabeth back into the casita, and the sun began to set.

"Could I make you a nice cup of tea Mrs. Branscombe?" he asked, evoking a smile from Elizabeth.

"I like the sound of that," she said softly. "Yes, please, but not too hot."

"It's almost dark and I understand that there have already been a few night-blooming cereuses that opened last night at Tohono Chul Park and that more are expected to open tonight," Cary said. "It's now 8:15." He glanced at his cellphone. "I'll go out take a peek at ours."

In a moment, he returned. "Hey, we're in luck! I can see it starting to open," he said. "I'll go switch on the outdoor floodlights."

Cary hurried to a wall switch mounted just inside the door to the casita and activated two floodlights mounted on the eaves of the roof overhanging the patio. He wheeled Elizabeth out to the edge of the brick patio.

"Oh my God, I can see it!" she exclaimed.

The plant was only a few feet away from where she sat in her wheelchair.

Cary pulled up a chair and sat beside her. "Shall we watch as it opens?"

"I wouldn't want to miss it," responded Elizabeth.

The two sat mesmerized as the white flower slowly unfurled its petals.

"You can see why they call it The Queen of the Night," said Cary. "By around midnight the flower reaches full bloom—perhaps to a width of four to six inches—and then when the sun comes up tomorrow it will have closed and begun to wilt."

"Maybe it's prophetic," commented Elizabeth. "I had a feeling about that plant when you showed it to me on the day I arrived."

She grasped his hand. "Cary, I'd love to watch this with you until it's finished blooming, but I'm getting so tired, and I still have one task ahead of me. Could you take me to my bedroom, please?"

He promptly obliged. Elizabeth opened the drawer of her nightstand and withdrew two white envelopes. She handed both to Cary.

"I want you to open these when I'm no longer here," she said. "You don't have to open them in any order. Just whenever you want."

Cary struggled to hold back his emotions. "Thank you. I will," he promised.

They returned to the patio, and Elizabeth asked Cary to help her onto one of the two chaise lounges. He then positioned the other one alongside her.

"I think I can go to sleep right here," she said. "It's a warm night and all I need is something light to put over me. And I can look out at the stars. It's such a beautiful, clear night."

Cary returned with a linen sheet and gently placed it over her. She beckoned him to take his place on the chaise lounge beside her and hold her hand. As they clasped fingers, he opened his mouth to speak—but before he could get the words out, he saw that Elizabeth had fallen asleep.

After a time, Cary dozed off. He slept soundly, not waking until the birds began chirping just before sunrise. When he looked over at Elizabeth, he immediately saw that she was too still. Her chest didn't rise and fall with breath.

He jumped up and went over to her. He took her wrist in his hand and sought a pulse. There was none. Her skin felt cold. He removed the nasal cannula which provided her with oxygen.

Cary's mind went blank. He felt numb as he pulled his cellphone from his pocket and entered Katie's emergency number, relating the situation in a too-calm voice he barely recognized as his own.

"I'll be there in twenty minutes," the nurse said. "In the meantime, you should call 911 and explain that Elizabeth appears to be deceased. That she's been in hospice care and that I'm on my way." She paused. "I'm very sorry for your loss."

Cary followed her instructions, then wandered like a sleepwalker into the casita to shut off the oxygen concentrator.

When he saw Elizabeth's room, filled with her books and belongings, Cary could no longer hold back the tidal wave of grief. The tears flowed down his cheeks as he sat on her bed and wept.

When his tears subsided, it occurred to him that he should notify Barb and Lee, which he did shortly after Katie arrived.

Barb embraced him while Lee patted his shoulder.

"I need to return these," Cary said as he slipped the borrowed gold band off his finger and reached into his pocket for the one Elizabeth had worn.

"Elizabeth and I were married for less than a day, but in some ways, it felt like a lifetime," said Cary.

"We're here for you, Cary," Lee said. "Whatever you need."

Cary returned to the chaise lounge where Elizabeth's body lay, and which Katie had covered with the sheet.

"I believe she felt no pain," said Katie. "She just quietly passed in her sleep."

Cary nodded, unable to speak.

"We'll help you with all the formalities," she said. "The police will be arriving shortly to fill out reports. When they're done, you'll be allowed to contact the funeral home, assuming that Elizabeth made advance arrangements."

"Yes, she did," said Cary, clearing his throat. "She was very practical. Elizabeth wanted to be cremated and have her ashes scattered over the Catalinas. She planned that with the funeral home."

"We can help you with that, and I know that you have a lawyer friend. He can fill in with those things that we aren't set up to do," said Katie.

By midday almost everything that was required had been done. Cary had managed by relying on sheer adrenaline to carry him through. He fed the dog and phoned Xander and Meg to inform them of Elizabeth's death. He called Dr. Rosenfeld, Rayne, Matt, Paul Giroux, and Marie. He remembered to email Mackenna to tell her that she could now release her story.

Then he packed up all of Elizabeth's clothing and personal possessions and took them to a women's shelter, according to her wishes. She had told him that he could keep anything he wanted, but he chose only one thing: the framed photo of a young Elizabeth standing beside her horse.

He stopped at Bogie's to say goodbye to Jake, but ordered only a ham sandwich, which he barely ate. On his way home, he stopped to bring Aunt Joan the sad news and inform her of his plans.

Cary knew he couldn't stand to live alone in the casita for even another day. It was too painful. Memories of Elizabeth lingered everywhere, especially in the kitchen and on the patio where they had shared so many wonderful meals and conversations. After returning home, he walked to the main house and alerted Barb that he would be departing for Boston the next morning.

He would leave the furniture and everything else, including dishes, linens, etc. This would enable Barb to rent the casita furnished, or simply keep or sell whatever she wished. He thanked her again for being the best landlady he ever had.

Returning to the casita, he set about packing.

By midnight, Cary was exhausted. But before he could collapse, he remembered that he had one more responsibility. It was to inform Guinevere's online followers.

His message read:

Yesterday, our beloved Guinevere departed this earth, leaving

a void that cannot be filled.

Despite a wide difference in our ages, Guinevere graced me with a life experience that will always be with me.

In the last year, since starting her blog, she was moved by the many messages and queries she received from those seeking counsel and always placed emails from her advice seekers ahead of all other correspondence.

Guinevere was the love of my life. I shall miss her more than any person or anything that I have ever known.

Rest in peace, my love.

(signed) her husband, Lancelot

Chapter
Twenty

Life is Change

A NEIGHBOR'S ROOSTER awakened Cary at daybreak. He hurriedly prepared for his departure.

Cary had packed a carton with food for himself and Annie, which he loaded into the bed of his pickup truck along with a couple of suitcases and his laptop.

He pulled a tarp over the load in case of rain and then returned to the casita to make coffee, which he poured into a thermos.

With everything clean and in order inside the casita, Cary headed back to the truck with Annie at his side.

He had made a bed for her consisting of a cushion and a small blanket where she could ride comfortably on the passenger seat and look out the window should she be so inclined.

The two envelopes Elizabeth had left for him lay in the truck's glove compartment. He decided to open one.

He chose the envelope that lay on top. Inside was a sheet of note paper containing a poem. It had apparently been written within the last couple of days.

The poem was in Elizabeth's hand, all in block letters.

Falling Leaf

On the darkest of nights
you are my shining star high in the sky.

My tree of life,
giving me strength and purpose.

Now I am a falling leaf parting the branch,
carried toward a new direction by the winds of time.

I leave you with this blessing;
May the universe always be as kind and loving
to you as you have been to me.

Upon reading the words, Cary began to cry. He broke down, overcome with grief. After a minute or two, he took hold of himself, wiped his eyes, and turned to the dog, petting her and saying that they needed to get started.

Meg was expecting him. She said he was welcome to stay in their guest cottage as long as he wished.

Within moments, they were on the road, traveling on Interstate 10 by way of Las Cruces, New Mexico, then taking Interstate 25 and connecting with Interstate 80 in Cheyenne, Wyoming. From there, it was I-80 all the way to Boston.

In an attempt to lift his spirits, Cary played CDs. His eclectic tastes took him from Jason Isbell's "24 Frames" to the "Ode to Joy" from Beethoven's Symphony No. 9.

When the crescendo came, it prompted a vision of Elizabeth. He saw her in her wedding dress ascending to Heaven. It was too much for him and made him feel even sadder. So he turned to talking to the dog and letting his feelings flow. Surely, Annie would empathize.

Later, he tuned in to local radio stations. He liked listening to the farm news reports; somehow, they soothed his raw emotions and provided a welcome distraction.

When they stopped for the night, Cary would bring in the luggage and supplies, walk and feed Annie, then head for the nearest truck stop or fast-food outlet and bring back his dinner, often sharing some of it with Annie.

Starting with their first night on the road, at bedtime, Annie jumped up on the bed and quickly snuggled in beside Cary. This provided him with a great sense of comfort. She was all he had now.

On the second day of their journey, Cary underwent a change. He thought it was time to stop feeling sorry for himself. Instead, as he drove, he focused on his plans for continuing his education. He knew that was what Elizabeth wanted for him.

Cary had already vetted the Bachelor of Science in physics program at the University of Massachusetts Boston and was assured that his credits from the community college in Tucson would be transferable. A trip to the UMass registrar's office lay in his immediate future.

He would need a part-time job or work-study as he did not want to dip into the education fund that Elizabeth left him.

He reviewed in his mind the course curriculum, which covered chemistry, physics, quantum mechanics, and higher math.

So it went, mile by mile, with Cary inching toward a more positive attitude.

When he reached Boston, it was a warm and sunny day. In spite of heavy traffic, he made his way to the address—a Tudor-style house on a tree-lined street. Both Meg and Errol were on hand to welcome him.

Meg greeted Cary with a big hug and then turned her attention to the dog. She let Annie know that she was a dog person by the way she approached her and petted her.

Errol moved with the aid of a walker, so it was Meg who guided Cary to the guest cottage where he was shown a fully furnished, one-bedroom brick structure with a fireplace and built-in reading or study area.

The grounds surrounding the cottage were well landscaped and cared for. Everywhere there were mature trees—mostly evergreens and some elms—along with flowering plants and lush green grass. Cary explored his new home and was overwhelmed to discover that everything was provided, including dishes, towels, bedding, and a mini-refrigerator fully stocked with a week's supply of food. There were also several cans of dog food and treats for Annie. Meg had thought of everything.

Before she handed Cary the key, Meg invited him to join them for dinner and bring along Annie, who would be fed in the kitchen before joining the others in the dining room.

Over dinner that evening, they talked about Cary's life with Elizabeth and plans for his education. Although Errol had been in emeritus status for many years, he still kept up with his interests, among them renewable energy.

He advised Cary that if he gained admission to UMass Boston and was seeking part-time employment, he should try first at MIT. That could be in building maintenance or custodial work—anywhere there was an opening. Errol stressed that was important if MIT was where Cary ultimately wanted to study for his advanced degree.

He informed Cary that their house was equipped with Wi-Fi and that it could be accessed in the cottage. Like many large employers, MIT listed all its job openings online. Check the listings online as soon as you can, he urged Cary.

When Cary returned to the cottage that evening, he booted up his laptop, connected to the Internet, and pulled up the job listings at MIT. One that caught his attention was a posting for a part-time custodial worker who could also be available on weekends with occasional night work required.

The next morning, after leaving a meeting with an admissions counselor at UMass, he headed to the employment office at MIT and filled out a job application. He was informed that he would be contacted after his application had been processed.

A few days later, Cary was notified that he would be admitted to the Bachelor of Science in physics program at UMass beginning with the start of the fall semester.

As an out-of-state student, his tuition would be more costly, but the counselor worked up a package for him that included some scholarships, a part-time work-study job in the library, and some other perks that brought the net amount down to an affordable figure.

Cary had resolved that he wouldn't draw on the $161,000 that Elizabeth left him unless there were no other options.

Thanks to his call center job, he had managed to save some money during the past year, and he paid his tuition by writing a check on his Tucson bank account.

Before he left the UMass campus that morning, he obtained a list of the textbooks he would need and went to the student bookstore and bought all of them. He planned to read ahead and be well prepared for the start of the fall semester.

The next day, while he was deep into his texts, his phone chimed. A woman was calling from human resources at MIT about Cary's application for part-time work. Could he come in for an interview at 8:30 a.m. the next morning?

Cary was interviewed by Corbin Miller, the assistant director of environmental services. There was an opening on the evening shift in janitorial that needed filling immediately. There were also some other slots open on the daytime shift on weekends. Cary jumped at the opportunities.

In the months ahead, Cary fulfilled his ambitions. Meanwhile, he also took time to learn as much as possible about the physics department at MIT.

He learned that often on weekends, professors worked in their labs, sometimes into the wee hours. Whenever he could, he accommodated requests for assistance in moving supplies or equipment. If he was going out on his lunch break for a sandwich, he would always offer to bring back a takeout order for a professor or graduate assistant still working.

Other opportunities arose, such as attending public forums on issues related to renewable energy and often networking with the presenters.

Several weeks after he arrived in Boston, Meg phoned to inform him that Mackenna's article in the *Sketch* was in print. She invited Cary to come and have a look. He was eager to read the story and immediately headed to the main house.

After finishing the lengthy feature article, he told Meg that Mackenna had gotten all the facts right, and that the quoted material was accurately reported. It came as a great relief to him to know that Elizabeth's reputation and legacy had been treated with honesty and dignity.

Late one evening while preparing an assigned paper for class, he allowed his curiosity to temporarily take over. He interrupted his work and, on his laptop, he clicked on Elizabeth's *Ask Guinevere* website.

The site had remained intact, and Cary discovered that a number of fans had left condolence messages after he had posted news of Elizabeth's passing. More than a dozen comments had been posted, many from followers expressing heartfelt feelings about how they had derived benefit from the column and had looked forward to every new posting.

Among them was a message from a fan describing herself as a widow in Carmel, California, who owned a large house on the oceanfront. She invited Lancelot to join her—which put a brief smile on his face, even as he shook his head.

On another day, while en route to class, Cary turned on the radio. The deejay was playing Willie Nelson.

The music began slow and moody. Cary took little notice until something he heard seemed familiar.

He felt Elizabeth's presence. Willie was singing "The September Song," one of her favorites.

It was about the days growing shorter as the calendar months roll by between May and September. And how the vocalist sought to spend those special moments with his beloved.

He blinked away tears and switched off the radio.

Meanwhile, the research atmosphere at MIT had become even more stimulating than Cary had anticipated. He envisioned the day when he could number himself among the student body.

He would often talk with Errol about his experiences on campus. He told him how he would sometimes talk briefly with researchers when he cleaned their labs.

Errol counseled patience. He told Cary that quite often an applicant for admission wouldn't be accepted on the first try but had a better chance on his second or third.

Many factors were considered, Errol told him, not only one's grade average at the undergraduate level, but also letters of recommendation and volunteer work experience, especially if it was in the public or community interest.

Between the start of the fall semester and the Christmas holidays, Cary was a human dynamo. He was everywhere and often survived on little sleep. Despite that, he was able to maintain a straight A average in his classes at UMass.

Meg was a godsend. She volunteered to look after Annie and not only fed her twice a day but often asked her household helper, Elena, to walk the dog.

One day, Meg knocked on the door of the cottage to bring Cary some egg salad sandwiches that Elena had prepared. As she stepped inside, Meg noticed the framed photograph of Elizabeth standing alongside her horse.

"Elizabeth was quite the beauty," she said with a sigh. "Unfortunately, she had been forbidden by her mother to date anyone who she didn't approve of, which was almost every man." Meg's lips tightened. "It was Dorothea's way of getting back at her daughter for refusing to take part in debutante balls, which Elizabeth considered snobbish."

Meg exhaled a deep breath and turned from the photo. "But she found you. It might have been decades later, but I do think you were fated to be together, Cary. And you made her so happy."

The words warmed his still-fragile heart. After Meg departed, Cary decided that this was an appropriate time to open the second envelope that Elizabeth had left for him. He removed it from a desk drawer where he had kept it and broke the red wax seal.

The message had been hand-printed in Elizabeth's elegant calligraphy.

Life is never incomplete if it is an honorable one.
At whatever point you leave life,
if you leave it in the right way, it is whole.

—Seneca

Not that it was necessary, but this quotation further defined Elizabeth's character. She was a woman of principle, which Cary had sensed the first day he met her.

Cary dwelt on the quotation for a few minutes, then reminded himself of his obligations and headed for his weekend janitorial job at MIT.

Almost always, when he returned home, he would hit the books, usually until he fell asleep at his desk. If there were any spare hours between working, classes, and studying, Cary used the time to attend lectures that were open to both MIT faculty and the public. After a time, he became a familiar face among those in the renewable energy movement.

He routinely turned down invitations to parties. There was also no time for TV.

At least once a month, he would talk by phone with Matt, often asking him questions for which he sometimes couldn't otherwise get answers.

Often Errol would invite Cary to join him for a chat in his study. There, seated in leather chairs near the fireplace, Errol shared some of his more notable experiences.

He recalled the time when he joined a team of NASA scientists on a visit to Huntsville, Alabama, where they met with the former Nazi rocket scientist Werner von Braun. Errol said he had reservations about meeting with von Braun despite the fact that von Braun was then working for our government.

When the holiday season arrived, Cary found himself invited to the St. Laurent family's Thanksgiving dinner which brought Andrea and her husband and the grandchildren to Boston.

Then, as Christmas neared, he began to feel lonely. Classes were out for the holidays, and he had some earned vacation days from his part-time job. He remembered that he had an open invitation to visit Mackenna.

Although he hadn't been in contact with her since notifying her of Elizabeth's death, he had thought about her from time to time. Deciding not to put it off any longer, he phoned, leaving a message that over the holidays he had a break in his studies, and was thinking about making a trip up the coast.

Within an hour, Mackenna returned his call and asked if he was free the day before Christmas.

He said yes and that he would look forward to the visit. She told him to plan on having lunch, and that she would prepare the meal. Cary had a good feeling about his visit as he drove toward Bangor on a cold winter day amid light flurries of snow.

Her directions were excellent. When he arrived, he found her home was a cabin at the end of a wooded lane.

Cary got out of his truck, breathing in the aroma of burning pine logs. Smoke snaked upward from the cabin's chimney. Mackenna was at the front door to greet him. She took his watch cap and down parka and seated him on a much-used leather sofa near the fireplace.

The cabin was old and rustic, with symbols of the season all around. There was a skinny Norway spruce Christmas tree with small handmade straw ornaments hanging by red ribbons from the branches. A tree stump, its bark intact, acted as a coffee table.

"It's cold outside. This will warm you up," Mackenna said as she handed Cary a steaming mug of hot chocolate. "I hope you don't mind the whipped cream."

As Cary sipped from the mug, he glanced around the living room, taking in the décor. An upright piano stood against one wall. There were prints, paintings and other wall hangings, all reflective of good taste.

Cary felt comfortable and at home—in a way he hadn't for a long time.

"I'm glad you're here," Mackenna said with a smile that lit up her attractive, intelligent face. "Tell me how your day has gone and everything that's happened in your life since I last saw you."

Epilogue

In the months that followed, Cary traveled to Maine on weekends when he could arrange for two days off. When he couldn't, Mackenna drove to Boston and brought her work with her.

Because Meg appreciated the sensitivity with which Mackenna had written the *Sketch* article, the two quickly became friends. As a result, Meg was very supportive of Cary's new relationship with Mackenna.

Later, when Mackenna moved to Boston to live with Cary, Meg and her husband continued to make their guest cottage available rent-free.

In turn, Mackenna made herself accessible to the couple for trips to medical appointments, grocery shopping, and any other help that she could offer.

While no longer enjoying a tenured academic position, Mackenna picked up part-time work teaching at a nearby community college. She also helped Cary by proofreading his term papers for his courses at UMass.

As busy as they were, the two occasionally found time to hike in nearby woods or attend a concert or theater performance.

Cary maintained his straight A grade average and had letters of recommendation when he applied for admission to MIT. These included letters from his professors at UMass and from chairs of committees and environmental organizations where he had volunteered. Also from Matt, his mentor in Tucson.

To his disappointment, he did not get accepted, but Errol encouraged him to continue working on his master's degree at UMass and apply to MIT again the next year.

Errol's sage advice proved correct. The following year, with additional recommendations and with Cary by then a familiar face at public forums and seminars on the MIT campus, he was accepted.

As a graduate student, his placement included assignment as lab assistant to a professor whose field of interest was renewable energy.

Then came four more years of work and study until he received his PhD. It was a challenging time, with the Trump years, Covid-19, climate change, and the beginnings of inflation.

In the final year of his doctoral studies, Cary interviewed with a number of large corporations as well as several well-financed startups.

After talking it over with Mackenna, Cary signed with a startup in Austin, Texas, whose focus was renewable energy. He was offered a generous sign-on bonus, a lab of his own, an assistant, and a block of founder's stock.

En route to Austin, they stopped in Tucson so Cary could visit relatives and old friends.

His first call was to Xander, who was now raising a family with Sedona. He also called on Paul Giroux, who he found in distress. The corporation that owned Fairfield had promoted him to the position of regional director. His new assignment would take him to an office in the Los Angeles area. Neither Paul nor his wife and children wished to relocate there, and Paul was deliberating whether to resign rather than accept the move.

When Cary and Mackenna were settled in Austin, one night Mackenna delivered Cary a dinner she had prepared after he informed her that he and his assistant would be working late in the lab. After passing through security and heading down a corridor leading to Cary's lab, she was surprised when she noticed lettering on one of the office doors. It read "Paul Giroux, Vice President, Human Resources."

Using the $161,000 legacy from Elizabeth combined with Cary's sign-on bonus, the couple managed to put together a down payment on a starter home during the peak of the inflationary period.

Not long after, Mackenna gave birth to twins—Alexander and Elizabeth.

Their memories of Elizabeth are kept alive by the framed photo of

Elizabeth and her horse, which enjoys a place on the mantelpiece in their living room.

Alongside it stands a bud vase that always holds a fresh flower.

The Branscombes reside in Austin to this day and remain very much in love.

Acknowledgments

With appreciation to friends and the professionals who provided support and assistance with this book.

Thanks to Colin Ingram, Marian Sanders, Steve Merski, Sue Siegel, and Jane Doherty for being Beta readers and to Nancy Nicholas and April Eberhardt, each of whom furnished overall assessments.

Kat Ross provided early editing, and later Suzanne Barnhill contributed more detailed editing and formatting.

Worthy of special mention are Mary Theresa Hussey for her expertise and guidance related to women's fiction and Jane Friedman for answering questions when no one else seemed up to the task.

Proofreaders extraordinaire were Dale Rodebaugh and Margaret York. Judy Gatrell helped immeasurably with her word processing proficiency.

Eleanor Kohloss, a friend and professional artist, engaged her exceptional talents to transform my visions into charming line drawings to help tell the story.

And special appreciation for friends Rick and Sybil Kinonen for graciously allowing me the use of their in-town mobile home on those occasions when I needed a quiet place to write without interruption from phone calls, doorbells, and other distractions.

I am indebted to Acorn LLC co-publishers, Holly Kammier and Jessica Therien, for recognizing the potential in my novel and taking on an octogenarian author.

Also thanks to Evelyn Lawhorn for coordinating the many steps in production that were required to advance the manuscript into print and to Senior Publishing Coordinator Jessica Hammett for contributing her many talents.

If not for my husband, George, this book would have remained only an idea. He served as my in-house editor and provided the research. It was his counsel and encouragement that kept me going. My love and admiration for him could be better expressed only by the Elizabeth who lives in this book.

Sondra Rice Newman's love for reading gave her an early start in writing, beginning with poetry and later with column contributions to a weekly newspaper.

A Michigan native, she attended Wittenberg University in Springfield, Ohio.

Balancing her literary interests, Sondra played a key role in managing her family's restaurant and fast-food franchises. Her civic engagement includes serving on a municipal planning commission and holding elected office.

Her debut novel *Silver Dreams* was published in 2006. Sondra currently lives in Tucson, Arizona, with her husband George, a retired newspaper reporter.